PENGUIN BOOKS

The Dressmaker

Rosalie Ham is the author of *The Dressmaker*, which is being made into a film starring Kate Winslet. Rosalie was born and raised in Jerilderie, New South Wales, and now lives in Melbourne, Australia. She holds a master of arts in creative writing and teaches literature.

The Dressmaker

ROSALIE HAM

PENGUIN BOOKS

PENGUIN BOOKS

An imprint of Penguin Random House LLC
375 Hudson Street
New York, New York 10014
penguin.com

First published in Australia by Duffy & Snellgrove 2000
Published in Penguin Books 2015

LIBRARY OF CONGRESS CATALOGING-IN-PUBLICATION DATA

Ham, Rosalie.
The dressmaker : a novel / Rosalie Ham.
pages cm
ISBN 978-0-14-312906-6
1. Fashion designers—Fiction.   2. Man-woman
relationships—Fiction.   I. Title.
PR9619.4.H343D84 2015
823'.92—dc23
2015011963

Printed in the United States of America
1   3   5   7   9   10   8   6   4   2

Set in Bembo STD

This is a work of fiction. Names, characters, places, and incidents either are the product of the author's imagination or are used fictitiously, and any resemblance to actual persons, living or dead, businesses, companies, events, or locales is entirely coincidental.

*'The sense of being well-dressed
gives a feeling of inward tranquillity
which religion is powerless to bestow.'*

MISS C. F. FORBES
QUOTED BY RALPH WALDO EMERSON
IN *SOCIAL AIMS*

The Dressmaker

*T*ravellers crossing the wheat-yellow plains to Dungatar would first notice a dark blot shimmering at the edge of the flatness. Further down the asphalt, the shape would emerge as a hill. On top of The Hill sat a shabby brown weatherboard, leaning provocatively on the grassy curve. It looked as if it was about to career down but was roped to a solid chimney by thick-limbed wisteria. When passengers approaching Dungatar by train felt the carriage warp around the slow southward curve, they glanced up through the window and saw the tumbling brown house. At night, light from the house could be seen from the surrounding plains – a shaky beacon in a vast, black sea, winking from the home of Mad Molly. As the sun set, The Hill cast a shadow over the town that stretched as far as the silos.

❦

One winter night, Myrtle Dunnage searched for the light from her mother's house through the windscreen of a Greyhound bus. Recently she had written to her mother but when she received no reply, she summoned the courage to phone. The curt voice at the telephone exchange had said, 'Molly Dunnage hasn't had a phone on for years, she wouldn't know what a phone was.'

'I wrote,' said Tilly. 'She didn't reply. Perhaps she didn't get my letter?'

'Old Mad Molly wouldn't know what to do with a letter either,' came the retort.

Tilly decided she would go back to Dungatar.

I

Gingham

A cotton fabric varying in quality depending on
the type of yarn, fastness of colour and weight. Can
be woven into a range of patterns. A durable fabric
if treated appropriately. Various uses, from grain
bags and curtains to house dresses and suits.

———————

Fabrics for Needlework

*S*ergeant Farrat patted his policeman's cap, picked a thread from his lapel and saluted his neat reflection. He strode to his shiny police car to begin his evening drive around, knowing all was well. The locals were subdued and the men asleep, for there was a chance of victory the next day on the football field.

He stopped his car in the main street to peruse the buildings, silver-roofed and smoky. Fog tiptoed around them, gathering around gateposts and walls, standing like gossamer marquees between trees. Muffled conversation wandered from the Station Hotel. He studied the vehicles nosing the pub: the usual Morris Minors and Austins, a utility, Councillor Pettyman's Wolseley and the Beaumonts' imposing but tired Triumph Gloria.

A Greyhound bus rumbled and hissed to a standstill outside the post office, its headlights illuminating Sergeant Farrat's pale face.

'A passenger?' he said aloud.

The door of the bus swung open and the glow from the interior beam struggled out. A slim young woman stepped lightly into the fog. Her hair was lush about her shoulders, and she wore a beret and an unusually cut overcoat. 'Very smart,' thought the sergeant.

The driver pulled a suitcase from the luggage boot and carried it to the post office porch, leaving it in the dark corner. He went back for another, then another, and then he pulled something else out – something with a domed cover with 'Singer' printed in gold letters across its side.

The passenger stood holding it, looking over to the creek then up and down the street.

'Oh my pretty hat,' said Sergeant Farrat, and shot from his car.

She heard the car door slam so turned on her heel and headed west, towards The Hill. Behind her the bus roared away, the taillights shrinking, but she could hear the footsteps approaching.

'Myrtle Dunnage, my, my.'

Myrtle quickened her pace. So did Sergeant Farrat. He inspected her fine boots – *Italian?* he wondered – and her trousers, definitely not serge.

'Myrtle, let me help you.'

She walked on, so the sergeant lunged, wrenching the domed box from her hand, spinning her around. They stood and stared at each other, the white air swirling around them. Tilly had grown into a woman while Sergeant Farrat had aged. He raised one pale hand to his mouth in embarrassment, then shrugged and headed for his car with the luggage. When he'd thrown the last of Myrtle's suitcases onto the back seat, he opened the passenger door for her and waited. When she was in he swung the car about and headed east. 'We'll take the long way home,' he said. The knot in the pit of Tilly's stomach hardened.

They glided through the fog and as they rounded the football oval, Sergeant Farrat said, 'We're third from the top of the ladder this year.'

Tilly was silent.

'You've come from Melbourne, have you?'

'Yes,' she answered flatly.

'Home for long?'

'Not sure.'

They drove back through the main street. When they passed the school hall she heard the childhood cries of Friday afternoon softball games and shrieks and splashes from swimming carnivals at the creek. When Sergeant Farrat turned the library corner towards The Hill, she smelled the library's waxed lino floor, and saw a flash of wet blood on the dry grass outside. Memories of being driven to the bus stop all those years ago by the same man rose up, and the knot in her stomach turned.

Finally the police car ground its way to the top of The Hill and stopped. She sat looking at her old home while the sergeant looked at her. Little Myrtle Dunnage had alabaster skin and her mother's eyes and hair. She seemed strong, but damaged.

'Does anyone know you're coming, Myrtle?' asked the sergeant.

'My name is Tilly,' she said. 'Everyone will know soon enough.'

She turned to look at Sergeant Farrat's expectant face in the foggy moonlight. 'How is my mother?' she asked.

He opened his car door. 'Your mother . . . doesn't get out these days,' he said, and climbed from the car. The fog resting around the veranda moved like frills on a skirt as the sergeant moved through it with Tilly's suitcases. He held the heavy dome. 'You've a lovely sewing machine, *Tilly*,' he said.

'I'm a seamstress and dressmaker, Sergeant Farrat.' She opened the back door.

He clapped his hands. 'Excellent!'

'Thanks for the lift.' She closed the back door on him.

As he drove away, Sergeant Farrat tried to remember the last time he'd visited Mad Molly. He hadn't seen her for at least a year, but knew Mae McSwiney kept an eye on her. He smiled. 'A dressmaker!'

❦

Molly's house was dank and smelled like possum piss. Tilly felt along the dusty wall for the light switch and turned it on, then moved through the kitchen to the lounge room, past the crusty old lounge suite to the fireplace. She put her hand to the ash. It was stone cold. She made her way over to her mother's bedroom door, turned the knob and pushed. A dull lamp glowed in the corner by the bed.

'Mum?'

A body stirred under piled blankets. A skeleton head wearing a tea cosy turned on a grubby kapok pillow. The mouth gaped like a charcoal hole, and sunken eyes gazed at her.

Molly Dunnage, mad woman and crone, said to her daughter, 'You've come about the dog, have you? You can't have him. We want to keep him.'

She gestured at a crowd of invisible people around her bed. 'Don't we?' She nodded at them.

'This is what they've done to you,' said Tilly.

A mitten, stiff and soiled, came from under the blankets. Molly looked at her skinny wrist. 'Half past four,' she said.

❦

Tilly unpacked the bottle of brandy she'd bought for her mother and sat on the back veranda looking down at the dull forms of Dungatar at slumber. She wondered about what she had left behind her, and what she had returned to.

At dawn she sighed and raised a glass to the small grey town and went inside. She evicted snug families of mice from between the towels in the linen press and spiders from their lace homes under light shades. She swept dust, dirt, twigs and a dead sparrow from the bath and turned on the taps to scrub it. The water ran cold and brown and when it flowed clear and hot, she filled the bath, then added lavender flowers from the garden. She tugged her mother from her crusty bed and pulled her tottering towards the bath. Mad Molly cursed, scratched and punched Tilly with Daddy Long Legs limbs, but soon tired and folded easily into the water.

'Anyway,' she snapped, 'everyone knows red jelly stays harder longer,' and she cackled at Tilly with green gums and lunatic eyes.

'Give me your teeth,' said Tilly. Molly clamped her mouth shut. Tilly pressed Molly's forearms across her chest, pinning her, then pinched her nostrils until Molly opened her mouth to breathe. She prised the teeth out with a spoon and dropped them into a bucket of ammonia. Molly yelled and thrashed about until she was exhausted and clean and, while she soaked, Tilly stripped the beds. When the sun was high she dragged the mattresses out onto the grass to bake.

Later she tucked Molly's scrawny frame back into bed and spooned her sweet black tea, talking to her all the while. Molly's answers were maniacal, angry, but answers just the same. Then she slept, so Tilly cleaned out the stove, gathered kindling from the garden and lit a fire. Smoke ballooned up the chimney and a possum in the roof thumped across the beams. She threw open all the doors and windows and started flinging things out – an ancient sewing machine and a moth-eaten dress stand, a wringer washing machine shell, old newspapers and boxes, dirty curtains and stiff carpet pieces, a couch and its ruined chairs, broken tables, empty tin cans and glass bottles. Soon the little weatherboard house stood stump deep in rubbish.

When Molly woke, Tilly walked her all the way down to the outhouse where she sat her on the toilet with her bloomers around her ankles and her nightie tucked up into her jumper. She tied her hands to the toilet door with her dressing gown cord so that she would not wander off. Molly bellowed at the top of her old lungs until she was hoarse. Later, Tilly heated tinned tomato soup and sat her mother in the sun – emptied, cleaned and wrapped in jumpers, gloves, cap, socks, slippers and blankets – and fed her. All the while Mad Molly prattled. Tilly wiped her mother's sauce-red mouth. 'Did you enjoy that?'

Her mother replied formally, 'Yes thank you, we always do,' and smiled graciously to the others attending the banquet, before vomiting over the strange woman she thought was feeding her poison.

Again Tilly stood on the veranda, the breeze pressing her trousers against her slim legs. Below her, smoke circled from beneath a copper in the McSwineys' yard at the base of The Hill beside the tip. Strangers assumed the bent railway carriages and dented caravans were part of it, but it was where the McSwiney family lived. Edward McSwiney was Dungatar's night cart man. He could negotiate every outhouse, every full dunny can in Dungatar – even on the blackest, windiest nights – without spilling a drop. During the day he also delivered things, riding around on his cart with his middle son Barney and a bunch of kids hanging off the back.

Little Myrtle used to watch the McSwiney kids playing: the oldest boy, a few years younger than herself, then three girls and

Barney, who was 'not quite finished'. He was crooked, with an upside-down head and a club foot.

❧

The town itself rested in the full glare of the morning sun. The railway station and the square, grey silo sat along the railway line, whose arc held the buildings against the bend of the Dungatar creek, like freckles on a nose. The creek had always been low, choked with willows and cumbungi weed, the flow sluggish and the water singing with mosquitos. The pioneer founders of Dungatar had allowed a flood plain along its inner curve, which was now a park of sorts with a community hall in the middle, Mr and Mrs Almanac's low damp cottage at the eastern end opposite their chemist shop, and the school at the western edge, where Prudence Dimm had taught the children of Dungatar for as long as anyone could remember. The main road followed the curve of the park, separating it from the commercial strip. The police station was situated out along the road to the east, halfway between the cemetery and the town's edge. It was not a busy road and there were few shops at its kerb, the chemist shop, then the Station Hotel, and then A and M Pratt, Merchant Supplies – a general store which sold everything anyone needed. The post office, bank and telephone exchange were housed together in the next building, and the last, most western building was the shire office and library combined. The houses of Dungatar, dotted behind the commercial strip, were dissected by a thin gravel road that ran to the football oval.

The green eye of the oval looked back up at Tilly, the cars around its edge like lashes. Inside, her mother stirred and called, and the possum thumped across the ceiling again.

Tilly went to the dress stand lying on the grass. She stood it up and then hosed it down, leaving it to dry in the sun.

On Saturday mornings the main street of Dungatar sang to the chug of farm trucks and solid British automobiles bearing smart pastoralist families. Younger children were passed into the care of older siblings, and sent to the park so mothers could shop and gossip. Men stood in clumps talking about the weather and looking to the sky, and thin-skinned, thick-boned women in floral sunfrocks and felt hats sat behind trestle tables selling raffle tickets.

Sergeant Farrat made his way past a young man slouched behind the wheel of a dusty Triumph Gloria and across the road towards Pratts. He encountered Mona Beaumont on the footpath outside.

'Good morning, Mona,' he called. 'I see you have your brother safely at home.'

'Mother sa-ays we can let the dreadful hired help go. That Mr Mac-Swiney . . .' Mona had a way of making words flat and long so Sergeant Farrat always used his most melodious vowels when he spoke to her. 'Not too hasty, Mona. There's a fair chance William will be snapped up by one of our eligible spinsters before long.' He smiled mischievously. 'You might find he's busy elsewhere.'

Mona shrank a little sideways and picked at the pilling on her cardigan cuff. 'Mother sa-ays the girls around here are un-refined.'

Sergeant Farrat looked at Mona's tweed beret sitting on top of her head like a dead cat, her posture laden and graceless. 'On the contrary, Mona, history has made us all independent, these are progressive times – it's an advantage to be adept, especially in the fairer sex . . .'

Mona giggled at the sex word.

'. . . take for example the Pratt women: they know nuts and bolts and powders that are lethal to maggots in flystruck merinos, also stock feed and the treatment for chicken lice, haberdashery, fruit preservatives and female intimate apparel. Most employable.'

'But Mother says it's un-refined –'

'Yes, I'm aware your mother considers herself very refined.'

He smiled, tipped his cap and entered the shop. Mona dragged a crumpled handkerchief from her cuff, held it to her open mouth and looked about, perplexed.

Alvin Pratt, his wife Muriel, daughter Gertrude, and Reginald Blood the butcher worked cheerfully, industrious behind their counters. Gertrude tended to groceries and dry goods. She tied every package with string, which she snapped with her bare fingers: a telling skill the sergeant thought. Mrs Muriel Pratt was the expert in haberdashery and hardware. People whispered that she was more suited to hardware. The smallgoods and butchery were in the far back corner of the shop, where Reginald carved and sawed carcasses and forced mince into sheep intestine, then arranged his sausages neatly against circles of trimmed loin chops. Mr Alvin Pratt had a courteous manner, but he was mean. He collected the account dockets from the counter three times a day and filed the debts alphabetically in his glass office. Customers usually turned their backs to him while Gertrude weighed up rolled oats or fetched Aspros, because he would pull files from big wooden drawers and slowly turn the blue-lined pages while they waited.

Sergeant Farrat approached Gertrude, large and sensible in navy floral, ramrod straight behind her dry goods counter. Her mother, dull and blank, leaned on the counter beside her.

'Well, Gertrude? Muriel?'

'Very well thank you, Sergeant.'

'Off to see our footballers win their final this afternoon I hope?'

'There's a lot of work to finish up here before we can relax, Sergeant Farrat,' said Gertrude.

The sergeant held Gertrude's gaze a moment. 'Ah Gertrude,' he said, 'a good mule's load is always large.' He turned to Muriel and smiled. 'If you'd oblige me with some blue-checked gingham and matching bias binding? I'm going to run up some bathroom curtains.' They were used to the sergeant's bachelor ways; he'd often purchased materials for tablecloths and curtains. Muriel said he must have the fanciest linen in town.

At the haberdashery counter Sergeant Farrat gazed at the button display while Muriel measured and ripped off five yards of gingham, which he took from her to fold, stretching it against his uniform, sniffing its starchy newness while Muriel spread wrapping paper on the counter.

Gertrude looked down at her copy of *Women's Illustrated* beneath the counter. 'DRAFT YOUR OWN COW GIRL SKIRT' cried the cover and a pretty girl twirled, unfurling a gay, blue and white checked gingham skirt, cut on the cross with bias binding bows to garnish. She smiled a sly, secret smile and watched Sergeant Farrat – a stout figure carrying a brown bundle under his arm – walk out the front door and across the street towards the Triumph. The Beaumonts' car was parked beside the park. Someone sat in the driver's seat. She stepped towards the door but Alvin Pratt called from the rear of the shop, 'Ger-TRUDE, a customer at chaff!' So she walked between the shelves beneath slow ceiling fans to the rear, where Miss Mona and Mrs Elsbeth Beaumont of Windswept Crest stood against the glare of back lane gravel. Mrs Beaumont 'had airs'. She was a farmer's daughter who had married a well-to-do grazier's son, although he wasn't as well-to-do as Elsbeth imagined on her engagement. She was a small, sharp, razor-thin woman with a long nose and an imperious expression. She wore, as ever, a navy linen day dress and her fox fur. Circling her sun-splotched wedding finger was a tiny diamond cluster next to a thin, gold band. Her daughter stood quietly beside her, wringing her handkerchief.

Muriel, laconic and unkempt in her grubby apron, was speaking to Elsbeth. 'Our Gert's a handsome, capable girl. When did you say William got back?'

'Oh,' said Gertrude, and smiled. 'William's back, is he?'

Mona spoke, 'Yes, and he's –'

'I'm waiting,' snapped Mrs Beaumont.

'Mrs Beaumont needs chaff, love,' said Muriel.

Gertrude pictured her with a chaff bag hanging from her nose. 'Do you like oats mixed with your chaff, Mrs Beaumont?'

Elsbeth inhaled, the dead fox about her shoulders rising. 'William's horse,' she said, 'prefers plain chaff.'

'I bet you're not the only woman glad to see your son back,' said Muriel, and nudged her.

Elsbeth glanced sideways at the girl leaning over a bin shov-elling chaff into a hessian sack and said loudly, 'William has a lot of hard work ahead of him at the property. Catching up will settle him and then he can truly work towards our future. But the property won't be everything to William. He's travelled, mixed with society, very worldly these days. He'll need to look much further than here to find suitable . . . *companionship*.'

Muriel nodded agreement. Gertrude stood next to the women, the chaff against her knees. She leaned close to Elsbeth and brushed at something on her shoulder. Fox fur floated. 'I thought something had caught on your poor old fox, Mrs Beaumont.'

'Chaff most likely,' said Elsbeth, and sniffed at the general store.

'No.' Gertrude smiled innocently. 'I can see what it is. Looks like you need a box of napthalene. Shall I fetch you one?' And she reached again, pinched some moth-eaten fox fur and let it float in front of them. The sharp eyes of the women circling Elsbeth Beaumont focused on the bald patches on the mottled, thinning pelt. Mrs Beaumont opened her mouth to speak, but Muriel said dully, 'We'll charge the chaff, as usual.'

❦

William Beaumont Junior had arrived back to Dungatar the night before, only hours before Tilly Dunnage. He'd been attending Agricultural College in Armidale, a small inland town. When William stepped from the train his mother flung herself at him, squashed his cheeks between her palms and said, 'My son, you've come home to your future – and your mother!'

He now sat waiting for her and his sister in the family car, the *Amalgamated Winyerp Dungatar Gazette Argus* crumpled in his lap. He stared down the main street at the hut on The Hill, watching smoke curl from the chimney. The hut had been built long ago by a man who supposedly wanted to spot advancing bushrangers. He dropped dead soon after its completion, so the council acquired it and the surrounding land, then dug the tip at the base. When they sold The Hill and dwelling, they sold it cheap. William fancied for a moment that it would be nice to live up there on top of The Hill, detached but seeing everything. He sighed and turned east to the flat plains, to the cemetery and the farming country beyond the police station at the edge of the town, past the crumbling brick-rendered shop façades and warped weatherboards covered in peeling paint.

'My future,' muttered William determinedly. 'I will make a life worth living here.' Then self-doubt engulfed him and he looked at his lap, his chin quivering.

The car door opened and William jumped. Mona climbed neatly into the back seat. 'Mother says to come,' she said.

He drove to the back of Pratts, and, while he was loading the chaff into the boot, a big girl standing in the huge open doorway smiled at him: a grinning expectant girl standing beside her plain mother against a backdrop of fishing rods and lines, lawn mowers, rope, car and tractor tyres, garden hoses and horse bridles, enamelled buckets and pitching forks in a haze of grain dust.

As they drove away Mona blew her nose and said, 'Every time we come to town I get hay fever.'

'It doesn't agree with me either,' said Elsbeth, looking out at the townfolk. The women from the street stall, the shoppers and proprietors were gathered in clumps on the footpath to look up at The Hill.

'Who lives at Mad Molly's now?' said William.

'Mad Molly,' said Elsbeth, 'unless she's dead.'

'Someone's alive – they lit her fire,' he said.

Elsbeth swung around and glared out the rear window. 'Stop!' she cried.

Sergeant Farrat paused outside the shire office to peer up at

The Hill, then turned to look down the street. Nancy Pickett leaned on her worn broom outside the chemist shop, while Fred and Purl Bundle wandered down from the pub to join sisters Ruth and Prudence Dimm outside the post office building. In his office above, Councillor Evan Pettyman picked up his coffee cup and swung his leather shire president's chair to gaze out the window. He jumped up, spilling his coffee, and swore.

In the back streets Beula Harridene ran between the housewives standing on their nature strips in brunch coats and curlers. 'She's back,' she hissed. 'Myrtle Dunnage has come back.'

At the tip, Mae McSwiney watched her son Teddy standing in the backyard looking up at the slim girl in trousers on the veranda, her hair lifting in the breeze. Mae crossed her arms and frowned.

❦

That afternoon, Sergeant Farrat stood at the table concentrating, his tongue earnestly searching for the tip of his nose. He ran a discerning thumb across the sharp peaks of his pinking shears, then crunched them through the gingham. As a child, little Horatio Farrat had lived with his mother in Melbourne above a milliner's shop. When he'd grown up he joined the police force. Just after the graduation ceremony, Horatio approached his superiors with drawings and patterns. He'd designed new Police uniforms.

Constable Farrat was immediately posted to Dungatar, where he found extremes in the weather and peace and quiet. The locals were pleased to find their new officer was also a Justice of the Peace and, unlike their former sergeant, didn't join the football club or insist on free beer. The sergeant was able to design and make his own clothes and hats to match the weather. The outfits didn't necessarily compliment his physique, but they were unique. He was able to enjoy their effect fully during his annual leave, but in Dungatar he wore them only inside the house. The sergeant liked to take his holidays in spring, spending two weeks in Melbourne shopping, enjoying the fashion shows at Myers and David Jones and attending the theatre, but it was always lovely to get home. His garden suffered without him, and he loved his town, his home, his office. He settled at his Singer, pumping the treadle with stockinged feet, and guided the skirt seams beneath the pounding needle.

Tooting car horns and a rousing cheer floated from the football oval where young men stood in the grandstand drinking beer. Men in hats and grey overcoats gathered near the dressing sheds, barracking, and today their wives had abandoned their knitting to watch every move the teams made. In the deserted refreshment shed, the pies burned to a cinder in the warming oven and kids squatted behind the hot-dog boiler picking the icing from the tops of the patty cakes. The crowd barked and horns blasted again. Dungatar was winning.

Down at the Station Hotel, Fred Bundle also caught the sounds floating through the grey afternoon and fetched more stools from the beer garden. Once Fred's body had been alcohol-pickled and his skin the texture of a sodden bar cloth. Then one day he'd been serving behind the bar and had opened the trap door intending to tap another keg. He reached for the torch, stepped back and vanished. He'd fallen into the cellar – a ten-foot plummet onto brick. He tapped the keg, finished his shift and closed up as usual. When he didn't come down for bacon and eggs the next morning, Purl went up. She pulled back the blankets and saw her ex-rover's legs were purple and swollen to the size of gum tree trunks. The doctor said he had broken both femurs in two places. Fred Bundle was a teetotaller these days.

Out in the kitchen, Purl hummed and rinsed lettuce, sliced tomatoes and buttered pieces of white high top for sandwiches. As a hostess and publican's wife, Purl believed it was essential to be attractive. She set her bottle-blonde hair every night and painted her fingernails and lips red and wore matching hair ribbons. She favoured pedal-pushers and stiletto scuffs with plastic flowers. Drunks removed their hats in her presence and farmers brought her fresh-skinned rabbits or homegrown marrows. The ordinary women of Dungatar curled their top lips and sneered. 'You do your own hair, don't you, Purl – I don't mind paying for a decent set myself.'

'They're just jealous,' Fred would say, pinching his wife's bottom, so Purl stood in front of her dressing table mirror every morning, smiled at her blonde and crimson reflection and said, 'Jealousy's a curse and ugliness is worse.'

The final siren blared and the rising club song carried from the oval. Fred and Purl embraced behind the bar and Sergeant Farrat paused to say, 'Hooray.'

❦

The siren did not reach Mr Almanac in his chemist shop. He was absorbed, shuffling through photo packages newly arrived from the developing lab in Winyerp. He studied the black-and-white images under the light from his open refrigerator, which held many secrets: Crooks Halibut Oil, pastes, coloured pills inside cotton-mouthed jars, creams, nostrums and purgatives, emetics, glomerulus inhibitors, potions for nooks and creases, galley pots, insecticidal oils for vermin-infested hair, stained glass jars and carboys containing fungi for female cycles or essence of animal for masculine irritations, tin oxide for boils, carbuncles, acne, styes, poultices and tubes for weeping sinuses, chloroforms and salts, ointments and salines, minerals and dyes, stones, waxes and abrasives, anti-venom and deadly oxidants, milk of magnesias and acids to eat cancers, blades and needles and soluble thread, herbs and abortifacients, anti-emetics and anti-pyretics, resins and ear plugs, lubricants and devices to remove accidental objects from orifices. Mr Almanac tended the townsfolk with the contents of his refrigerator, and only Mr Almanac knew what you needed and why. (The nearest doctor was thirty miles away.) He was examining the square grey-and-white snapshots belonging to Faith O'Brien . . . Faith standing, smiling with her husband, Hamish, at the railway station; Faith O'Brien reclining on a blanket next to Reginald Blood's black Ford Prefect, her blouse unbuttoned, her skirt kicked up and her slip showing.

Mr Almanac growled. 'Sinners,' he said, sliding the photographs back into the blue-and-white envelope. He reached a stiff crooked arm to the back of the refrigerator to a jar of white paste. Faith had been in, whispering to Mr Almanac that she 'had an itch . . . down there,' and now he knew her lusty husband wasn't the cause of her discomfort. Mr Almanac unscrewed the lid and sniffed, then reached for the open tin of White Lily abrasive cleaner on the sink at his elbow. He scooped some onto his fingers then plunged them into the potion and stirred, screwed the lid back on and put the jar at the front of the top shelf.

He closed the door, reached with both arms to the edge of the fridge and grabbed it. With a small grunt the stiff old man pulled his stooped torso faintly to the left, then the right, and gathering momentum rocked his rigid body until one foot rose, the other followed and Mr Almanac turned and tripped across his dispensary, halting only when he bumped against the shop counter. All the counters and shelves in Mr Almanac's chemist shop were bare. Everything on view was either in wire-strengthened glass cases or on high-sided benches like billiard tables so that nothing could fall and break when Mr Almanac bumped to a halt against them. Advancing Parkinson's disease had left him curved, a mumbling question mark, forever face-down, tumbling short-stepped through his shop and across the road to his low damp home. Collision was his friend and saviour when his assistant Nancy was absent from the shop, and his customers were used to greeting only the top of his balding head, standing behind his ornate and musical copper-plated cash register. As his disease advanced, so had his anger over the state of Dungatar's footpaths, and he had written to Mr Evan Pettyman, the shire president.

Mr Almanac waited, stuck and coiled against the shop counter until Nancy came. 'Yoohoo . . . I'm here, boss.' She gently guided him by the elbow to the front door, pushed his hat tightly onto his bent head and wound his scarf around his neck, tying a knot at the nape to sit where his head used to belong. She curled over in front of him and looked up into his face. 'Close game today, boss, only beat 'em by eight-goals-two! There'd be a few minor injuries, I'd say, but I told 'em you got gallons of liniment and crepe bandage.'

She patted the arched cervical vertebra pushing on his white coat and shuffled with him to the curb. Mrs Almanac sat in her wheelchair in the front gate opposite. A quick glance up and down the street and Nancy gave her boss a shove, and he chugged straight over the rise in the middle of the bitumen and down to Mrs Almanac, who held a cushion out at arm's length. Mr Almanac's, hat came to a soft halt deep in the cushion and he was safely home.

Out at Windswept Crest, Elsbeth Beaumont stood at her Aga in her homestead kitchen lovingly basting a roasting pork joint – her son loved the crackle. William Beaumont Junior was at the oval, laughing with the men in the change rooms, standing in the steamy air with naked blokes and the smell of sweat and stale socks, Palmolive soap and liniment. He felt easy, bold and confident among the soft ugly intimacy of the grass-stuck grazed knees, the songs, the profanity. Scotty Pullit was smiling next to William, sipping from a tin flask, springing on the balls of his feet. Scotty was fragile and crimson with a bulbous, blue-tipped nose and a wet, boiling cough from smoking a packet of Capstans a day. He'd failed both as a husband and a jockey but had stumbled on success and popularity when he stilled some excellent watermelon firewater. His still was set up at a secret location on the creek bank. He drank most of it but sold some or gave it to Purl for food, rent and cigarettes.

'And how about the first goal of the third quarter! Had it in the bag for certain then, mate, just a question of waitin' for the siren, all over bar the shouting . . .' He laughed then coughed until he turned purple.

❧

Fred Bundle snapped the top off the bottle with a barman's finesse and tilted its mouth to the glass, black fluid pouring thickly. He placed the glass on the bar in front of Hamish O'Brien and picked through the coins sitting wetly on the bar cloth. Hamish stared at his Guinness, waiting for the froth to settle.

The first wave of football revellers neared, singing down the street then tumbling into the bar, trailing chilled air and victory, the room now full and roaring. 'My boys!' cried Purl, and spread her arms to them, her face alive with smiles. A young man's profile caught her eye – most did – but this was a face from her past, and Fred had helped her bury her past. She stood, arms spread, watching the young man drink from his beer glass, the footballers singing and jostling about her. He turned to look at her, a smudge of foam sitting on his nose. Purl felt her pelvic floor contract and she steadied herself against the bar, her eyebrows crumpled together and her mouth creased down. 'Bill?' she said. Fred was beside her then. 'William resembles his father rather than his mother – wouldn't you say, Purl?' He cupped her elbow.

'It's William,' said the young man, and wiped the foam from his nose, 'not a ghost.' He smiled his father's smile. Teddy McSwiney arrived at the bar beside him. 'Is there a ghost of a chance we'll get a beer, Purl?'

Purl drew in a long, unsteady breath. 'Teddy, our priceless full forward – did you win for us today?' Teddy launched into the club song. William joined him, and the crowd sang again. Purl kept a close eye on young William, who laughed readily and shouted drinks when it wasn't his turn, trying to fit in. Fred kept a close eye on his Purly.

From the end of the bar Sergeant Farrat caught Fred's eye and pointed to his watch. It was well after six pm. Fred gave the sergeant the thumbs-up. Purl caught the sergeant at the door as he paused and put his cap on. 'That young Myrtle Dunnage is back, I see.'

The sergeant nodded and turned to go.

'Surely she's not staying?'

'I don't know,' he said. Then he was gone and the footballers were fastening Masonite covers to the glass doors and windows – night air raid covers left over from the war. Purl went back to the bar and poured a fat foamy pot of beer, placed it neatly in front of William and smiled lovingly at him.

At his car Sergeant Farrat looked back at the pub, standing like an electric wireless in the mist, light peeping around the edges of the black-outs and the sound of sportsmen, winners and drinkers singing inside. The District Inspector was unlikely to pass through. Sergeant Farrat cruised, his wipers smearing dew across the windscreen, first down to the creek to check Scotty's still for thieves then over the railway line towards the cemetery.

Reginald Blood's Ford Prefect was there, steamy windowed and rocking softly behind the headstones. Inside the car Reginald looked up over Faith O'Brien's large breasts and said, 'You're a fine-grained and tender creature, Faith,' and he kissed the soft beige areola around her hard nipple while her husband, Hamish, sat at the bar of the Station Hotel sucking on the beige foam of his pint of Guinness.

3

There was a gap in the McSwiney children after Barney, a pause, but they had got used to him and decided there wasn't much wrong really, and started again fairly quickly. In all there were now eleven McSwiney offspring. Teddy was Mae's firstborn, her dashing boy – cheeky, quick and canny. He ran a card game at the pub on Thursday nights and two-up on Fridays, organised the Saturday night dances, was the SP bookie, owned all the sweeps on Cup Day and was first to raffle a chook if funds were needed by anyone for anything. They said Teddy McSwiney could sell a sailor sea-water. He was Dungatar's highly valued full forward, he was charming and nice girls loved him, but he was a McSwiney. Beula Harridene said he was just a bludger and a thief.

He was sitting on an old bus seat outside his caravan, cutting his toenails, looking up from time to time at the smoke drifting from Mad Molly's chimney. His sisters were in the middle of the yard bobbing up and down over soap-sud sheets in an old bath tub that also served as a bathroom, a drinking trough for the horse and, in summer when the creek was low and leech-ridden, a swimming pool for the littlies. Mae McSwiney flopped some sodden sheets over the telegraph wire slung between the caravans and spread them out, moving the pet galah sideways. She was a matter-of-fact woman who wore floral mumus and a plastic flower behind her ear, round and neat with a scrubbed, freckled complexion. She took the pegs from her mouth and said to her oldest boy, 'You remember Myrtle Dunnage? Left town as a youngster when –'

'I remember,' said Teddy.

'Saw her yesterday, taking wheelbarrows full of junk down to the tip,' said Mae.

'You speak to her?'

'She doesn't want to speak to anyone.' Mae went back to her washing.

'Fair enough.' Teddy held his gaze to The Hill.

'She's a nice-looking girl,' said Mae, 'but like I said, wants to keep to herself.'

'I hear what you're saying, Mae. She crazy?'

'Nope.'

'But her mother is?'

'Glad I don't have to run food up there any more. I'm overworked as it is. You'll be off to get us a rabbit for tea now, Teddy boy?'

Teddy stood up and hooked his thumbs in his grey twill belt loops and inclined a little from the waist as if to walk off. He stood that way when he schemed, Mae knew.

Elizabeth and Mary wrung a sheet, coiled like fat toffee between them. Margaret took it from them and slapped the wet sheet into the wicker basket. 'Not fricassee rabbit again, Mum!'

'Very well then, Princess Margaret, we'll see if your brother

Teddy can find us a pheasant and a couple of truffles out there in the waste – or perhaps you'd like a nice piece of venison?'

'As a matter of fact I would,' said Margaret.

Teddy emerged from the caravan with the twenty-two slung over his shoulder. He went to the yard behind the vegie patch and caught two slimy golden ferrets, put them into a cage and set off, three tiny Jack Russells at his heels.

❦

Molly Dunnage woke to the sound of a fire crackling nearby and the possum thumping across the ceiling overhead. She wandered out to the kitchen, balancing against the wall. The thin girl was at the stove again, stirring poison in a pot. She sat in an old chair beside the stove and the girl held a bowl of porridge out to her. She turned her head away.

'It's not poisoned,' said the girl. 'Everyone else has had some.' Molly looked about the room. No one else was there.

'What have you done to all my friends?'

'They ate before they left,' said Tilly, and smiled at Molly. 'There's just you and me now, Mum.'

'How long are you staying?'

'Until I decide to go.'

'There's nothing here,' said Molly.

'There's nothing anywhere.' She put the bowl down in front of her mother.

Molly scooped a spoonful of porridge and said, 'Why are you here?'

'For peace and quiet,' said the girl.

'Fat chance,' said Molly, and flipped the spoonful of porridge at her. It stuck like hot tar to Tilly's arm, burning and blistering.

❧

Tilly tied a hanky across her nose and mouth and stretched an empty onion sack over her large straw hat, then gathered it about her neck with a bit of string. She shoved her trouser legs into her socks and pushed the empty barrow down to the tip. She climbed down into the pit and searched through the sodden papers and fetid food scraps, the flies seething about her. She was wrestling with a half-submerged wheelchair when she heard a man's voice.

'We've got one of those at home, in full working order. You can have it.'

Tilly looked up at the young man. Three small brown and white dogs sat beside him, listening. He held a cage of writhing ferrets, and a gun and three dead rabbits dangled about his shoulders. He was a wiry bloke, not big, and wore his hat pushed back on his head.

'I'm Ted McSwiney and you're Myrtle Dunnage.' He smiled. He had straight white teeth.

'How do you know?'

'I know a lot.'

'Your mother, Mae isn't it, looked in on Molly from time to time?' asked Tilly.

'From time to time.'

'Tell her thanks.' Tilly dug deeper, throwing fruit tins, dolls' heads and bent bicycle wheels aside.

'You tell her when you collect the wheelchair,' he called.

She went on digging.

'So you can come out of there now. That is, if you want to,' he said.

She stood and sighed, waving away the flies from her onion

sack. Teddy watched her scramble up through the rubbish on the far side of the pit, the side nearest the trench where his father emptied the night cans. He made his way around and was at the top of the bank when she got there. She straightened, looked up into Teddy's face and overbalanced. He grabbed her, steadied her. They looked down into the bubbling brown pool.

She pulled free of him. 'You gave me a fright,' she said.

'I'm the one should be frightened of you, isn't that so?' He winked, turned and whistled away along the bank.

At home Tilly tore off all her clothes and threw them into the flaming wood stove then soaked in a hot bath for a very long time. She thought about Teddy McSwiney and wondered if the rest of the town would be as friendly. She was drying her hair by the fire when Molly tottered out from her room and said, 'You're back. Want a cup of tea?'

'That'd be nice,' said Tilly.

'You can make me one too,' said Molly, and sat down. She picked up the poker and prodded the burning kindling. 'See anyone you know at the tip?' she sniggered.

Tilly poured boiling water from the kettle into the teapot and got two mugs from the cupboard.

'You can't keep anything secret here,' said the old woman. 'Everybody knows everything about everyone but no one ever tittle-tattles because then someone else'll tell on them. But you don't matter – it's open slather on outcasts.'

'You're probably right,' said Tilly, and poured them sweet black tea.

In the morning an ancient wheelchair of battered cane, cracked leather and clanking steel wheels sat outside Tilly's back door. It was freshly scrubbed and reeked of Dettol.

4

The next Saturday brought the match between Itheca and Winyerp. The winner would play Dungatar in the grand final the following week. Tilly Dunnage had maintained her industrious battle until the house was scrubbed and shiny and the cupboards bare, all the tinned food eaten, and now Molly sat in the dappled sunlight at the end of the veranda in her wheelchair, the wisteria behind her just beginning to bud. Tilly tucked a tartan Onkaparinga rug over her mother's knees.

'I know your sort,' said Molly, nodding and steepling her translucent fingers. As food had nourished her body and therefore her mind, some sense had returned to her. She realised she'd have to be crafty, employ stubborn resistance and subtle violence against this stronger woman who was determined to stay. Tilly smoothed Molly's wayward grey hair and slung her dillybag over her shoulder, pushed a large-brimmed straw hat down on her head, put on dark glasses and pushed the chair off the veranda and over the buffalo tufts and yellow dandelions.

At the gateposts they paused and looked down. In the main street the Saturday shoppers came and went or stood about in groups. Tilly drew breath and pushed on. Molly held the wicker armrests and bellowed all the way to the bottom of The Hill. 'So you *are* going to kill me,' she cried.

'No,' said Tilly, and wiped her sweaty palms on her trousers. 'The others were happy to let you die; I saved you. It's me they'll try to kill now.'

When they rounded the corner to the main street they stopped again. Lois Pickett, fat and pimply, and Beula Harridene, skinny and mean, were manning the Saturday morning street stall.

'What is it?' asked Lois.

'It's a wheelchair!' said Beula.

'Someone pushing . . .'

Next door, Nancy stopped sweeping her footpath to peer at the figures rolling through the shadows and shine.

'It's her. It's that Myrtle Dunnage – the nerve,' said Beula.

'Well!'

'Well well well –'

'And Mad Molly!'

'Does Marigold know?'

'*No!*' said Beula, 'Marigold doesn't know *anything*!'

'I'd almost forgotten.'

'How could you!'

'The nerve of that girl.'

'This'll be a treat.'

'The hair . . .'

'Not natural . . .'

'They're coming . . .'

'The clothes!'

'Oooaaa . . .'

'Shssss . . .'

As the outcasts rolled towards them, Lois reached for her knitting and Beula straightened the homemade jams. Tilly came to a stop with her knees pressed together to stop them shaking and smiled at the ladies in their elastic stockings and cardigans. 'Hello.'

'Oh, you gave us a start,' said Lois.

'If it isn't Molly and this must be young Myrtle back from . . . where was it you went to, Myrtle?' said Beula, peering hard at Tilly's dark glasses.

'Away.'

'How are you these days, Molly?' asked Lois.

'No point complaining,' said Molly.

Molly studied the cakes and Tilly looked at the contents of the hamper: tinned ham, spam, pineapple, peaches, a packet of Tic Tocs, a Christmas pudding, Milo, Vegemite and Rawleigh's Salve were all arranged in a wicker basket under red cellophane. The women studied Tilly.

'That's the raffle prize,' said Lois, 'from Mr Pratt for the Football Club. Tickets are sixpence.'

'I'll just have a cake, thank you, the chocolate sponge with coconut,' said Tilly.

'No fear – not that one, we'll get septicaemia,' said Molly.

Lois folded her arms. 'Well!'

Beula puckered her lips and raised her eyebrows.

'What about this one?' asked Tilly, and bit her top lip to stop herself from smiling.

Molly looked up at the brilliant sunshine, boring like hot steel rods through the holes in the corrugated iron veranda roof, 'The cream will be rancid, the jam roll's safest.'

'How much?' said Tilly.

'Two –'

'Three shillings!' said Lois, who had made the chocolate sponge, and cast Molly a look that'd start a brushfire. Tilly handed over three shillings and Lois shoved the cake towards Molly, then recoiled. Tilly pushed her mother inside Pratts. 'Daylight robbery,' said Molly. 'That Lois Pickett scratches her scabs and blackheads then eats it from under her nails and she only puts coconut on her cake because of her dandruff, calls herself a cleaner, does Irma Almanac's house and you just wouldn't buy anything Beula Harridene made on principle, the type she is . . .'

Muriel, Gertrude and Reg froze when Tilly wheeled Molly through the door. They stared as she picked over the sad fruit and vegetable selection and took some cereals from the shelves and handed them to her mother to nurse. When the two women moved to haberdashery, Alvin Pratt rushed from his office. Tilly asked for three yards of the green georgette and Alvin said, 'Certainly,' so Muriel cut and wrapped the cloth and Alvin held the brown paper package to his chest and smiled broadly at Tilly. He had brown teeth. 'Such an unusual green – that's why it's discounted. Still, if you're determined enough you'll make something of it. A tablecloth perhaps?'

Tilly opened her purse.

'First you'll be settling your mother's unpaid account.' His smile vanished and he offered one palm.

Molly studied her fingernails. Tilly paid.

Outside, Molly jerked her thumb back and said, 'Trumped-up little merchant.'

They headed for the chemist. Purl, barefoot and hosing the path, turned to stare as they passed. Fred was down in the cellar, and as the hose swept over the open trapdoors he yelled and his head popped up at footpath level. He too watched the women pass. Nancy stopped sweeping to stare.

Mr Almanac was behind his cash register. 'Good morning,' said Tilly to his round pink head.

'Good day,' he mumbled to the floor.

'I need a serum or a purgative, I'm being poisoned,' cried Molly.

Mr Almanac's bald dome shifted to form corrugations.

'It's Molly Dunnage, I'm still alive. What about that poor wife of yours?'

'Irma is as well as can be expected,' said Mr Almanac. 'How can I help you?'

Nancy Pickett came through the doorway carrying her broom. She was a square-faced woman with broad shoulders and a boyish gait. She used to sit behind Tilly at school, tease her, dip her plait into the inkwell, and follow her home to help the other kids bash her up. Nancy was always a good fighter and would happily flatten anyone who picked on her big brother Bobby. She looked straight at Tilly. 'What are you after?'

'It's in my food,' whispered Molly loudly. Nancy leaned down to her. 'She puts it in my food.'

Nancy nodded knowingly. 'Right.' She took some De Witt's antacid from a table nearby and held it under Mr Almanac's face. Mr Almanac raised his veiny hand, patted his fingertips over the cash register keys and pressed down hard. There was a clash, a ring and a thunk and Mr Almanac wheezed, 'That'll be sixpence.'

Tilly paid Mr Almanac, and as she passed Nancy she said in a low murmur, 'If I do decide to kill her I'll probably break her neck.'

❦

Purl, Fred, Alvin, Muriel, Gertrude, Beula and Lois, and all the Saturday morning shoppers and country folk watched the illegitimate girl push her mad mother – loose woman and hag – across the road and into the park.

'Something's burning my back,' said Molly.

'You should be used to it by now,' said Tilly.

They walked to the creek and stopped to watch some duck-lings struggling after their mother against a mild torrent and a flotilla of twigs. They passed Irma Almanac, framed by her roses, warming her bones in the sunlight at her front gate, a stiff faded form with a loud knee rug and knuckles like ginger roots. The disease that crippled Mrs Almanac was rheumatoid arthritis. Her face was lined from pain – some days even her breathing caused her dry bones to grate and her muscles to fill with fire. She could predict rain coming, sometimes a week ahead, so was a handy barometer for farmers – they often confirmed with Irma what the corns on their toes indicated. Her husband did not believe in drugs. Addictive, he said. 'All that's needed is God's forgiveness, a clean mind and a wholesome diet, plenty of red meat and well-cooked vegetables.'

Irma dreamed of moving through time like oil on water. She longed for a life without pain and the bother of her bent husband, stuck fast in a corner or hounding her about sin, the cause of all disease.

'You've always had lovely roses,' said Molly. 'How come?'

Irma lifted her eyebrows to the petals above but did not open her eyes. 'Molly Dunnage?' she said.

'Yes.' Molly reached over and prodded Irma's bruised and kidney-shaped fist. Irma winced, drew her breath in sharply.

'Still hurt, does it?'

'A little,' she said, and opened her eyes. 'How are you, Molly?'

'Awful, but I'm not allowed to complain. What's wrong with your eyes?'

'Arthritis in them today.' She smiled. 'You're in a wheel-chair too, Molly.'

'It suits my captor,' said Molly.

Tilly leaned down to look at her and said, 'Mrs Almanac, my name is –'

'I know who you are, Myrtle. Very good of you to come home to your mother. Very brave too.'

'You've been sending food all these years –'

'Don't mention it.' Irma cast a warning look towards the chemist shop.

'I wouldn't want it mentioned either, you're a terrible cook,' said Molly. She grinned slyly at Irma. 'Your husband's mighty slow these days. How did you manage that?'

Tilly placed an apologetic hand, lighter than pollen, on Mrs Almanac's cold, stony shoulder. Irma smiled. 'Percival says God is responsible for everything.'

She used to have a lot of falls, which left her with a black eye or a cut lip. Over the years, as her husband ground to a stiff and shuffling old man, her injuries ceased.

Irma glanced over at the shoppers on the other side of the street. They stood in lines, staring over at the three women talking. Tilly bade her farewell and they continued along the creek towards home.

✿

With Molly safely parked at the fireside, Tilly sat on her veranda and rolled herself a cigarette. Down below, the people bobbed together like chooks pecking at vegetable scraps, turning occasionally to glance up at the house on The Hill, before turning hurriedly away.

Miss Prudence Dimm taught the people of Dungatar to read, write and multiply in the schoolhouse across the road from the post office, which her sister Ruth ran. Prudence was also the librarian on Saturday mornings and Wednesday evenings. Where she was large, white and short-sighted, Ruth was small, sharp and sunburned, with skin the texture of cracked mud at the bottom of a dried-up puddle. Ruth shared night shift on the telephone exchange with Beula Harridene but was solely responsible for loading and unloading the Dungatar letters and parcels onto the daily train, as well as sorting and delivering them. She also deposited everyone's savings for them, cashed cheques, and paid their household and life insurance.

On the big, leather couch at the post office, Nancy Pickett lay with her head in the soft curve of Ruth's thin thigh. Beside them the exchange stood quiet, an electric wall of lights and cords and plugs and earphones. Bougainvillea branches scraped hard against the window. Nancy woke, lifted her head and blinked, crinkly goose pimple white and naked, nipples erect like light switches. Ruth stretched and yawned. A branch snapped outside, as Beula crept along the wall of the post office.

'Beula!' hissed Nancy.

Nancy scrambled behind the exchange to dress. Ruth leapt to sit at her post, snapped on the overhead light and called, 'Morning, Beula.'

Outside, Beula dropped into a mattress of jagged thorns and broken branches. Nancy skipped the short distance down the lane and popped through loosened palings in a fence, then scrambled through her open window and landed silently on the red-rose linoleum. Her mother, Lois, lay in her bed scratching at the black-heads lumped over her nose, yesterday's underwear beneath the pillow.

Nancy padded softly to the bathroom and splashed water on her face, grabbed her purse and made for the kitchen where Bobby was mixing powdered Denkovit and warm water to feed his lambs. Nancy had given him a dog for Christmas – she thought it might stop him sucking his thumb. But recently, while defending the house and all in it, his dog had been bitten by an attacking brown snake and died. In his spare time Bobby played football and rescued animals, including several tortoises, a goanna, a blue-tongue lizard and some silkworms the school kids had tired of.

'Morning, sis.'

'I'm late, Mr A will be waitin'.'

Bobby poured warm, liquid Denkovit into empty beer bottles on the sink. 'You haven't had breakfast. You've got to have something, it's not good to start the day without breakfast.' He stretched rubber teats over the mouths of the bottles.

'I'll have milk.' She grabbed a bottle from the Kelvinator door and shook it, then raised the bottle to her lips and drank. She dumped the bottle back in the refrigerator door and inched her way through the hungry pets crowding the back porch – three lambs, two cats, a poddy calf and a joey, some pigeons, magpies, chooks and a lame wombat.

As she unlocked the chemist shop door she saw Beula Harridene advancing. Her shins were scratched and a purple petal clung to her cardigan. Nancy stepped into her path, smiled and said, 'Morning again, Mrs *Harriden*.'

Beula looked directly back at Nancy and said, 'One of these –'

Suddenly she gasped, slapped a hand over her mouth and bolted. Nancy was both pleased and puzzled. She unlocked the chemist door, stood by the mirror to run a comb through her hair and saw why Beula had run – a white milk smear rimmed her lips. She smiled.

❦

By eight fifty on Monday morning Sergeant Farrat had bathed and dressed in his crisp navy uniform. His cap was perched gaily to one side, his navy skirt was taut across his thighs and generous buttocks, and the seams at the back of his pale nylon calves were straight as a new fence line. His new checked gingham skirt hung starched and pressed on the wardrobe doorknob behind him. He was vacuuming the last of the telltale threads into the bladder of his upright Hoover.

Beula Harridene stood on the porch, her face pressed to the window, squinting into the dimness. She banged on the door. The sergeant switched off his cleaner and wound the cord precisely up and down the handle catches. He removed his skirt and hung it with his gingham skirt in the wardrobe, then locked the door. He paused a moment to run his hands over his nylon stockings and admire his new lace panties. Then he put on his navy trousers, socks and shoes. He checked his image in the mirror and made his way to the office.

Outside, Beula hopped from one foot to the other. Sergeant Farrat glanced up at the clock and unlocked the front door. Beula fell in blabbering.

'Those dogs barked all Saturday night, stirred up by those hoodlum footballers, and since you haven't silenced them I've phoned Councillor Pettyman this morning and he says he'll see to it, and I've written to your superiors again – this time I told them everything. What's the point of having a law enforcer if he enforces the law according to himself, not the legal law? Your clock's set wrong, you open up late and I know you lock up early Fridays . . .'

Beula Harridene had bloodshot-beige eyes that bulged. She had an undershot chin and rabbit-size buck teeth, so her bottom lip was forever blue with bruised imprints and froth gathered and dried at the corners of her unfortunate mouth. The sergeant concluded that because her bite was inefficient she was starving, therefore vicious, malnourished and mad. While Beula went on, and on, Sergeant Farrat placed a form on the counter, sharpened a pencil and wrote, 'Nine O-one Monday 9th October . . .'

Beula stamped her feet. '. . . *And*, that daughter of Mad Molly's is back – the murderess! And that fancy William Beaumont's been hanging around town too, Sergeant, neglecting his poor mother and the property, hanging about with those hoodlum footballers, well let me tell you if he's got any queer ideas we'll all suffer, I know what men get up to when they go away to cities, there are men dressed as women and I know –'

'How do you know, Beula?'

Beula smiled. 'My father warned me.'

Sergeant Farrat looked directly at Beula and raised his pale eyebrows. 'And how did he know, Beula?'

Beula blinked.

'What is your particular problem today, Beula?'

'I've been assaulted, this very morning, I've been assaulted by a pack of marauding children –'

'And what did these children look like, Beula?'

'They looked like children – short and grubby.'

'In school uniform?'

'Yes.'

As Beula talked the sergeant wrote. 'Sergeant Horatio Farrat, Dungatar police station, reports an official complaint made by Mrs Beula Harridene. Mrs Harridene has been the victim of marauding schoolchildren, two boys and a girl, who early this morning were seen fleeing from outside Mrs Harridene's residence having attacked her premises. Mrs Harridene accuses the said three schoolchildren of throwing bunches of seed pods onto her corrugated iron roof, having stolen the bunches of seed pods from the jacaranda tree located on her nature strip.'

'It was those McSwineys! I saw them . . .' She continued to screech, sweating, a sweet pungency permeating the room and small droplets of spittle flying, landing on Sergeant Farrat's logbook. He gathered the form and his book and took a step back. Beula clutched the counter, swaying, her teeth puncturing her lower lip.

'All right, Beula. Let's go see Mae and Edward, look over a few of their kids.'

He drove Beula to her house. First they established that wind must have blown away all the bunches of seed pods from the guttering surrounding her roof. Next Sergeant Farrat drove in search of the said accused criminals. Nancy was leaning on her broom chatting while Purl hosed the footpath. Irma was at her front gate. Lois and Betty were at Pratts' window, their arms through wicker basket handles. Miss Dimm was standing in her school yard, waist deep in a pool of children. Opposite, Ruth Dimm and Norma Pullit paused while unloading mailbags from the small red post office van.

Everyone saw Beula drive past squawking away at poor old Sergeant Farrat and everyone smiled and waved back as the sergeant tooted his way through the main street.

❧

It was a fine sweet Monday out at the McSwineys': there was an easterly blowing, which meant that their happy ramshackle home was downwind of the tip. Edward McSwiney sat on the car seat in the sunshine mending drum nets, threading new wire through bent and torn chicken wire and round and around rusty steel frames. Three small kids ran about cornering squawking, flapping fowls, then took them to the chopping block where Barney, awkward, stood with an axe. The blade was stuck with blood-tipped feathers, Barney's shirt was red-splattered. He was crying, so Princess Margaret handed him the poker and sent him to stoke the fire under the boiling chook-filled copper while she wielded the axe. Mae grabbed the hot floating chickens from the copper to pluck them, then Elizabeth lay them on a tree stump and tore the entrails from their pink and dimpled carcasses.

The Jack Russells started yapping urgently, turning circles and making eye contact with Mae. She studied them for a moment. 'Wallopers,' she said.

Edward was a quiet, steady man, but at the sound of 'Wallopers', he leapt as though he'd been bitten and ran with his drum net. The chook herders, two small girls in bib and brace and a lad in striped pyjamas, ran to the front gate. The toddler fetched a bag of marbles and the girls a stick each. The taller lass drew a circle in the dirt with her stick, the toddler emptied his marbles into it and both knelt down earnestly. The other lass touched up the lines of an ancient hopscotch game chiselled into the raw red clay in front of the gateposts, and began to bounce through the squares on one foot. By the time the black Holden eased to a halt at the gate, the children were deep in play. Sergeant Farrat tooted. The children ignored him. He tooted again. The taller lass slowly opened the gate. Edward ambled back and sat down innocently on the seat by the caravan.

Beula leapt from the car and Sergeant Farrat offered the three bawling children a bag of boiled lollies. They grabbed a handful each and ran to their mother, who was advancing with the bloodied axe in her hand. Margaret and Elizabeth walked on either side of her, red-tinged feathers floating with them, Elizabeth red to her elbows and Margaret carrying a lighted tree branch. Beula stopped before them.

'Top of the morning to you,' said the friendly policeman. He smiled again at the three children. They smiled back, their cheeks bulging, and sweet saliva spilled and coated their chins.

'Would these three littlies here be the children you saw, Beula?'

'Yes,' cried Beula 'they're the scoundrels.' She lifted her hand to slap them. Sergeant Farrat, Edward, Mae and the daughters all took a step forward.

'It was two girls and a boy then, Beula?'

'Yes, it was, now that I see them.'

'And the school uniforms?'

'Obviously they took them off.'

'I don't go to school yet,' said the toddler. 'Neither does Mary. Victoria goes next year but.'

'Are you looking forward to school, Victoria?' asked Sergeant Farrat.

The three children answered as one. 'Na, rather go tip fishin'.'

Sergeant Farrat looked at the short, grubby lineup in front of him. They looked back at the bag of lollies he held at his chest. 'You've all been tip fishing this morning, have you?'

They answered now in turns. 'Na, bugger-all there today. We go Fridays – garbage day.'

'We've been catchin' chooks today.'

'Creek fishn' tomorra, to catch fish.'

'Round off your words, stop dropping your G's and sound your vowels,' said Mae sternly.

'They're lying!' Beula was puce, damp and pungent. 'They threw seed pods on my roof.'

The children looked at each other. 'Not today we didn't.'

'Would you like us to?'

Beula jumped up and down, screeching and spitting, 'It was them, it was them.' The kiddies looked at her. The small boy said, 'You sure got shit on your liver today, Mrs, you musta sunk a power of piss last night.'

Mae smacked young George over the right ear. The rest of the group looked hard at their shoes. 'I'm sorry,' said Mae, 'they learn that sort of talk at school.'

Sergeant Farrat explained the benefits of nipping mischievous behaviour in the bud, of setting examples. Mae crossed her arms. 'We know all that, Sarge, but what are you going do about it?'

Sergeant Farrat turned to Beula. 'Miss Harridene, would you be satisfied with the screams if I took these children behind the caravan to teach them a lesson, or would you prefer I brutally thrash them within an inch of their lives here and now in front of everyone?'

The McSwineys doubled over, hooting with laughter. Sergeant Farrat handed Victoria the bag of lollies, and Beula lurched away to the car. She kicked and smashed a headlight then got in slamming the door so that the windows in the railway carriages and caravans rattled. She leaned over to the driver's seat and put her palm firmly on the horn, holding it there.

Sergeant Farrat drove her through the front gate then stopped the car. He turned to her and moved close, leaning across her to place his hand on the door handle. He breathed warmly, tenderly into her face. She shrank against the door. Sergeant Farrat spoke softly, 'I'm not going your way, Beula, it's an offence to waste police force petrol. I'll let you out here.' He flipped the door handle.

Above them on The Hill, Tilly Dunnage paused at her digging to watch Beula Harridene spill onto the ground from the black car. She smiled and went back to turning the soft soil for her vegetable patch.

$\mathcal{D}$own in the town, William parked the Triumph Gloria outside Pratts and strode across the footpath in the morning sun. He smiled at Muriel stacking horseshoe magnets and picture hooks, tipped his hat to Lois scratching and searching for tinned peas and waved at Reg and Faith in his butchery. Faith was waiting for Reg to slice her two porterhouse steaks, humming, *I've got you . . . under my skin.*

'Like that song, do you?' said the handsome butcher, flashing his bone-white teeth at her.

Faith blushed and placed her hand at her ample bosom, the gold rings on her fingers winking.

'You've got a lovely voice,' said the butcher, dropping his long, sharp knife into the metal holder hanging at his hip. His chest was broad under his starched white shirt and his blue-striped apron sat neatly across his flat waist.

'Can I do anything else for you, Faith?'

She could hardly speak. She pointed to the small-goods and said, 'A Devon Roll, please.'

In the office Gertrude was bent behind the glass partition, dusting.

'Excuse me,' William said.

Gertrude straightened and smiled broadly at William. 'Hello William.'

'Hello . . .'

'Gertrude, I'm Gertrude Pratt.' She held out her small round hand but William was looking about the shop.

'Could you tell me where I can find Mr Pratt?'

'Certainly,' breathed Gertrude, and pointed towards the back door. 'He's just . . .' but William had already walked away. He found Mr Pratt unstacking boxes from the McSwineys' horse cart.

'Ah,' said William, 'just the chap.'

Mr Pratt looped his thumbs into his apron strings and bowed. 'Remittance son returneth,' he said, and laughed.

'Mr Pratt, a word?'

'By all means.'

Mr Pratt opened the office door and said to his daughter, 'Gertrude, the Windswept Crest account.' He bowed again, ushering William past.

Gertrude handed a thick file to her father, who said, 'Excuse us now, Gert.' As she left she brushed against William, but his attention was on the thick account file Mr Pratt held to his chest. 'I was after some coils of fencing wire and a dozen bundles of star pickets . . .'

His voice trailed away. Alvin was shaking his head from side to side in a very definite manner.

Gertrude stood by the smallgoods counter. She watched the young man sliding the rim of his hat around and around in his fingers and shifting his weight, his thin dark face growing long and limp. When her father smirked at him and mouthed, 'Three hundred and forty-seven pounds ten shillings and eight,'

William sat heavily in the office chair and his tweed jacket suddenly looked big about his shoulders.

Gertrude went to the ladies' rest room and applied red lipstick.

They stood at the front door, William frowning at the footpath, Mr Pratt smiling out at the sunny winter day. Gertrude sidled up to them. 'Nice to see you home, William,' she purred.

He glanced at her. 'Thank you . . . and thank you, Mr Pratt, I'll see what I can do . . . goodbye.' William walked slowly to his car and sat behind the wheel, staring at the dashboard. Mr Pratt turned his attention to his daughter, watching William with dreamy eyes. 'Get on then, Gertrude, back to your work,' he said, and stalked off muttering, 'The idea . . . a great calico bag of water, not a chance of unloading her to anyone. Least of all William Beaumont . . .'

Muriel came to stand beside her daughter. 'The footballers' dance is Saturday fortnight,' she said.

❧

The sign stuck to the library door said, 'Open Wednesday and Saturday afternoons. Enquire at Shire Office.' Tilly peered down the main street and saw the people to-ing and fro-ing and decided she'd come back Wednesday. As she turned away she caught sight of the school across the road. The playground was full of skipping girls, boys playing footy and small children playing hoppy. Miss Dimm came out to the pole and pulled the rope, her arm pumping and the bell at the top singing, and the children disappeared into the classroom. Tilly wandered across the road to the park, looked over at the low benches under the peppercorns where she used to sit for lunch, and smiled at the worn dirt patch in front of the veranda, where the children still assembled each morning. She found herself at the edge of the creek so she sat on the bank and slipped her sandals off. She stared at her toes through the amber surface. Bits of gum leaf floated past, insects skimmed by and small raindrops spat onto the water.

They used to march to class in a crooked line, shunting with lifted knees and military arms to the beat of the bass drum. Stewart Pettyman played the drum, a big, solid ten-year-old banging away with a worn stick. Beside him a small schoolgirl chimed in time on the musical triangle while Miss Dimm called, 'AAH-ten-shon, RIGHT turn, QUICK MARCH.'

They kept time behind their small chocolate seats in the classroom until Miss Dimm cried, 'HALT! Be seated and don't scrape your chairs!' Then shuffle shuffle clunk and silence. They sat with their arms folded, waiting.

'Myrtle Dunnage, you're on ink-well duty again for fighting after school yesterday. The rest of you get out your pencils and exercise books.'

'But I did it yest–'

'Myrtle Dunnage, you will be on ink-well duty until I say so.' Miss Dimm chopped Myrtle's fingers with her rusty steel ruler and cried, 'I did not tell you to uncross your arms!' The white crease from the ruler was still on her fingers when she started to mix the ink. She stood at the wash trough to mix the black powder with water then moved from desk to desk very slowly, carrying the jug. It was difficult to pour the blue–black ink into the wells. She wasn't allowed to drip any on the desk and it was hard to tell which wells were full. Ink bubbled to the top of Stewart Pettyman's, rimming the white marble lip, so he bumped the desk. The ink spilled, running down the desk top onto his bare knees.

'Miss Dimm, she stained me, she stained me with the ink.'

Miss Dimm came, cuffed Myrtle over the head and dragged her from the room by her plait. The other kids leaned on the glass windows laughing out loud. Myrtle sat for the rest of the morning on the veranda where everyone in the whole town could see her.

After school she ran as fast as she could but they caught up with her. They held her and gave her Chinese burns, then they held her arms out and Stewart ran at her, head down like a charging bull so his head banged her in the tummy. She bent in half, lost her breath and fell to the ground, holding her stomach. The boys pulled her pants down and poked at her, then smelled their fingers. The girls sang, 'Dunny's mum's a slut, Dunnybum's mum's a slut, Myr-tle's a bar-std, Myr-tle's a bar-std.'

❧

Marigold Pettyman sat by the light of the radiogram with an icepack balanced on her curlers waiting for her husband, Evan. The six o'clock news muttered gently beside her, *'And now for the weather. Light rain is expected.'*

'Oh Lord,' said Marigold, and reached for the small brown bottle on the lamp-stand table. She shook three tablets into her palm and swallowed them in one, leaned back and rubbed her temples. Marigold was a shrill, whippet-like woman with a startled bearing and a nervous rash on her neck. When she heard the key in the screen door lock she sat bolt upright and called anxiously, 'Is that you, Evan?'

'Yes, dear.'

'You'll take off your shoes and shake your coat for dust before you come in, won't you?' Evan's shoes thumped onto the veranda boards and there was the clank of wooden coat hangers meeting. He unlocked the kitchen door and stepped into the kitchen which was scrubbed and disinfected to surgery standard, its floor slippery and brilliant.

Evan Pettyman was a round man with yellow hair and complexion and small quick eyes. He was a man who touched women, leaned close to talk, licked his lips and at dances pressed his partners tightly, ramming his thigh between their legs to move them around the floor. The ladies of Dungatar were polite to Councillor Pettyman – he was the shire president and Marigold's husband. But they turned their backs when they saw him coming, busied themselves with a shop window or suddenly remembered something they had to do across the road. Men avoided the councillor but were cordial. He'd lost his son and had a lot on his plate, with Marigold the way she was – 'highly strung'. He was a good councillor who got things done. He also knew how every man earned his keep.

Marigold had been just a shy, innocent little thing when Evan came to Dungatar. Her father was the shire president then, and when he died he left her a lot of money, so Evan swept her off her feet. Her nerves started to go, and slowly got worse, and she had never been the same after their son Stewart was so tragically killed.

Evan passed directly through to the bathroom where he removed his clothes and placed them in the washing basket and closed the lid. He showered then put on the starched pyjamas left sitting on the bench with the freshly laundered dressing gown and as-new woollen slippers.

'Good evening my pet,' said Evan, and pecked her cheek.

'Your dinner's in the refrigerator,' she said.

Evan ate at the kitchen table. Sliced cold devon, tomato – seeds removed, beetroot – the liquid soaked from the neat round slices, a neat dome of grated carrot, and a halved boiled egg. There were two slices of white bread, buttered to the edges. Since there might be crumbs Marigold had spread newspaper around Evan's chair. He peeled and ate a home-grown orange over the sink, careful to put all the pips in the bin. Marigold tidied up after him. She scrubbed his knife, fork and plate in boiling suds, littered the sink with Vim, rubbed, rinsed and dried the area thoroughly then disinfected all the handles and knobs where Evan might have left prints. Evan washed his face and moustache in the bathroom and returned to the kitchen.

'It's going to rain tomorrow,' Marigold said shrilly. 'The windows will need cleaning when it stops and all the door-knobs and window latches need a good soaking as well.'

Evan smiled down at her and said, 'But, my pet, it's not time –'

'It's spring!' she cried, and held the icepack to her temples. 'I've already washed the walls and skirting boards and dusted the ceilings and cornices, I can get on with the doors and the window sills if you'd just remove all the knobs and latches.'

'You could save yourself some trouble, pet, just wash around them, I'm very busy.'

Marigold bit her fist and hurried back to the radiogram and closed her eyes, the icepack back on her curlers.

Evan filled her hot-water bottle. 'Beddie-bies,' he said, and poured tonic into a spoon for her. She closed her mouth and turned her head away.

'Come, Marigold, your tonic.'

She closed her eyes and shook her head from side to side.

'All right, my pet,' said Evan, 'I'll get up early and remove the doorknobs and window latches before breakfast.'

She opened her mouth and he spilled her medicine onto her tongue, then helped her to bed.

'It's twenty years since Stewart fell out of the tree . . .' she said.

'Yes, dear.'

'Twenty years since I lost my boy . . .'

'There there, dear.'

'I can't see him.'

Evan adjusted the photo of their dead, smiling son.

'Twenty years . . .'

'Yes, dear.' Evan poured a little more tonic and gave it to her. When she slept Evan undressed, then leaned over her, licking his lips and rubbing his hands together. He pulled back the bed-clothes and removed Marigold's nightie. She was limp but he positioned her as he wanted her, legs splayed, arms over her head, then he knelt between her thighs.

❦

The next morni3ng Marigold Pettyman stood safe from the dangerous rain at her kitchen sink with her saveloy-red hands deep in steaming suds, earnestly scrubbing all the doorknobs and window latches.

7

On Friday evening the footballers and a farmer or two were bunched at the far end of the bar, studying a diagram of the football oval that was pinned over a punctured picture of Bob Menzies on the dartboard. The names of the players were pencilled in at the various positions on the layout. The experts stood around it shaking their heads.

'Crikey.'

'Blimey.'

'Coach's gone troppo.'

'Nar – he's got a plan, tactics, according to Teddy.'

'Teddy just wants your money.'

'A quid.'

'Coach's right – Bobby is big, that's what matters.'

'He's better placed in the centre.'

'Injury.'

'Has he gotten over his dog dyin' yet?' The men shook their heads and turned their attention back to the game plan.

'Gunna's roving.'

'Stroke of genius that is, half-time swap, bring on Bobby and they won't see a ball down their end for fifty minutes.'

There was a general rumble of approval. The men turned from the diagram, their hands shoved deep in their pockets.

It was a serious evening. The tense footballers and their supporters lined up at the bar. A foaming beer sat waiting at every spot. They pondered the skirting board behind the bar, sipping. When the amber tide had sunk to one gulp above the glass bottom the men looked knowingly at each other, sculled, clapped and rubbed their hands, secured their hats and made for the door. They were needed at the footy oval. Purl looked at Fred and pressed her red fingernails to her red lips. 'Shouldn't you be going, Fred?'

'Purlywurly, we have a celebration to prepare for.'

She went to him and lay her head down on his, 'I love them boys, Fred . . .' Fred reached two thin arms around his Purly's waist and nuzzled so deep into her cleavage that only the tops of his ears were showing. 'Weywuvootoo,' he said.

❦

Spectators lined the white boundary fence watching the players run and shout, desperate echoes in a cold dusk. Sincerity and determination spurred the brave athletes, though fear was in their hearts. The supporters worried about the bets they'd laid – not that they had any doubts about Dungatar's victory.

Every available man, kid and dog gathered to watch the grand final training, to listen to the coach's pep-talk in the dressing sheds afterwards and rub Oil of Wintergreen on the players' thighs and calves. There was a heartfelt 'Hear hear' from the clever captain Teddy McSwiney and his grateful team-mates in recognition of the coach's magnificent efforts, then they sang the club song in a sombre way, slapped each other's backs, shook hands and went home to grilled chops, mashed potato and peas before bed.

❧

The supporters went back to the pub. The last champions from Dungatar to seize the football cup were now war veterans hiding next to radiograms in dim lounge rooms, but tomorrow they would leave their armchairs and drag their shell-shock, emphysema and prosthetics to the white railing by the goalposts even if it killed them. Purl was so sick with worry that she was tempted to bite her nails. The supporters along the bar frowned at their beers. Hamish O'Brien and Septimus Crescant usually argued. Tonight they sat quietly.

'Gawd,' said Purl, 'just look at all of us!' She smiled brightly at them. No one smiled back. 'How about the new girl in town?' she said conspiratorially.

The line of pale faces along the bar looked blankly at her.

'One more to fight off,' said an ancient whiskered sheep drover.

'Our own dandy and full forward has his eye on her,' said a shearer.

'Who?' They felt the night breeze on their backs and smelt Teddy McSwiney as soon as he opened the door. He'd been wasting a lot of talc about his person ever since that woman got off the bus.

'The new sheila,' said the shearer.

'Myrtle Dunnage,' said Purl.

'That'd be Tilly,' said Teddy, and winked at Purl.

'She inherit any of her mother's loose ways?' said the drover.

Teddy pulled his clenched fists from his pockets and thrust out his chest.

'Steady on, steady on,' said Fred.

'Boys!' said Purl.

'I hear she's a good looking sheila,' said the shearer. Purl put a beer in front of him and took his money. 'I suppose you could say that,' she said, and sniffed.

'She is,' said Teddy, and grinned.

'More like our Purl, is she?' said the drover, and looked at her with a lewd expression.

Fred looked the drover in the eye, '*My* Purl,' he said, and screwed a bar cloth over the sink until it squeaked.

'She's yours *now*,' said the shearer, and finished his beer. The drinkers turned their backs to him and his glass sat empty in front of him. Teddy moved to stand behind the shearer, his fists low but ready.

'I remember her!' said Reginald, and snapped his fingers, 'That's Mad Molly's bastard girl. At school we used to –'

'Shut it, Reg!' Teddy leapt back and raised his fists, dancing. The men turned.

The shearer sprang, 'Hello, bit of a dark past here as well, better drop in for a chat with Beula on my way home . . .'

Teddy was on the shearer fast as a bullet, his singlet gathered at his Adam's apple and his shoulders pinned to the tiles with Teddy's knees, a fist poised.

'*Stop*,' shrilled Purl. 'Teddy, you're our full forward.'

Teddy paused.

'Might be worth your while to keep your mouth shut from here on in, I'd say,' said Fred, and pointed to the shearer, then to the old drover.

The shearer spoke. 'Might be worth Teddy's while to get an early night. All I have to do is sneeze and I'd send him through the glass door there.' Reg and the other men stepped forward, circling the shearer.

'Please, Teddy,' said Purl tearfully.

Teddy stood and dusted himself off. The shearer stood and looked down on him. 'Not much chance I'll get another beer here tonight – may as well go home to bed.' They watched him saunter to the door, put on his hat and disappear into the dark. All eyes turned to Teddy.

'I'll just finish me beer,' he said, showing his palms in surrender. He walked home through the rolling fog. Sergeant Farrat, cruising past in his police car, slowed, but Teddy waved him on. Later he lay in his bed staring through the caravan window, pondering the square yellow glow from Tilly's window up on The Hill.

❦

The Dungatar supporters suffered four long quarters of a close and dirty battle with Winyerp, urging their warriors on with bloodcurdling oaths and well-founded threats. Towards the end of the fourth quarter the players were exhausted, wet and heaving for breath, blood seeping from their mud-caked limbs. Only Bobby Pickett remained clean – the crease still in his shorts and his guernsey dry – but somehow he'd lost a front tooth.

With thirteen seconds left of time-on, Winyerp kicked a goal to even the score. Teddy McSwiney, miles out of his position, went under the pack at the ball-up, scooped up the ball as it fell between the leaping legs and ran with it. He shrugged off reaching hands as though he was covered in hot Vaseline, bounced his way towards the four tall poles and kicked a wobbly left footer that slipped off the side of his boot to bounce low and dribble towards the goalposts. It toppled through for a point as the final siren sounded, the red, green and mud-coloured pack lunging through the posts over it.

Dungatar 11-11-77
Winyerp 11-10-76

The sound of blaring car horns lifted the sky and the crowd screamed with lust, revenge, joy, hate and elation. The earth shook to the sound of clapping and stamping while the tight bleeding wave of sportsmen raged back across the oval like a boiling clump of centipedes into the arms of the waiting fans. No team was ever happier, no town ever noisier. As the sun set the club song amplified over the plains of Dungatar and the entire town bounced down to the Station Hotel.

Penny bangers shuddered the doorjambs and skyrockets flew, setting crops alight two miles away. Purl was dancing behind her bar in white shorts and a striped football guernsey, fishnet stockings and football boots laced all the way up to her knees. Fred Bundle wore a mud-stained goal umpire's coat, and two white flags adorned with tinsel and flower-shaped cellophane shot roofwards from a red and blue beanie. He looked like a small elk at Christmas. The rabble were in various stages of undress and inebriation – embracing indiscriminately, singing, dancing onto the footpath or swinging down from the balcony on the unfurled fire hydrant hose. Some chose a quiet corner to knit, chat, breast-feed. Reginald – a meat cleaver wedged in his hat – played the fiddle, while Faithful O'Brien stood by her microphone bantering with three young women in the corner – the McSwiney girls wearing rouge, their stocking tops and pettycoat lace draped over their crossed thighs. They had flowers in their hair – blue roses – and were smoking cigarettes and giggling. The sergeant danced on the bar wearing top hat, tails and tap shoes. Skinny Scotty Pullit thrust his watermelon firewater at everyone, saying, 'Suck this, special drop.' Teddy took a sip. His lips turned into a big O and the fire burned all the way down into his gullet. He reached for more. Septimus Crescant was handing out leaflets about his Flat Earth Society. He encountered William looking fearful with his arms crossed against Gertrude, who was beaming closely down on him. Elsbeth sat at his side, displeased, with Mona beside her bursting to dance but afraid. William took a leaflet then eased away from Gertrude, moving with Septimus to the bar. When they arrived Septimus took his hard hat off and threw it on the green-marbled linoleum. The top of his head was flat, his dome straight enough to set a bowl of jelly on. 'Very sturdy,' he said, stepping onto the hat.

'Why do you wear it?'

'There was an accident when I was a babe in arms – a fall. I'm no good at heights at all. I moved here because of the terrain and because it's a long way from the edge. It's a fraction above sea level as well, so we won't be flooded when the end comes – the water will run away from us down to the edge. And of course there's The Hill.'

'The end?'

A dart whistled past the men. It landed between Robert Menzies' eyes. 'A toast!' called Sergeant Farrat. 'To today's second place getters in the art of balling by foot. To Winyerp.'

There was silence while everyone swallowed.

'And now a proud toast for our noble, brave and victorious sportsmen, the Dungatar First Football Team.' Then there was a deafening noise, whistling and applause. The team were lifted onto shoulders and marched around the bar, with the club song sung again, and again, and again.

❧

When Beula Harridene passed the hotel just before dawn the party was still in progress. Bleary people were strewn about the footpath in pockets and piles, bushes shimmered to the sound of frottage, men were being led home by the hand and Scotty Pullit sat upright at the bar, asleep. Purl stretched alongside him, also asleep. Fred sat next to them sipping a hot cup of Horlicks.

8

*R*uth Dimm leaned against the wheel guard of her post office van in the morning sun and squinted along the railway tracks. Hamish O'Brien walked down the platform carrying a dripping watering can, drenching the petunias, which were bunched like frilly socks on the veranda posts. In the distance, a long tooooooot sounded. He stopped, checked his fob watch then stared off towards the soft sounds, chuff chuff chuff chuff. The ten past nine Thomson and Company SAR raced towards Dungatar at a top speed of 32 mph, all steam and clatter and thumping.

It drew towards the station, the long connecting rods slowing beside the platform, the pumping pistons easing, steam ballooning white and grey, then the giant black engine screeched, halted, rumbled and sighed. The flagman waved, Hamish blew his whistle and the guard threw the great canvas bags of mail to land at Ruth's feet. Next he dragged a cowering liver-coloured kelpie pup on a lead over to Ruth. It had a tag stuck to its collar that said, 'Please give me a drink.'

'This fer Bobby Pickett?' asked Hamish.

'Yes,' Ruth was rubbing the puppy's velvet ears, 'from Nancy.'

'Hope it's not as scared of sheep as it is of trains,' said the guard, and slid a tea-chest from his hand cart onto the gravel next to the van. Hamish and Ruth looked down at it. It was addressed to Miss Tilly Dunnage, Dungatar, Australia, in big, red letters.

The train pulled away and they watched it until it was a puff of grey smoke on the horizon. Hamish turned his beefy face to Ruth. Tears sat sideways in the cream-coloured folds beneath his blue eyes. He shoved his pipe between his teeth and said, 'It's the diesel taking over you see . . .'

'I know, Hamish, I know . . . ,' said Ruth, '. . . progress.' She patted his shoulder.

'Damn progress, there's naught that's poetic about diesel or electric. Who needs speed?'

'Farmers? Passengers?'

'To hell with the blooming passengers. It's got naught to do with them either.'

❦

Because of the forthcoming footballers' dance and the Spring Race meeting the mailbags were filled with parcels – Myers catalogues, new frocks, materials and hats – but Ruth concentrated on the tea-chest with the red address. Its contents were scattered about her feet. Small parcels, calico-wrapped, tied and glued, wax-sealed tins and wads of folded material, that Ruth had never seen before. There were recipes and pictures of foreign food, photographs of thin, elegant ladies and angular men, mannequins smiling in front of famous landmarks of Europe. There were postcards from Paris written in French, opened letters postmarked Tangiers and Brazil, addressed to someone else in Paris, but now sent on for Tilly to read. Ruth found some unusual buttons and matching clasps in a jar, some odd-shaped buckles and yards and yards of fine lace in a wrapped bundle post-marked Brussels, and some books from America – *The Town and The City*, and one by someone called Hemingway. Ruth read a page or two of the Hemingway but found no romance so tossed it aside and removed the tape securing the lid on a small tin before prising it open. She pressed the tip of her long nose into the dried grey-green herb inside. It was sticky, sweet-smelling. She replaced the lid. Next she unscrewed the top from a jar that held a lump of moist brown-black glue-like matter. She scratched at its surface and tasted it. It smelled as it tasted, like molten grass. There was a small jar of fine greyish powder, bitter-smelly, and an old Milo tin containing what looked like dried mud. Someone had scrawled 'Mix with warm water' on the green label.

She held the button jar against her grey post office shirt and dropped it into her jacket pocket, then carried the Milo tin to her cupboard to hide it.

❦

They arrived at the base of The Hill, tired and laden. Molly carried on her lap a pile of groceries, a curtain rod and some material from Pratts. Tilly stood fanning herself with her straw hat. A large, piebald half-draft loped from around the corner dragging a four-wheeled flatbed cart and Teddy McSwiney perched on the corner, the reins looped loosely over his fists. 'Whoa-boy,' he said. The horse stopped beside Tilly and Molly. It sniffed at Tilly's hat, then sighed.

'Want a lift?' said Teddy.

'No thank you,' said Tilly.

Teddy hopped down from the cart and swept Molly Dunnage

from her chariot, bundles and all. He placed her neatly on the trailer in prime position.

'This cart's got the shit of Dungatar spilt all over it,' said Molly. Teddy pushed back his hat and heaved the wheelchair up onto the cart. He grinned at Tilly and slapped the boards behind Molly. She looked at his flat man's hand, resting in a dusty brown smear.

'Leg up?' he said.

Tilly turned to walk up The Hill.

'Safer for Molly if you ride with her.'

'It'd suit her if I fell off,' said Molly.

Teddy leaned in close to Molly and said, 'I'm not surprised.' Tilly placed two hands behind her on the cart and heaved her neat bottom onto the boards beside her mother. Teddy clicked and lightly flipped the reins over the horse's back. They lurched forward, Molly's eyes fixed on the warm round equine rump folding and bobbing two feet from her sensible lace-ups. The horse lifted and swished its tail, whipping at hovering flies, the fine sharp strands of tail hair prickling her shins. He smelled delicious, like hot grass and greasy sweat.

Teddy flicked the reins again. 'We won the grand final, did you hear?'

'Yes,' said Tilly.

'What's the horse's name?' said Molly.

'Graham.'

'Ridiculous.'

They rolled resolutely up, sunshine on their faces and the smell of horse and night cart pungent. Graham stopped at the gatepost in front of the tilted brown house. Tilly headed for the clothes line and Teddy scooped up Molly again and bore her to the front veranda. She put her arms around his neck and fluttered her sparse, grey eyelashes at him. 'I've got a packet of Iced VoVos – care for a cuppa?'

'How could I resist?'

❧

They sat in silence in the kitchen, the VoVos pink and neat on Molly's best plate.

Molly poured the spilt tea from her saucer into her cup. 'I like normal tea. Don't you?'

Teddy looked into his cup. 'Normal tea?'

'She made normal tea for you – she makes me drink tea made from grass and roots. Have another bicky.'

'No thanks, Molly, better leave some for Tilly.'

'Oh she won't eat them. She eats birdseed and fruit and other things she has sent from the city. She gets things from overseas too, from places I've never heard of. She mixes things up – potions – says they're herbs, "remedial", and she pretends to be an arty type, so why would she want to stay here?'

'Arty types need space to create.' He drained his tea, wiped his mouth on his sleeve and leaned back.

'You're just trying to sound as if you understand her.'

'Girls like her need a bloke like me about.'

Molly shook her head. 'I don't want her. She used to think I was her mother but I said to her, "Any mother of yours could only live in a coven,"' then she took her teeth out and put them on her saucer. Tilly came inside and dumped a pile of stiff linen on the table between the conspirators. It smelled of dry sunshine. Molly lifted her teeth to Tilly. 'Rinse those for me,' she said, and looked apologetically at Teddy. 'It's the coconut see.' Tilly ran her mother's teeth under the tap.

'Do they still have those dances here Saturday nights?' lisped Molly innocently. Tilly placed the dentures on the saucer in front of her, then began folding, snapping pillowcases and towels dangerously close to Teddy's left ear.

Teddy leaned forward. 'Footballers' dance this Saturday, we won the grand final –'

'Oh, how lovely.' Molly smiled sweetly at Tilly. Then she looked at Teddy, raised her eyebrows and mouthed a gummy, 'Take her.'

'The O'Brien Brothers provide the music.' He looked to Tilly, who continued folding and smoothing the hard cotton into square piles.

'I hear the O'Brien Brothers are rather good,' said Molly.

'Bonza,' said Teddy, 'Hamish O'Brien on drums, Reggie Blood on fiddle, Big Bobby Pickett plays electric guitar and Faith O'Brien tickles the ivories and sings. Vaughan Monroe and the like.'

'Very flash,' said Molly.

Tilly folded, slap fhutt fhutt slap.

'How about it, Til? Fancy a spin around a polished floor with the handsomest-born dancer in town?'

She looked straight into his twinkling blue eyes. 'I'd love it, if there were such a person.'

❦

Nancy settled on the couch beside the exchange with the eiderdown and pillows. Ruth brought the steaming cup of brown liquid to her. They sniffed it, held it and looked at it.

'It's not Milo,' said Nancy.

'No,' said Ruth. 'Prudence says she must be a herbalist. She read it in a book.'

'I've got salts from Mr A's fridge in case we're sick.' Nancy patted her shirt pocket. 'You go first.'

'Nothing happened when we ate the green, weedy stuff.'

'Slept like babies,' said Nancy.

Ruth looked at the brown drink. 'Come on, we'll drink together.'

They sipped, screwed up their noses. 'We'll just have half,' said Ruth, 'see if anything happens.'

They sat wide-eyed and waiting. 'Anything happening to you?' said Nancy.

'Nothing.'

'Me neither.'

They woke to rapping at the back door. Ruth looked about, touched herself. She was all right, still alive. She went to the door. 'Who is it?'

'Tilly Dunnage.'

Ruth opened the door an inch. 'What do you want?'

'I've lost something, or rather, I never actually got it.'

Ruth's eyes widened. Behind her Nancy crept to stand behind the door.

'It was powder,' said Tilly, 'brownish powder.'

Ruth shook her head. 'We haven't seen it, don't know anything about a tin of powder at all.'

'I see,' said Tilly. Ruth's lips were brown.

Ruth frowned. 'What sort of powder was it?'

'It wasn't important.' Tilly walked away.

'Not poison or anything?'

'It was fertiliser for my plants,' replied Tilly, 'South American Vampire bat dung – the best, because of the blood they suck.'

'Oh,' said Ruth.

As Tilly left (wondering where she could get some more

henna) she could hear retching and feet scurrying about inside. The bathroom light flicked on.

☙

As Tilly was strolling towards Pratts she met Mae at the library corner. Mae was on her way home with pegs and milk.

'Good morning,' she said.

'Morning,' said Mae, and kept walking. Tilly turned to the big red flowers hurrying away and called, 'Thank you for looking out for Molly.'

Mae stopped and turned. 'I didn't do anything, thought that was obvious.'

'You hid the fact that she was . . .' Tilly couldn't bring herself to say the words lunatic or mad because that's what they had used to call Barney. Once some people had come to the school to take him away and lock him up, but Margaret had run and gotten Mae. Someone was always with Barney, even now.

'It's better to keep to yourself around here, you should know,' said Mae, and walked back to Tilly. 'Nothing ever really changes, Myrtle.' She strode away again, leaving Tilly stunned and sobered.

☙

The next day was still and the low clouds sat like lemon butter on toast, keeping the earth warm. Irma Almanac sat on her back porch watching the creek roll away, carrying traces of spring with it. Tilly pushed her mother along the creek bank towards her.

'How are you today?'

'There's rain coming,' Irma replied, 'only enough to settle the dust, though.' The two women sat together on the porch while Tilly made tea. Irma and Molly chatted, carefully avoiding the tender topics they shared – absent babies, brutal men. They talked instead about the rabbit plague, the proposed vaccination for whooping cough, communism and the need to drain kidney beans before and after boiling and before they go into soup because of possible poisoning. Tilly placed some cakes in front of Irma.

'Speaking of poison . . . ,' muttered Molly.

'I made you some special cakes,' said Tilly.

Irma picked one up in her swollen, lumpy fingers and tasted it. 'Unusual,' she said.

'Ever eaten anything Lois Pickett's made?'

'I believe I have.'

'You should be right then,' said Molly.

Irma chewed and swallowed. 'Tell me, why did a beautiful and clever girl like you come back here?'

'Why not?'

🎵

They left well before lunch. Irma felt light and pleased and was sharply conscious of the day's details – the quiet sky and the creek smell, rotting cumbungi and mud – and the warmth of her buffalo grass lawn, mosquitos singing and a faint breeze moving her hair about her ears. She could hear her bones scraping inside her body but they no longer hurt and the aching had stopped. She was eating another cake when Nancy popped her head around the door. 'Here you are, eh?' Irma jumped, then stiffened to wait for the rush of red-hot pain to take her breath away, but it didn't come. Nancy was cross, her brow creased, her hands on her hips. Behind her, Mr Almanac's bald dome taxied slowly through the door frame like the nose of a DC3. Irma giggled.

'You wasn't out the front to stop Mr A here so he'd have

gone bang into the front door if I hadn't rushed over.' Nancy patted Mr A's head.

Tears were streaming down Irma's face and her buckled old body was jigging with laughter. 'I'll just leave it open in future,' she said, and almost whooped and slapped her thigh.

Mr Almanac fell into his chair like a rake falling onto a barrow. 'You're a fool,' he said.

'Right then, I'll leave you to it,' said Nancy, and swaggered out.

'Those Dunnage women have been here,' muttered Mr Almanac.

'Yes,' said Irma cheerfully, 'young Myrtle took my frocks away. She's going to put bigger buttons on them, easier for me to manage.'

'She can never make up for it,' he said.

'She was only a child –'

'You don't know anything,' he said.

Irma looked at her husband, sitting with his face bowed close to the table, his features all hanging like teats on a breeding bitch. She started to laugh again.

❦

That week Teddy McSwiney called up to The Hill three more times. On his first visit he brought yabbies and fresh eggs that Mae had just collected, 'She said if you ever need any, just sing out.' Tilly was relieved but still found urgent work to do in the garden and left him and mad Molly to eat the yabbies – freshly caught, cooked, peeled, wrapped in lettuce and sprinkled with homemade lemon vinegar. He left her share of yabbies in the refrigerator. She ate them late that night before bed, licking the juice from the plate before putting it in the sink.

On the second occasion, Teddy arrived with two Murray cod fillets marinated in a secret sauce and sprinkled with fresh thyme. Tilly went to work on her vegetable patch, but the smell of frying cod brought her inside. The fish melted over their tingling tastebuds and when there was nothing left on their plates, Tilly and Molly put down their fish knife and fork side by side and gazed at the empty plates. Tilly said coolly, 'That was delicious.'

Molly burped and said, 'That's better. You shouldn't be rude to him, his mother saved my life.'

'His mother left food Mrs Almanac made. *I* saved your life.'

'He's a kind young man and he'd like to take you to the dance,' said Molly, and blinked fetchingly at him. He smiled graciously at Molly and raised his glass.

'I don't want to go,' said Tilly, and took the plates to the sink.

'That's right, stay here and torture me, get under my feet, make sure I don't go for help. It's my house, you know.'

'Not going.'

'Not important,' said Teddy, 'she'll only upset my regular partners . . . and everybody else.' He watched Tilly's shoulders stiffen.

⚜

Molly sulked for two days. She didn't look at Tilly and she wouldn't eat. She woke Tilly three times in one night to say, 'I've wet my bed.' Tilly changed the sheets. When she came into the kitchen on the third afternoon with a basket full of dry sheets Molly rolled swiftly at her, scraping a deep gash across her shin with the sharp edge of the footrest.

Tilly said, 'I'm still not going dancing.'

❦

He saw her through binoculars as she sat reading on the veranda step, so hurried up The Hill carrying wine, six blood-red and wrinkly home-grown tomatoes, some onions, parsnips and carrots (still dirt warm), a dozen fresh eggs, a plump chicken (plucked and gutted) and a brand-new cooking pot.

'It came from Marigold's bin,' he said. 'She wouldn't know what to do with it.'

Tilly raised one eyebrow at Teddy. 'Indefatigable, aren't you?'

'It's called a pressure cooker. I'll show you.' He walked past her into the kitchen. Molly wheeled herself to her place at the head of the table, poked a napkin into her collar and smoothed it down the front of her new frock. Teddy began to prepare a chicken-in-wine pot roast. When Tilly stepped into the kitchen Molly said, 'I had a surprise this morning, young man, a phonograph was delivered to me from the railway station. Would you like to listen to some music while you cook?'

Teddy looked at Tilly, his eyes teary and a handful of chopped onions on the board. Tilly hung her sun hat on a nail on the wall and put her hands on her hips.

'She'll do it after she's set the table,' said Molly.

Tilly placed a record on the turntable.

Teddy talked, 'Have either of you read about this new play in America called *South Pacific*? It hasn't been on here yet. I've got a mate can get me a record of it soon as it hits the shores. Would you like one, Molly?'

'It sounds very romantic.'

'Oh, it is, Molly,' said Teddy.

'I hate romance,' Tilly said. Billie Holiday began to sing a song about broken hearts and painful love. Later over the chicken-and-wine pot roast Tilly played some sort of jazz, the likes of which Teddy had never heard and was too afraid to ask about so he said, 'George Bernard Shaw died.'

'Is that so?' asked Tilly. 'JD Salinger's still alive, though, could you ask your friend to get me a copy of *The Catcher in the Rye*? It hasn't been published yet.' Her sarcasm hung in the air.

Molly looked at her, then picked up her steaming bowl of chicken stew and tipped it onto her thighs. The terylene frock Tilly had finished for her that day melted onto her crepe thighs. Tilly froze.

'Now look what you've made me do,' laughed Molly, who then started to shake, shock whistling softly through her thin elastic lips.

Teddy whipped the skirt away from her thighs before it stuck. He looked at Tilly, still frozen at the table. 'Butter,' he snapped. Tilly jumped. He pulled his hip flask from his pocket and poured whisky into the old woman. Then she passed out. He carried her to her bed then left, but was soon back to sit with Tilly. She said nothing, just sat at her mother's bedside looking grim. Barney arrived with a bottle of cream from Mr Almanac and handed it to Teddy. 'I did what you said, I said it wasn't for Mad Molly.'

'Did you say her name?' snapped Teddy.

'You told me not to.'

'So you didn't say her name?'

'No. I said your name, and he said, you gotta put it on tomorra.' Tilly looked at Barney standing in her doorway. 'Tomorra,' he said again. 'He told me to tell you, tomorra.'

Teddy rubbed his brother's shoulders gently. 'All right, Barney.' He turned to Tilly, 'You remember my brother?'

'Thank you for bringing the cream,' she said. Barney blushed and looked at the wall beside him.

When they had gone she sniffed Mr Almanac's cream and threw it away, then gathered some herbs and creams from a trunk under her bed and made a paste to apply. Molly lay in bed naked from the waist down, while two palm-sized red blotches ballooned on her thighs and filled with clear liquid. Tilly emptied her mother's bedpan several times a day, dressed her wounds and did as the old woman bid. The blisters subsided to leave two smarting marks.

9

*O*ut at Windswept Crest, Elsbeth sat rigidly at the bay window, fists clenched, eyes brimming. Mona slunk about the corners of the kitchen wiping shiny surfaces, peeping into the oven and checking container lids while casting sideways glances at her mother.

William was at the pub leaning on the bar, thinking about his mother and the fact that it was tea time. The youths about him drained their beers and zigzagged towards the door, heading for the hall. Scotty Pullit slapped his back. 'Come on, twinkle toes, let's go give the girls a thrill,' and he walked away, bent and coughing.

William stopped outside the post office, jangling some coins in his pocket, looking at the public telephone. He had still not recovered from his meeting with Mr Pratt and the thick file labelled 'Windswept Crest'. Scotty Pullit appeared beside him again and handed him his bottle of clear, boiling watermelon firewater. William took a swig, coughed and gasped then followed Scotty and the other footballers, farmers' sons and daughters into the hall. Inside, balloons and streamers were slung from bearer to bearer. He wandered to the refreshment table, where he and the boys drank punch and smoked. Local girls in twos and threes fluttered to corner tables, twittering and chatting.

The O'Brien Brothers tuned their instruments. Hamish rumbled around his drum kit while his wife stood at the piano, stretching her fingers and humming. Faith was squeezed into a fire engine–red rayon taffeta frock. Her dark brown curls were piled on her head with flowers, à la Carmen Miranda, and plastic roses dangled from her ears. A matching ring covered three knuckles. She wore too much foundation makeup and powder. 'The brassy section,' hissed Beula. She plopped her broad bum and billowing skirt onto a tiny stool, cleared her throat and warbled a flat scale up to a painful high C. Beside her, Reginald – 'Faith's fiddler' – was tearing his bow over the violin strings, struggling to match Faith's notes. Bobby Pickett plucked at his Fender, smiling through his missing tooth as the feedback screamed. Faith tap-tapped the microphone, 'One two one two,' then blew. A shrill electric scream bounced off the rafters. William winced and put his fingers in his ears.

'Good evening and welcome to the Saturday Night shimmer and shuffle with Faithful O'Brien's Band –'

'Och, the Blood and O'Brien *Brothers* Band!' called Hamish.

Faith rolled her eyes, put her hands on generous hips and said through the microphone, 'Hamish, we've been through all this before. None of you are brothers.'

A cymbal clash from Hamish and the musicians struck the first phrase of 'God Save the King'. Everyone stood to attention. It reminded William of his mother so he grabbed Scotty's bottle of watermelon firewater and took a swig to quell his conscience. When the anthem was over, a line of footballers boldly led a girl each to the dance floor, then turned with arms raised, eyes to the picture rail. The band launched into 'Buttons and Bows' and the couples bounced sideways as one, setting sail in a clockwise direction around the hall. Faith O'Brien's family band warmed to a jaunty rendition of 'Sunny Side of the Street'. A lumpy farmer was snatched from William's side by a lass from a neighbouring acreage and they swirled onto the dance floor awash with swaying full skirts, seamed stockings, kicking flat heels and petticoats peeping. Here and there, a frayed wool skirt-suit from ten years ago manoeuvred sedately through the circling frills.

Gertrude Pratt strolled through the door, her cardigan hanging from her shoulders and her purse over her arm. She cruised towards the refreshment table. William turned to grind his Capstan out in the sawdust and leave but found instead that he was facing Gertrude. He looked at the full-faced girl with the soft brown eyes and, smiling apologetically, raised an arm, pointing at the door behind her, saying, 'I was just about to go home . . .'

She stepped forward, took his raised hand in hers and spun him off into the dancers.

William hadn't danced since lessons with Miss Dimm when he was fifteen and awkward. The girl in his arms reminded him of then, except she was surprisingly light on her feet, soft to touch and smelled of perfume. He could feel her hips twist, the warm flesh of her waist move under his palm, her luxurious brown hair against his cheek. He stumbled, trod on her toes and bashed his knees against hers so she held him tighter, closer, and he felt her soft breasts flatten against his lapels. After a while he was reassured by the friendly girl in his arms. She felt like the wake of passing angels, they could have been in heaven.

At the end of the bracket he went to fetch punch. He found Scotty at the refreshment table and drank lavishly from the watermelon firewater bottle. Scotty looked over at Gertrude. 'Reckon she might cost a few bob to run, that one,' he said.

'Well,' said William forlornly, 'I daresay her father's using my money to run her now.' He wished he could somehow get some of it back or raise a loan, just to get started. He wondered if . . . he reached for the watermelon firewater again then made his way over to the table where Gertrude Pratt sat waiting for her punch. 'It's very warm in here,' she said.

'Yes,' said William.

'Shall we go for a stroll outside?' She took William's hand.

❧

The dancers stood poised like frozen champions on trophies, waiting. Barney McSwiney turned Faith's black-spotted pages and the band searched for a common note, thunking, plinking. They saw Tilly Dunnage arrive on the arm of Teddy McSwiney, star full forward, as the two young people stepped inside the door. Then Faith spotted them and the band seized; all heads turned to look. Somewhere a balloon burst.

Tilly kept her eyes to the middle distance. She knew it was a mistake, it was too soon, too bold. A feverish nausea swamped her, guilt, and she said to herself, *It wasn't my fault*, but moved to step back anyway. Teddy held her firm, his arm strong about her waist.

'I can't stay,' she whispered, but he moved forward, steering her across the floor. Couples stood aside and stared at Tilly, draped in a striking green gown that was sculpted, crafted about her svelte frame. It curved with her hips, stretched over her breasts and clung to her thighs. And the material – georgette, two-and-six a yard from the sale stand at Pratts. The girls in their short frocks with pinched waists, their hair stiff in neat circles, opened their pink lips wide and tugged self-consciously at their frothy skirts. The wallflowers sunk further into the wall and a wave of admiring nudges kicked through the young men.

She maintained a stiff expression all the way to the empty table at the side of the hall, right up near the band. She sat while he took her shawl and hung it softly over the back of the chair. Her shoulders were white against the green and a long curl escaped down her neck and hung between her shoulder blades.

Teddy went to the refreshment counter. The crowd of men allowed him through. He bought her a punch, himself a beer and sat down next to her. They looked up at the band. The band looked back. Tilly raised a single eyebrow to Faith. Faith blinked and turned to her keyboard, and in a second the din had resumed. The band ground its way into, 'If You Knew Suzie, Like I Knew Suzie, (Oh Oh)'.

Teddy leaned back, slung one shin over his knee and stretched an arm across the back of Tilly's chair. She was trembling. He nudged her. 'Let's dance.'

'No.' She kept her face to the band all night. She pressed the guilt down again until it churned in her stomach. She was used to it, used to forgetting and enjoying herself then suddenly remembering, suddenly feeling unworthy. No one came near the star full forward or his partner that night. She was glad; it was easier that way.

❦

When it was clear William would not be home for tea Mona read for a while, floodlit beneath yellow lamplight in the corner. The quiet, dull drone of the radiogram wound through the house. Elsbeth Beaumont remained, silhouetted in the bay window with the bright moonlight edging the line of her nose.

Mona said, 'I think I might go to bed now, Mother.' Her

mother ignored her. Mona closed the bedroom door behind her firmly. She crossed to her dressing table and picked up her hand mirror. She closed the blinds, adjusted her bedside lamp, slid off her limp rayon panties and lifted her skirt. She perched on the edge of her bed holding a mirror angled to her and studied the purple black fronds of her groin, smiling at the dark fig puckers. Then she undressed slowly, watching herself in the mirror, letting her petticoat straps fall from her shoulders to tumble about her ankles. She caressed her breasts, and ran her hands over her throat. Then, beneath her terylene bedspread, Mona Beaumont reached her quiet, evening orgasm.

※

On the banks of the Dungatar creek William, erect and eager, rubbed hard up against Gertrude Pratt's warm round thigh. Reaching for his fly he could think of only one thing to say. 'Gertrude, I love you.'

'Yes,' said Gertrude, and opened her legs a little wider. Gertrude Pratt won William Beaumont by allowing him to insert the middle finger of his right hand between the shifting crepe moisture of her purple inner labia minor to where the tightness closed, not quite to the bud.

※

William arrived at Windswept Crest flushed and grateful. His mother still sat in the bay window, the early-morning light behind her. 'Good morning, Mother,' he said.

She turned to him with tears seeping down her linen cheeks, dripping onto the marcasite peacock pinned to her breast. 'I've been waiting for you all night.'

'S' not necessary, Mother.'

'You've been drinking.'

'I'm a man, now, Mother, and it's Saturday night – at least it was.'

Elsbeth sniffed and dabbed her eyes with her hanky.

'I had . . . fun. Next time I'll insist Mona come with me,' he said, and whistled off to his room.

❦

Teddy McSwiney walked Tilly home and saw her to her door.

'Good night,' she said.

'It wasn't so bad, was it?'

She pulled her shawl about her shoulders.

'I can look after you . . .' He smiled and leaned towards her.

She had tied her tobacco into her scarf and turned away to search for it in the folds.

'. . . that is, if you want me to.'

She stuck a rolling paper to her lip and held her tobacco tin. 'Good night,' she said, and opened the back door.

'They'll just have to get used to you,' he said, and shrugged.

'No,' she said, 'I'll have to get used to them.' She closed the door behind her.

II

Shantung

A fabric woven plainly with irregular wild silk yarn,
having a textured effect. Its natural cream colour is
often dyed in strong colours, producing a vibrant effect.
Slightly crisp to handle and with a soft lustre.
Suitable for dresses, blouses and trims.

———

Fabrics for Needlework

10

Sergeant Farrat sat nipple-deep in steaming water, the alarm clock ticking and the hot tap dripping. At the edges of his wet pink body floated sprigs of rosemary (to stimulate clarity of mind) and lemon grass (for added fragrance). He'd lathered raw duck egg into his hair and snotty streaks of it slid down his forehead, merging at the ends of his white eyebrows with the aloe vera pulp face mask. A cup of camomile tea and a note pad rested on the soap stand suspended across the bath in front of him. He sucked on a pencil, pondering the frock sketched on the note pad. It needed a feather – a peacock feather perhaps.

The alarm clock rang. He had an hour before Beula would arrive, full of hate and accusations about the goings on at the dance. He held his nose and sank into the brown water, scrubbing the beauty preparations from his submerged body. He struggled out of the bath, his bottom squeezing against the enamel, and stood, his tomato scrotum hanging long and steaming. He reached for a towel and padded dripping to his bedroom to dress and prepare for the week ahead.

❦

When Beula Harridene arrived and started banging at his office door, the sergeant was leaning on the counter peering at the small instructions in his knitting catalogue, *Quaker Girl*, for a pattern of an Italian jumper designed by BIKI of Milan. He was muttering, 'No. 14 needles cast on 138 sts., work 3½ ins in k. 1, p. 1 rib Inc. thus: K. 21, (k. 11, inc. in next st) 8 times . . .' A thread of fine wool stretched over his fat index finger, and two thin metallic needles rested in his palms, held aside. Sergeant Farrat had on his police uniform and thin, pale pink socks and delicate apricot ballet slippers tied gently around his firm ankles with white satin. He ignored Beula and continued to ponder the stitches petalled beneath the needles, then the pattern. Finally he put them down, pirouetted to his bedroom and put on regulation socks and shoes. Then he unlocked the office door and resumed his position behind the desk while Beula fell in behind him yakking.

'. . . and the fornication that occurred in this town on Saturday night – Sergeant Farrat – was vile and repulsive. My word there'll be trouble when I tell that Alvin Pratt about his daughter –'

'Do you knit, Beula?'

Beula blinked. He turned the catalogue and pushed it towards her. She looked down at the pattern, her chin receding into her neck.

'I need you to write down for me in plain English what these abbreviations really mean.' He leaned to her ear and whispered, 'Code. I'm trying to de-code a message from HQ. Top secret, but I know you're good at secrets.'

❦

At the chemist shop Nancy gently positioned Mr Almanac so that he faced the open front door. She gave him a small shove and he trotted inertia-powered, favouring the left. Nancy threw her hands to her ears and grimaced. Mr Almanac collided with a table, ricocheted and came to rest against the wall like a leaning ladder.

'Why don't you let me go get the mail today, Mr A?'

'I enjoy my morning walk,' he said.

Nancy worked his stiff body out the door onto the footpath and faced him the right way, then gently prodded him forward.

'Stick to the middle crack.' She watched his headless, stooped body totter away then ran inside and picked up the phone.

Ruth stood by her electric kettle steaming open a fat letter addressed to Tilly Dunnage. She heard the buzz and went to her exchange. Picking up the headphones, she twisted the cone to her mouth, stretched the cord and plugged into the chemist shop. 'Nance?'

''S' Nance, yep, he's on his way.'

Ruth went back to her kettle, held the envelope over the steam, eased the last of the seal free and slipped the letter out. It was written in Spanish. She put it back in her delivery bag, collected Mr Almanac's mail and moved to the door. Unlocking it, she slapped up the blinds, flipped the 'OPEN' sign, and went out to stand on the footpath. Mr Almanac shuffled towards her straight down the line.

'Morning.' She placed her hand on his shiny dome. He marked time with his feet until the 'Stop' signal from his brain made its way to them.

'Good morning,' he said, an elastic line of saliva settling

between his shoes. Ruth placed a brown-paper-and-string bundle under one stiff arm, inched him about-face and pushed at his shoulder blades with an index finger. He shuffled off again.

'Stay on that middle line now.'

Outside the chemist shop a block away, Nancy stopped sweeping and waved to her friend. Reginald skipped into the chemist, beckoning Nancy to follow.

'What can I do for you, Reg?'

Reg looked pained. 'I need something for a . . . rash,' he whispered.

'Show me,' said Nancy.

Reg grimaced. 'It's more like chafing, raw . . .'

'Oh,' said Nancy, and nodded knowingly, 'something soothing.'

'Soothing,' said Reg, and watched her open Mr Almanac's fridge. 'I'll take two big jars,' he said.

❦

Muriel was rubbing a polishing cloth back and forth over the petrol bowsers in front of the shop when Beula Harridene marched up to her, red and bothered.

'Hello, Beula.'

'That Myrtle Dunnage, or Tilly she calls herself now, went to the dance Saturday night.'

'You don't say.'

'With that Teddy McSwiney.'

'You don't say?' said Muriel.

'You'll never guess what she wore, or almost wore: a green tablecloth she bought from you. Just wound it about her. Didn't hide a thing. Everybody was speechless with disgust. She's up to no good again that one, worse than her mother.'

'I dare say,' said Muriel.

'And guess who Gertrude was with, *all night*.'

'Who?'

Just then William drove slowly past in his mother's old black monstrosity. As they turned to watch he lifted two fingers on the steering wheel, inclined his hat and glided on.

Muriel looked at Beula and folded her arms. Beula nodded. 'Mark my words, Muriel, he'll have her out behind the cemetery before you know it.'

❧

Lois was on her knees, one grimy arm wrist-deep in a bucket of warm soapy water, the floor around her wet and shiny. She was a squat woman with an adipose apron that bounced on her thighs when she walked. Her short grey hair featured a permanent cocky's crest and scattered snowy flakes of sticky scalp all over her shoulders. She was sweating, salt water dripping from the end of her blood-rushed nose, yet she had washed just one square yard of Irma Almanac's floor.

Irma was heading for her spot, her rusty knuckles working the wheels of her chair, her bones grating like chalk on a blackboard. As she inched towards the fire hearth, her axle squeaked.

'Where's your butter, Irmalove?' said Lois.

Irma inclined with her blue eyes to the fridge. Lois attacked the sprockets and joins of the wheelchair with butter then shunted it back and forth, back and forth. Not a squeak, but Irma winced and her eyes grew watery.

'Need some for your bones, Irmalove?'

Irma watched Lois wipe away at her floor. She wished she had the strength to tell her to put the chairs up on the table and wash under it – that patch of floor hadn't been washed since Lois had been hired to 'clean' the house years ago.

'How was the dance?' she asked.

'Well. I'm not gossipin' or anythink . . .'

'No.'

'. . . but that Myrtle Dunnage who calls herself Tilly these days, well she's got a nerve I tell you, turned up wearing a very bold frock – obscene – and followed Teddy McSwiney around all night. It's a bad lot it is, if you ask me. I'm not saying anythink just like I'm not saying anythink about Faif O'Brien and her goings on but that Tilly will cause more trouble, you just wait. Apparently young Gertrude Pratt and that William spent the whole night wif each other . . .'

'Gertrude, you say?'

'. . . and Nancy tells me that Beula told her that she finks Gertrude's getting married now. Can you imagine Elsbef?'

11

The morning sun shone on Sergeant Farrat's back as he sat on his back porch, eating breakfast. He held the tip of a banana, steadying the curve against a plate and slit it down the centre, then dissected it at one-inch intervals. He put his knife down and carefully peeled back the skin using a dainty dessert fork, then popped a small half moon into his mouth and chewed quickly. He'd heard about the green dress and wondered if he could ask Tilly for an ostrich feather. He ate some toast and marmalade, then brushed the crumbs from his outfit – a Rita Hayworth ensemble that he'd copied from a magazine picture of Rita's marriage to Aly Khan. He'd given his hat a bigger brim – 18 inches – and edged it with pale blue net and white crepe paper roses. He sighed; it would have been perfect for the Spring race meeting.

Up on The Hill, Tilly was bent over her machine sewing a six-inch zipper to the bodice of a deep amethyst frock, her expert fingers guiding the cloth over the grinding needle plate. Molly came into the kitchen, and as she moved towards the back door swept the salt and pepper shakers, a vase of dried herbs and an incense burner from the bench with her walking stick. Tilly continued to sew. Outside, Molly steadied herself against the veranda post and watched a figure approaching: a young man swinging his arms high to counter a club foot enormously booted at the end of his withered leg. At the gate he removed his battered hat and stood hot-smelling and grinning widely, despite a face rashed with yellow-topped red spots. His mouth was small and he had too many teeth. His jacket was tight and his shorts loose.

'Mrs Dunnage?'

'I know,' she said.

Barney's smile dropped. 'It's me, Barney.'

'Are we related?'

'No.'

'Thank heavens.'

'I'd like to see Tilly, please.'

'What on earth makes you think she'd like to see you?'

Barney blinked and swallowed. His face fell and he crushed his hat in his fists.

'Hello, Barney.' Tilly stood behind Molly. She smiled at him.

'Oh good,' he said, then noticed she wore only a short vivid blue silk petticoat. He stepped from one foot to the other and back again, dipping sadly on his club foot.

'Did Teddy send you?'

'Yes.'

'Barney . . .' She came down the step towards him, and he stepped back. 'Will you please go back and tell Teddy I said I didn't want to go to the races with him and I meant it?'

'Yeah, I know, but I thought you might like to go with me. Please.' He bobbed again, punching his hat.

As Molly opened her mouth Tilly turned and put her hand over it. 'I don't care if you kill yourself, Molly, I'm not going,' she said. Molly's burned thighs still smarted in a warm bath.

Tilly turned back to the crestfallen lad. 'It's not that I don't want to go with you –'

'Nonsense, it is. It's because you're a spastic,' chirped Molly.

Tilly looked at the ground and counted to ten then she looked back into Barney's hurt face, his small blue eyes brimming with tears. 'If you'd care to step inside to wait while I hem my frock, Barney? I'll only keep you a minute.' She turned back to her mother, 'You'll keep.'

'I'll hardly go rotten,' she said, and smiled at Barney. 'Come inside, laddy, I'll make you a cup of tea. Don't let her make anything for you, she's a sorceress. It must be a great nuisance dragging a club foot about with you – have you got a hump on your back too?'

❧

Sergeant Farrat stood at the mirror, stripped to his new Alston high-waisted rubber reducing wrap-around girdle, styled 'to inhibit the spare tyre while controlling the diaphragm'. He dressed carefully, then picked up his box Brownie camera, admiring his slimmer reflection. He caught sight of Rita Hayworth's ensemble flung across the bed behind him and frowned.

❧

The grandstand was full, everyone waiting for the next race. Elsbeth looked uncomfortable in the warm, horse-filled air. William Beaumont appeared with Gertrude Pratt on his arm and Alvin following. The spectators stopped fanning their race forms to watch. Mona gasped and Elsbeth's hand shot to the marcasite brooch at her throat. She turned away and raised her opera glasses and looked earnestly at the distant, empty barrier. Mona covered her mouth with her hanky and moved closer to her mother. William, Gertrude and Alvin made their way through the crowd and sat down next to Elsbeth. Alvin smiled broadly at Elsbeth and saluted her while Gertrude fixed her smile at some point past the tree tops and William smiled cordially at the staring people in the stand.

Then Alvin said, 'Have you placed a bet, Elsbeth?'

'I don't gamble,' she said.

Alvin gave a short laugh. 'I see, just here for a stickybeak then?'

Elsbeth took her binoculars away from her eyes and gave them to Mona.

Alvin continued happily, 'I think I'll have a wager on number thirteen, *Married Well*.'

The spectators started fanning their race forms again, slowly. Elsbeth screeched, 'That would naturally be, *on the nose*.'

Gertrude reddened, and William bit his bottom lip and stared at his shoelaces. Alvin stood up, cleared his throat and said very, very clearly, 'Since I was sure we would meet here, Mrs Beaumont, I took the opportunity to bring with me your unpaid accounts . . . of the last two years.'

He opened his jacket and reached inside to his pocket. 'I thought I'd save postage. You know how it is.' She snatched the fat wad of invoices from his hand. Gertrude stood and marched off through the parting crowd.

William stood up next to Alvin and glared at his mother. 'Bother you,' he said, and rushed through the straw hats, bretons and berets, the white gloved hands flapping their race forms madly in his wake.

❦

Tilly arrived at the kitchen table in her new dress and wide-brimmed straw hat. Barney stood rapidly, upending his chair. He swallowed. He had coconut and pink icing stuck to the tip of his extra long chin. Tilly stood backlit in the grey kitchen wearing the bright amethyst dress. It was made from shantung and had a low, square neck and firm bodice that continued down, pulling firmly across her thighs. At her knees, short tiers of gathered satin skirts kicked and swam. Her arms and legs were bare and Barney thought her black strappy sandals must be difficult to balance on.

'Barney,' said Tilly, 'I think it's only fair that you know something. Your brother sent you to ask me to the races so that he could take me from you when we get there, then he'll give you some money to get rid of you. Do you think that's right?'

'No. That's wrong. I made him give me the money already.' Teddy was waiting at the library corner in a very old but very shiny Ford when Tilly – her brilliant, silky dress shimmering in the sunshine – strolled by on the arm of bobbing Barney. They chatted intensely as they passed on the creek bank opposite him and continued to ignore him as he puttered beside them all the way down Oval Street to the football ground, which became a race track or cricket pitch off season. The women in their sensible floral cotton button-throughs with box cluster pleat skirts stopped to stare. Their mouths dropped and their eyebrows rose as they pointed and whispered, *Thinks she's royalty.* Tilly made her way to the stables on Barney's arm. Teddy walked beside them, smiling and tipping his hat to the gawking townsfolk. The three of them turned their backs to the crowd and leaned on the stable fence to watch the horses. Barney said, 'My best friend Graham, he's a horse.'

'So are you,' mumbled Teddy.

'I like horses,' said Tilly.

'Mum says I'm not quite finished. Dad said I'm only five bob out of ten.'

'People say things about me too, Barney.' Faint sibilant sounds reached them and Teddy heard Tilly say, very quietly, 'We could go home if you like.' He turned to face the women behind them. They were standing about in pairs and bunches, leaning together, glancing down at their own frocks – pale spun rayon prints, shoulder pads, swathed waists, prominent bust lines, high prim collars, three-quarter sleeves, tweed suits, gloves and dumpy, eye-veiling head-hugging hats.

It was the purple dress. They were discussing Tilly's dress.

'There's no need to leave,' said Teddy.

Gertrude Pratt came forward and stepped between Tilly and Barney. 'Did you make that dress?' she asked.

Tilly turned to look at her and said cautiously, 'Yes. I'm a dressmaker. You know Barney, don't you?' Tilly indicated Barney shuffling at Gertrude's back.

'Everyone knows Barney,' said Gertrude dismissively. Her eyes did not move from Tilly's face. It was an unusual face with downy alabaster skin. She looked like someone out of a movie and the air around her seemed different.

'Ah-ha, there you are, Gertrude!' It was Sergeant Farrat.

She turned to him. 'My, what a pretty umbrella.'

'Yes, lost property. William is looking for you, Gertrude. I believe you'll find he's over at the –'

Gertrude swung to face Tilly again. 'The sergeant means William Beaumont. William and I are engaged, almost.'

'Congratulations,' said Tilly.

'So you're a trained dressmaker?'

'Yes,' said Tilly.

'Where did you train?'

'Overseas.'

'Here he comes towards us now,' said Sergeant Farrat.

Gertrude moved quickly to intercept her boyfriend, grabbing hold of the tall young man to drag him away.

'You look extremely fetching, Tilly,' said Sergeant Farrat, beaming, but Tilly was watching Gertrude's young man and he was watching her.

'I remember him,' said Tilly.

'He used to wet his pants at school,' said Teddy.

William thought the tall girl with the unusual face and strong shoulders was striking. A McSwiney stood either side of her, like sentries at a luminous statue.

Gertrude tugged at William's arm. 'Is that . . . ?' he asked.

'Myrtle Dunnage and the McSwineys. They deserve each other.'

'I heard she was back,' said William, staring. 'She's quite beautiful.' Gertrude pulled his arm again. He looked down at his round, brown-eyed girlfriend, her eyes and nose red from crying, the sun in her face.

❦

That night Gertrude lay on the back seat of the car with her knees flopped open. William was elbow deep in her petticoats, his mouth jammed over hers panting through his nose when she wrenched her face away and said, 'It's time to go in.'

'Yes!' said William, and reached for his fly.

'*No!*' said Gertrude, and pushed at his shoulders. She struggled, feeling about in the dark with William still oozing all over her, sucking at her neck. She crawled out from under him and was gone. William was left engorged, panting and alone in his mother's car. He scratched his head, straightened his tie and sighed. He drove to the Station Hotel but there was no sign of life. The soft yellow light at the top of The Hill burned, so he drove towards it, stopping at the base to smoke a cigarette. Mona said the Dunnage girl had apparently travelled and was driving Miss Dimm spare, always at the library ordering in strange books. Ruth Dimm said she even received a French newspaper in the mail every month.

He drove home. His mother was waiting. 'Why?' she cried.

'Why not?'

'You can't marry her, she's a heifer!'

'I can if I like,' said William, and raised his chin.

Elsbeth stood looking at her only son and shrieked, 'You've been had – and it doesn't take too much imagination to work out how.'

William's voice rose to the Beaumont shrill. 'I want a future, a life –'

'You've got a life.'

'It's not mine!' William stomped off towards his room.

'*No!*' his mother wailed.

He turned. 'It's either her or Tilly Dunnage.'

Elsbeth collapsed into a chair. On his way past Mona's room, William called, 'And you should find someone too, sister.'

Mona's wet rubbing halted under her blankets and she bit the sheet.

William went to see Alvin Pratt the next day and by evening all had been arranged for William to marry down, thus reinstating his mother to her rightful place.

12

Marigold Pettyman, Lois Pickett, Beula Harridene and Faith O'Brien were standing at Pratts' vacant window. Alvin had removed the specials advertisements from the glass two days ago. Purl, Nancy and Ruth joined the gathering crowd. Finally Alvin, dusty and scone-coloured, leaned into his window, scooped away a few dead blowies and rested a catalogue open on a page featuring five richly illustrated wedding cakes. Beside it he placed a two-tiered, elaborately decorated and perfect wedding cake on a silver tray. He smiled lovingly at his beautiful creation before carefully closing the lace curtains hanging behind.

Inside, Muriel, Gertrude and Tilly leaned together over the haberdashery counter flicking through a magazine. Molly sat beside them in her wheelchair, watching out the door.

'Lois Pickett always looks like a tea-stained hanky,' she said.

Tilly gave her a black look.

'And we all know how unbalanced Marigold Pettyman is, these days.'

The wedding gown they were looking at was strapless with an overly clinched waist held by a bunchy satin sash which gave way to an overskirt of unspectacular beaded net. At the bodice top there was another bunch of satin, a bow, fit to camouflage any cleavage.

Gertrude pointed to a picture and said, 'That one, I like that one.'

'It's beautiful, Gert,' said Muriel, and stepped back to picture her daughter wearing the white wedding gown.

'It'll hide those thighs of yours,' said Molly. Tilly pushed her mother over to hardware and parked her in front of a shelf full of boxes of nails. Molly was right about the thighs, but Gertrude had a waist Tilly could emphasise, which would also help with her hips. Then there was the square bottom and shapeless down-pipe legs and matching arms, and under that cardigan Gertrude was hirsute, so bare skin was out of the question. She also had a pigeon chest. Tilly looked again at the gown. 'Oh no,' she said, 'we can do much better than that,' and Gertrude caught her breath.

❦

Teddy was leaning on the bar and Purl was telling him all about the wedding,

'. . . so of course Elsbeth's furious, Ruth said she hasn't posted the invitations yet but Myrtle Dunnage phoned Winyerp and ordered six yards of cloth and five yards of lace. It should arrive Friday.'

'Friday?' repeated Teddy.

'By train.'

Teddy arrived on the veranda at The Hill that evening and talked about the poor mail service around Christmas and how Hamish complained the new diesel trains were always late. Tilly leaned on the doorjamb, crossed her arms and raised one eyebrow.

'. . . and I understand it's a hasty decision, on William's part,' he said, 'a very hasty decision.'

'So you think Gertrude needs her wedding dress as soon as possible?'

'I don't, but I bet Gertrude thinks that so she can tell him as soon as possible that it's all stitched up.'

'Perhaps we should leave it to the trains, and fate.'

'No one would ever know how well you can sew.' He put his hands in his pockets and looked at the stars. 'And I happen to be driving to Winyerp tomorrow.' He looked at her. 'Molly might like the drive. Ever been for a ride in a car, Molly?'

'They don't look much chop to me,' she said.

Teddy said he'd be leaving about eight.

When he got to his car the next morning she was already sitting in it, lovely in her deep cloche and dark glasses. She looked at her watch and waved a fly away. 'Hello,' said Teddy. He left her alone and dropped her off at nine with a plan to meet her at the pub at noon. At lunch he shouted her a plate of vegetables and a stout and took her parcels for her, leaving her free all afternoon. He dropped her home at dusk. When she went inside she found Molly had dismantled her sewing machine entirely. It took her three days to find all the parts and put them back together.

A week before Christmas Tilly sat hunched over her sewing machine at the kitchen table, happy to be creating again. Molly was in her wheelchair beside the stove unravelling the jumper she was wearing, a crinkly nest of wool gathering over her knees. Tilly glanced at the woolly pile. 'Why are you doing that?' she said.

'I'm hot.'

'Move away from the fire.'

'I don't want to.'

'Please yourself.'

She pressed down firmly on the electric treadle. Molly reached for the stove poker and hid it under her knee rug then slowly pushed at her wheels.

Tilly's fingers guided the slippery surface beneath the speeding foot, the needle racing. Molly fumbled about under her knee rug, found the poker, raised it high and let it fall on Tilly's head just as Teddy rapped at the screen door. He heard a yelp, then someone stumbling.

He found Tilly standing in the corner holding the back of her head. Molly sat innocently by the fire unravelling thread from her jumper. On the floor by the table satin and lace lay heaped like cloud cushions.

'What happened?'

'She hit me,' said Tilly.

'I did not.'

'You did. You hit me with the poker.'

'Liar. You're just trying to have me put away. You're the dangerous one, you killed my possum.' Molly began to weep.

'He moved back to the tree because of the chimney smoke, you can see him any time you like.' She rubbed her head.

'If you weren't always stirring away at your cauldron.'

Teddy looked from one to the other, then went to Molly and rubbed her bony back and handed her his hanky. 'There, there,' he said.

Molly fell against him, howling. He handed her his hip flask. 'I've got just the thing.' She grabbed it and put it to her lips.

Teddy moved to Tilly and reached for her. 'Show me.'

'It's all right.' She pulled farther into the corner but he persisted. He pushed his fingers into her glorious hair and felt around her warm scalp. 'You've got an egg on your head.' He turned back to Molly just as she shoved his hip flask down the front of her nightie.

'Give me that.'

'Get it yourself.'

Teddy screwed his face up. Tilly dived down her mother's nightie with two hands, retrieving the flask and handing it to Teddy.

'It's empty,' he said.

Tilly heaped Gertrude's wedding dress back onto the table.

'I came to invite both of you for a Christmas drink to-morrow night, but . . .' He looked sideways at Molly and shook his flask one more time.

'I'd love to come,' said Molly then burped.

'I'm not going,' said Tilly.

'That's all right. He'll come and fetch me, won't you, sonny?'

⚜

He did come to fetch her and he brought roses to Tilly. A huge bunch of velvet-skinned, scarlet-black roses that smelled thickly of sugar, summer and misty creek water. Tilly was amazed.

'I risked my life to get these for you last night.'

'Which garden – Beula or Sergeant Farrat?'

Teddy winked. 'Come for a drink?'

'No.'

'Just one.'

'I really appreciate you taking Molly off my hands for an hour or so, I really do.'

'You can still come.'

'It'll be nice to be by myself.'

Molly was at the veranda step. 'Come on then,' she called, 'leave her to sulk.'

From the back step Teddy pleaded one more time. 'Come on, please? We're having a high old time down by the tip, pile of presents from Santa under the tree for the kids, all down there screeching about.'

She smiled, closed the door and said softly, 'That would break my heart.'

13

*E*lsbeth took to her bed and refused to have anything to do with the wedding plans. William despaired a little, but things just seemed to go ahead. Mr Pratt restored the credit account so he was able to think seriously about developing the property; buy some star pickets and mend a few fences to start with, a new tractor, next season's crop, there would be children, a family to raise, and Gertrude would adjust, learn . . .

He read her a sonnet – Shakespeare, number 130. 'What did you think of that, dear?'

'What?'

'It was Shakespeare, William Shakespeare.'

'Lovely.'

'Yes – what did you especially like about it, Gertrude?'

'Most poems are too long; that one wasn't.'

They were standing beneath a halo of moths skipping about the light globe above the Pratts' back door. William moved his hat brim around and around in his hands and said, 'Mona says the invitations are all ready to go . . .'

Mona had never dreamed she'd ever be anyone's bridesmaid. Since Elsbeth would not provide a guest list, Mona supplied

Gertrude with one – she simply named every relative and school chum William ever had.

'. . . I'd rather hoped for a small wedding, I hadn't realised –'

'Kiss me, William, you haven't kissed me in ages,' Gertrude pouted.

He pecked her on the cheek but she reached for him.

'Gertrude, I've got to tell you, to say, um, I know you've got your frock and everything –'

'It's a gown, William, a gown.'

'– and the arrangements are going so, well, quickly – you're doing an exemplary job it seems. I just wonder, because this is meant to be for life, I just . . . it was so hurried and . . . well, if you're not sure you'll be happy with me out there with Mother, and Mona, there'd be no harm waiting – until we're more secure, not so busy, after harvest . . . we can easily . . . I'd understand.'

Gertrude's chin contracted and dimpled and her eyes puckered like burst apricots. 'But you, I mean we . . . I'd never have . . . I thought you loved me. What about my reputation?' A light flicked on at the front of the house. Gertrude slumped to the wooden floor boards and sat among the old shoes and gardening tools with her hands over her face. William sighed and bent down to her. He rubbed her shoulder.

❧

He was studying his shoelaces when he sensed fussing at the church door. The guests turned to look and an ooh swept through the crowd. William closed his eyes and Faith played 'Here Comes The Bride'. William took a deep breath, then opened his eyes to look down the aisle. The deep lines across his brow fell away and the colour rose in his cheeks, his shoulders relaxed and he bounced on his toes. Nerves, it had all been nerves. She looked lovely. Her dark chestnut locks were swept up in a poised wave and held secure with a row of luscious pink roses, her eyes sparkling, velvet brown. Her neck looked slender and her skin peachy. She stood there in a fine silk taffeta gown, apricot pink, scoop necked – not too scooped – with sheer off-white tulle three-quarter-length sleeves. The bodice was wrapped firmly about her waist and gathered snugly around her hips, culminating in a large soft bow below her bottom, before falling to swing elegantly. Ribbons hung from the bow and trailed a full three yards as she walked slowly towards him, the silk taffeta flowing thinly about her legs. Gertrude Pratt looked curvy and succulent and she knew it. Mona crept behind her, hunched and trembling. Her hair fell in soft curls about her shoulders and was crowned with rusty dewy roses that complemented perfectly her scoop-necked gown of rust-orange silk taffeta. It was cut to emphasise the few curves Mona had. The silk gathered about her thighs and flared slightly at her knees. Her sloping shoulders supported an off-white tulle cowl which fell to a large bold loop at the small of her back. The bride and bridesmaid clutched enormous clusters of brightly co-loured roses. The women noted as they passed that the dress-maker was an absolute wizard with fabric and scissors. Gertrude looked at William beaming back at her and knew she was safe.

Elsbeth sat stone-faced in the front pew. She had risen from her bed only when William's chums from university and all her relatives arrived cheering and ra-rahhing about the jolly big occasion. Her fashionable cousin Una from Melbourne leaned to her and said, 'Exquisite,' then smiled approvingly. Elsbeth turned around doubtfully, then swelled. Her chin went up and she assumed her 'I-can-smell-dog-dirt-on-someone's-boot' expression. 'Yes,' she said to her cousin, 'my daughter-in-law's family are in business, they move in commercial circles.' Gertrude stood shining and assured on her proud father's arm at the altar. Muriel burst into tears, became flushed and breathless and was assisted outside where she removed her girdle. She missed the ceremony.

Afterwards the attractive bridal party stood in bursting sunshine and beamed at the clucking box Brownie shutters. Small girls in pretty dresses hung lace horseshoes on Gertrude's arm while Sergeant Farrat pumped William's arm with serious vigour for a long time – he was noting the fine detail on the gowns. Gertrude and William paused at the Triumph Gloria to wave at the stickybeaks – Purl and Fred, Lois, Nancy, Ruth and her sister Miss Dimm and Beula, all gathered along the fence in their housecoats and slippers. Muriel had wanted to include her lifelong friends and loyal customers in her only daughter's wedding day, but Gertrude said simply, 'We'll have Councillor and Marigold Pettyman and the Sergeant – but we needn't bother with the others.'

At the hall the guests boiled happily together at bleached damask tablecloths beneath crepe peonies and satin ribbon. The CWA ladies poured the champagne for the toast, beer for the men and wine for the women, and served cold chicken salad for tea followed by pavlova.

Tilly Dunnage arrived just in time for the speeches. She stood in the darkness outside the back door and peeped over the top of the seated guests. William rose from his seat to clink a spoon against his glass. He was flushed and jubilant and started, 'There comes a time in every chap's life . . .' He thanked his mother, his deceased father, his sister, Mr and Mrs Pratt, his beautiful, radiant bride, the army of caterers and friends helping with the refreshments, without whom none of this would have been possible, the Minister for his fine words, Sergeant Farrat and Miss Beula Harridene for the splendid flowers. He ended with, '. . . and that just about covers everyone, so without further ado, I will now propose a toast . . .' and fifty chairs scraped as one as the guests stood to join him in an upright toast to King and Country, the Prime Minister, The Happy Occasion and The Future. Hear hear.

Every female seated in the War Memorial Hall that afternoon had listened hard, waited with bated breath for the name of a seamstress or dressmaker. She wasn't mentioned.

❀

At home, Tilly sat by the fire with a glass of beer and a cigarette, thinking about her schooldays with dumpy little Gertrude, who had had to wear extra elastic in her plaits because her hair was so thick. At lunchtime Tilly would sit on a wood bench at the boundary of the playground and watch the boys play cricket. In the far corner little Gertrude, Nancy, Mona and some other girls would play hoppy.

A rubber cricket ball bounced and rolled past her. Stewart Pettyman called, 'Get it, Dunnybum, get it!'

Another boy called, 'No no, she'll take it into the girls' toilet again!'

'Yeah, then we can get her again!'

They all started shouting, 'Get the ball Dunnybum and we'll get you, get the ball Dunnybum and we'll fill your mouth with poo.' The girls joined in. Myrtle ran inside.

After school Myrtle ran, but he was waiting, blocking her way at the library corner. He grabbed her around the neck, dragged her down beside the library, held her by the throat against the wall and rubbed her fanny hard under her panties. Myrtle couldn't breathe and vomit rose. It burned in her nose.

When he finished he looked into her eyes, like a red devil. He was wet and smelled hot, like wee. He said, 'Stand really really still, Dunnybum, or I'll come around to your house tonight and I'll kill your mother the slut, and when she's dead I'll get you.'

Myrtle stood still, up against the wall. He walked backwards looking at her with his devil eyes. Myrtle knew what he was going to do, it was his favourite. He put his head down like a bull and ran ran ran at her as fast as he could, head first at her tummy, like a bull charging. Myrtle sucked in her tummy and closed her eyes – he could just kill her.

She decided to die.

Then she changed her mind.

She stepped sideways.

The boy ran head first, full pelt into the red brick library wall. He crumpled and fell onto the hot dry grass.

❦

Molly wheeled in. She'd grown fond of her chair and had decorated it. As she sat by the fire or in the sun on the veranda, she tied bits of wool thread and plaited ribbons over the armrests, wove climbing geraniums through the spokes, and shoved several small square knitted rugs about the seat-cushion. When the whim took her she would abandon her colourful wheelchair for her walking stick and wander around the house prodding about in crockery cupboards, dislodging curtain rails or scraping objects onto the floor from bench tops. She parked at the hearth next to the girl who was staring into the fire. 'How was the ball, Cinderella?' she asked.

'The gowns were wonderful.' She told herself she couldn't expect anything from this town. 'It was a wedding.'

'Shame.'

⚘

Gertrude stepped out of her wedding gown and hung it on a coathanger. She caught her reflection in the bathroom mirror – an unremarkable brunette with quiver-thighs and unbeautiful breasts. She let the tea-coloured silk negligee slide over her chilly nipples and looked in the mirror again.

'I am Mrs William Beaumont of Windswept Crest,' she said.

William was nonchalantly reading a book in bed, his striped flannel pyjamas unbuttoned down his chest. She slid in next to her husband and he said, 'Well,' then rolled over to switch off the light. She took a piece of towelling from her feminine sponge bag and manoeuvred it beneath her buttocks.

William found her in the dark. They embraced, kissed. His body felt hard yet flannel-soft. She felt spongy and slippery.

William lay on top of Gertrude and she opened her legs. Something warm and hard poked out from his pyjamas and nudged about her inner thighs. He started humping and puffing in her ear, so she shifted around under him until his penis found a damp patch in her pubic hair and he pushed.

⚘

He lay beside her. 'Did I hurt you, dear?'

'A little,' she said. It wasn't like it was described in *Married Life* at all. The discomfort was only momentary and localised, a rude and uncomfortable sensation. Once, when she was young, she'd shoved her hand down a hollow log for a dare. Her fingers got covered in something warm, runny-wet, sticky, prickly and gooey; broken eggs. A bird's nest in the log. That sensation had made her feel strangely affronted too.

'Well,' said William, and kissed her cheek. He felt it had been quite satisfying and all had gone well. He'd approached his prone bride as he'd approached the one small chocolate egg he received after eleven o'clock church each Easter Sunday. He'd peel the tinfoil back gently exposing a small area of chocolate. Then he'd break off one section to suck, savouring it. But William was always overcome and would shove the entire egg into his mouth quickly, gorging himself, and be left both satisfied, and strangely not.

'Are you happy?' asked William.

His wife replied, 'I'm happy now.' William found her hand and held it.

❦

Gertrude kept the small towel in place beneath her bottom for the rest of the night. In the morning she inspected the red and flaky smears closely, sniffed them then wrapped the towelling in brown paper and put it aside to drop in the bin at a discreet moment. When she stepped under the shower she was humming. The new Mrs Beaumont refused the offer of a breakfast tray in bed and arrived at the table immaculately groomed and beaming. Elsbeth and Mona found something serious to look at in their eggs and William splashed a newspaper about in front of him, but Gertrude was not blushing.

'Good morning, all,' she said.

'Good morning,' they chorused.

There followed an awkward silence.

'Gosh,' said Mona, 'one person at each side of the table now.'

'When will harvest be over?' asked Gertrude.

'As I said, dear, it depends on the weather.' He looked to his mother for support. Elsbeth was staring out the window.

'Can't you get a man to oversee it?'

'Well, dear, there's Edward McSwiney but I –'

'Oh William, that wretched man again!' Elsbeth banged her teacup in its saucer and crossed her arms.

Gertrude smiled sweetly. 'I really don't mind so much about our honeymoon, William, really I don't, it's just . . . an urgent trip to Melbourne is *necessary*. I need to purchase some new materials for curtains in our room –'

'They were perfectly adequate for me,' said Elsbeth.

'Anyone for more tea?' said Mona, turning the pot.

'Stop turning the pot – you'll wear a ring in the table,' snapped Elsbeth.

'New linen is needed and I need a few things to complete my trousseau, to start my new life properly.' Gertrude bit into her toast and poured salt onto the plate beside her egg. Elsbeth sent William a filthy squint-eye look and William sunk behind his newspaper again.

Mrs William Beaumont continued, 'There's Dad's account at Myer and he gave me a blank cheque.'

William turned crimson. The colour completely drained from Elsbeth's face and Mona cried, 'Oh, let's go! It's been years since we've been shopping!'

Gertrude frowned at the tarnished teaspoon, then whipped the top off her soft-boiled egg.

14

*T*illy sat in the shade of the thickening wisteria watching a long freight train move slowly away from the silo and crawl around to the south, disappearing behind The Hill. It rumbled away to the west, into a watery horizon. It was summer again, hot, that time of the year when Christmas and shearing season have come and gone, and the sun has ripened the crops. The sound of rolling steel, bumping, metal on metal, carries over Dungatar from the railway lines, as giant engines arrive to shunt grain trucks together beside the square, corrugated silo.

When the engines arrive children come to watch and play at the silo. Trains roll up pulling empty trucks to be filled with wheat, while others come from Winyerp and are already filled with sorghum. Winyerp sits smugly to the north of Dungatar in the middle of an undulating brown blanket of acres and acres of sorghum. The farms around Dungatar are golden seas of wheat, which are stripped, the header spewing the grain into semitrailers. The semis transport the grain and pour it into the silo. When the mountains of wheat are dry, a huge auger is plunged into their hearts and grain is spiralled up, then spilled onto a conveyor belt which takes it to the loading dock where it's poured into an empty rail truck, filling it to the top with the yellow grain. In the heat of the day, suffocating wheat dust clouds the silo. The grain trucks are left standing close by, waiting, until the engines roll into place and they are coupled and herded and attached to the end of the line of sorghum-filled trucks. Eventually the engines tow them away, brimming with dusty gold and brown seed, away from the vast grain belt where the sun shines most of the year and rain is too often scarce. The engines will stop again and again at silos and sidings to take on fuel or more grain trucks, dragging them to a distant port. Passengers in cars stopped at railway crossings count up to fifty trucks rumbling past.

The wheat will become flour or perhaps it will sail to overseas lands. The famous Winyerp sorghum will become stock fodder.

The town will be quiet again and the children will go back to the creek to play. The adults will wait for football season. The cycle was familiar to Tilly, a map.

☙

Molly inched out from the kitchen and poked Tilly with her walking stick. 'What are you staring at?'

'Life,' said Tilly, and picked up her cane basket. 'I'll be back soon.' She headed down The Hill.

'Don't bother,' called Molly. 'I'd rather my possum came back.'

Marigold Pettyman and Beula Harridene stopped talking to watch her approach. 'Think you can sew, do you?' sneered Beula.

'You copied those dresses from a *Women's Weekly*, I'm told,' said Marigold, as though it were a clever thing. 'You can do mending then?'

Tilly looked at the inglorious women. 'I can,' she said flatly.

She marched back up The Hill with her groceries, clenched fists and gritted teeth. She found Lois Pickett sitting on the step clutching a plump, crumpled paper bag. 'You've got a good view from up here,' she said, 'and a nice garden coming along.'

Tilly moved past her onto the veranda. Lois stood up. 'I heard you could sew, you made your dress you wore to the races and Muriel says you didn't even use a pattern for Gert's weddin' dress, just a dummy.'

'Come in,' said Tilly pleasantly.

Lois upended the paper bag and spread an ancient musty frock, stiff and greasy, across the kitchen table and pointed at the decayed armpits. 'Gone under here, see.' Tilly looked pained, shook her head and opened her mouth to speak but just then Purl Bundle called *Yoohoo* from the veranda and clicked straight through the door in her high-heeled scuffs and red pedal-pushers, all bright and blonde and barmaidy. She thrust several yards of satin and lace at Tilly and said, 'I'll have a line of night attire and lingerie that'll put some spring back into the old mattress, thanks.'

Tilly nodded. 'Good,' she said.

Lois asked, 'P'raps you could just cut the top off and make it a skirt?'

❦

That afternoon Molly sat scratching beneath the layers of her knee rugs and Barney lounged on the step at her feet, staring, his bottom lip fat and hanging, a look of pure wonder on his face. Tilly was driving golf balls between the tip and the McSwineys' with her number three wood. One of the balls whizzed past Miss Dimm, who'd rolled up over the hill-top, her face to the clouds and an arm reaching for the unseen obstacles. She held under one

arm a bolt of blue-and-white checked cotton and a paper bag full
of buttons, zippers and school uniform patterns, sizes 6–20. Miss
Dimm was extremely short-sighted and also very vain, so wore
her glasses only in the classroom. She'd always kept her hair in a
short page-boy bob and worn a white blouse tucked firmly into
a voluminous gathered skirt. She was enormously fat-bottomed
but very pleased with her tiny feet, so tiptoed everywhere in
dainty slippers tied with ribbons, and when she sat she settled her
crossed ankles prominently. She tripped up to the golf bag and
felt the clubs sticking out.

'Golf clubs,' said Tilly, and held one up.

'Oh,' said Miss Dimm, 'lucky you, you've got lots of
them! I'm looking for little Myrtle Dunnage.' She headed off
towards the house. On the veranda she stared directly at the
pink and blue tea cosy on Molly's head and said, 'I'm here on
behalf of the Dungatar Public School Parents and Teachers
Committee and I'd like to see little Myrtle Dunnage, please.'

'I bet you would,' said Molly, 'In fact I reckon you *should*
be able to see, then you'd know what we have to endure every
time we see you.'

'Come in, Miss Dimm,' said Tilly.

'Oh, there you are.' Miss Dimm turned to the sun-speckled
wisteria vine behind Molly and held out her hand.

They negotiated a fair price and all necessary fittings for nine
school uniforms and as she was leaving, Miss Dimm thanked
Molly's hat again, fell down the small step, regained her momentum and skipped away. Barney had collected the golf balls in
Tilly's wicker basket and was driving them off the crest with
Tilly's one iron when the homely teacher passed him, stumbled
and somersaulted out of sight, her lace petticoat flailing, slipper
ribbons spinning.

Teddy was on his way up when he was felled by Miss Dimm. 'Oh God,' he said, and scrambled towards her as she lay flat on her back with her skirt up over her face and her dimpled thighs, like purple brocade on lard, exposed to the world. Barney leaned over the crest.

'What do you think you're doing, numbskull?' Teddy stood and brushed the grass from his new plaid trousers.

'Playing golf,' said Barney, and held up a one iron.

'The balls are landing on my roof.'

'Good shot,' said Tilly, and shook his hand. 'You deserve a cup of tea.' She led him away.

Teddy blinked at his brother, thin and pimply and crooked, limping off with the most beautiful woman he'd ever seen. He helped Miss Dimm up. 'Come on, I'll lead you to the path.'

'Why, thank you . . . who are you?'

𝄢

Next morning Faith browsed through a *Women's Illustrated* while Tilly knelt in front of her, pinning her hem. The cover headline read, 'Dior's Extravagance sets women back ten years – Balenciaga rebels, Page 10'. Faith mouthed 'Bal – en – see – aga' and perused the fashion articles – tunic, soft, standaway collar, chemise, seersucker, denim, America, Anna Klein, Galanos, Chanel, Schiaparelli, Molyneux, other names she couldn't pronounce. 'Ruth said you get lots of parcels from the city,' she said, and looked down at Tilly, 'and postcards from Paris written in French from someone called Madelaine?'

Tilly stood and eased the bodice so that it sat higher over Faith's decolletage. Faith wrenched it down again.

Molly cleared her throat and in her best Elsbeth Beaumont voice said, 'She claims she used to care for Madame Madelaine

Vionnet, the famous Paris fashion designer.' She looked accusingly at Tilly. 'She probably *died*.'

'She was very old,' said Tilly through the pins in her mouth.

'Did she teach you to sew?' said Faith.

Molly aimed her nose at the picture rails. 'Apparently Madame Vionnet recommended our genius here to Balenciaga because of her unusual talent for bias cutting.' Molly made a sloppy fart sound with her tongue and vibrating lips.

'I've never heard of either of them,' said Molly.

'Elsbeth's cousin Una said Gertrude's wedding dress was very Parisian,' said Faith. 'I'm going to Paris, one day.' She looked dreamy.

'Who with?' Molly cackled mischievously.

'I can hem this while you wait, if you like.'

Faith glanced over at Molly.

Tilly persisted, 'Molly can sit on the veranda; would you like a cup of tea?' Faith nodded and removed her frock. She sat in her slip and stockings reading Tilly's catalogues, poring over the pictures. When Tilly handed her the skirt with the hemline finely stitched and perfect, Faith put aside the magazines. 'I shouldn't have gone to all this trouble really, it's just a silly old box cluster pleat that deserves to be chucked out. It'll probably end up on one of the McSwiney girls.'

Muriel came next. 'Make me something else that suits me, this time something I can wear to work but that looks real good, like my outfit for Gert's wedding.'

'With pleasure,' said Tilly.

※

When Ruth returned from the railway station with the mailbags the next morning, she and Nancy spilled the contents onto the post office floor and found Nancy's fat brown envelope. She opened it and flicked through her new magazine until she found the feature – colour photographs of a New York fashion parade highlighting the latest designs of Emilio Pucci and Roberto Capucci. They looked at the fashions and the angular girls with prominent cheekbones and dark lines on their eyelids and said, 'Aren't they something,' then Nancy headed for The Hill.

The rapping on the back door woke Tilly. Her bladder was full, she still had sleep in her eyes and her hair was wild about her shoulders when she opened it, folding a silk sarong about her. Nancy was distracted by her bare shoulders, so held the January edition of *Vogue* up in front of her and pointed to a model in an elegant tapered trouser suit in bright swirling colours. 'See her? That's what I want.'

Tilly was puzzled, so Nancy continued, 'You can get the fabric from your friends in Melbourne, and don't show anyone, I don't want copycats.'

'Oh,' said Tilly, 'the pant suit.'

'You've got a parcel and a postcard from Florence.' Nancy handed them to Tilly and left.

That evening Teddy sat on the veranda sipping a bottle of beer, smoking, watching Barney pull weeds from Tilly's vegetable patch and throw them into a wheelbarrow. When the barrow was full Teddy pushed it to the cart and pitched the grass aboard. Graham turned his head to see and when Teddy headed away again with the barrow, the horse sighed, shifted his weight and dropped his head again. Molly inched out from the kitchen and pulled an empty glass from under her knee rug, so Teddy drained the last of the beer into her glass and moved to the screen door. Tilly was standing at the window, hand-stitching something fine.

'Thought I might go for a walk, throw a line in at the creek, it's nice down there at dusk, we could – '

'I have a business to run,' she said, and smiled at him, a big, broad smile that went all the way to her eyes.

'Lovely,' he said.

*N*ancy was attaching a new brush to her old broom handle
and Muriel was wiping Pratts' front window with a wad of
turpentine-soaked newspaper. Beula Harridene rushed around
the corner, stopping between the two women. 'New outfits?'

The women grinned and nodded. 'You should get something made, that Tilly can do magic,' said Muriel.

'Obviously,' said Beula, 'if she made you think you look
good in that.'

Just then the Triumph Gloria rolled back into town. The
women stopped to look. William was driving with a stranger in the
seat beside him while Gertrude, Elsbeth and Mona sat in the back,
each wearing a new hat. Three large shiny-new suitcases were
strapped to the bumper rack of the car and several large tea-chests
were secured in a new trailer trundling along behind. As the big
old car rounded the curve of the main street, Evan Pettyman put
down his mid-morning cup of coffee and moved closer to his window to follow the Beaumonts' triumphant return. At the school
Miss Dimm put her glasses on to see what the large thing sailing
by was and Purl ceased shaking mats on the pub balcony to watch.

The people of Dungatar suddenly had something more to

expect and it swelled the air. The smart wedding party, their suitcases stuffed with Collins Street fashions, would soon discover that the women in town had striking new outfits, and every hemline was now in keeping with current European fashion.

On Saturday morning Elsbeth Beaumont and her daughter-in-law arrived at Pratts General Store wearing a new frock each with matching hat and gloves. At 9:00 am they stood between the dingy shelves in their Dior skirts, huge and domed in yards and yards of taffeta, their hems brushing the tops of Nugget boot polish tins and shoe white bottles and rattling the hanging shoe horns.

'Oh my,' said Muriel, 'just look at you.'

'Hello, Muriel,' said Elsbeth, a little clenched-of-dentures.

'Hello, Mother.' Gertrude leaned to receive a peck on the cheek.

'Good trip?' asked Muriel flatly.

'Oh, won-der-ful!' said Gertrude.

Elsbeth nodded in agreement, 'Maaarrvellous.'

Muriel came from behind her counter. Her shoes needed polishing and her hair needed brushing but she too wore a new outfit – a long sapphire grey, fine-weave linen tunic with an unusual inset neckline and a very straight calf-length skirt. At the back the tunic and skirt were wrapped over double and fastened with a martingale. The outfit was well tailored, chic and practical, and it suited her. Gertrude and Elsbeth were both surprised and miffed.

'Where's Father?' said Gertrude.

'"Father" can still be found out the back, Gert. If you call out "Hey, Dad" he'll still answer,' replied Muriel.

'Won't you tell him I've returned and that we need to speak to him.'

Muriel crossed her arms and looked squarely at her daughter.

'Reg,' she said. Reginald closed his mouth. 'Fetch Alvin for me, if you don't mind?' He placed the tray of entrails he was holding on the marble counter-top and left to find Alvin.

The new Gertrude continued, 'Elsbeth and I have great plans for lots of exciting things to do in the coming year. We're going to take *Doongatah* for the ride of its life. It'll be such fun, won't it, Elsbeth?'

Elsbeth squeezed her eyes shut and raised her shoulders in delicious joy. '*Such* fun!' she said.

Reginald returned, 'Beg pardon, *mams*, your "Father" is rushing at your command and will be here as soon as he possibly can,' and he bobbed ever so slightly.

'Thank you,' said Elsbeth graciously. Reg went back to his entrails and carcasses.

'Well hello hello hello,' boomed Alvin in his friendliest grocer's voice. He approached his daughter (off-loaded so successfully) with his arms wide, grabbed her waist and lifted her in a circle so that her Dior petticoats hooped and the air unsettled the dust. He placed her clumsily on the boards with a squeeze and a cough. She was heavier than he expected. 'My little girl.' He beamed and cupped her fulsome cheeks in his flour-dusted hands. Gertrude winced and shared an exasperated look with Elsbeth. She straightened her hat.

'Yes, I've noticed it,' said Alvin. 'New hat!' And he nodded at Muriel, who rolled her eyes.

'Daddy, Elsbeth and I want you to put this prospectus in the window in a prominent position and pin several more about the store. We've several Gestetnered copies and there'll be reminders in the local paper –'

'We've formed a Social Club,' announced Elsbeth. 'I'm secretary, Trudy's president and Mona will be our typist. We thought Muriel could be treasurer and –'

'*Trudy?*'

'Yes, Mother, you will call me *Trudy* from now on. Our first meeting is scheduled for Monday and is to be held at home, at Windswept Crest. We have all the dates of every event and we're going to gather the locals to organise functions, essentially fund-raisers . . . tea parties, croquet games, dances –'

Elsbeth corrected her, 'A *ball*, a fund-raising *ball*.'

'A ball, the biggest and best we've ever had –'

'And there'll be a theatrical Eisteddfod with a section created especially for EL-O-CU-SHUN,' emphasised Elsbeth.

'So!' said Gertrude, and nodded to Elsbeth. Elsbeth thrust the Gestetnered copies at Alvin. A neat pile of bold typed letters with 'TRUDY AND ELSBETH BEAUMONT invite THE PROGRESSIVE-MINDED LADIES OF DUNGATAH TO A MEETING', and there was a paragraph of fancy scrolled print beneath. Alvin placed his thumbs behind his apron straps. A pause settled over the group.

'Dunga*tah?*' said Alvin.

'Where's Mona?' asked Muriel.

'She's learning Dressage and Equestrian,' said Gertrude. 'We've a new man at the property.'

'Mona's terrified of horses,' said Muriel.

'Exactly! That's the point.' Trudy tsked and shook her head.

Alvin looked surprised. 'You have a new man?'

'His name is Lesley Muncan and he is a true gentleman,' announced Elsbeth, and sniffed at Alvin.

The smile on Alvin's face remained fixed. 'My my.' He looked the ladies up and down, from the waving feathers sprouting from their startling headdress to their pinched toes encased in stylish new shoes. 'Had a bit of a spree in Melbourne, eh?'

Gertrude smiled conspiratorially at Elsbeth, who squeezed her arm in camaraderie.

'I take it William will be in with his harvest cheque soon – as there is the matter of your outstanding account, *Mrs Beaumonts*, and I expect you've brought along all the receipts from your spree so shall we pop into the office and go through them together before I add them to your existing outstanding account?'

The smiles fell from the Beaumont women's faces. 'Daddy, I thought –' said Gertrude.

'I said you could buy *yourself* a small wedding trousseau,' said Alvin, then looked at Elsbeth and sniffed.

Elsbeth shoved the leaflets at Muriel and looked blackly at her new daughter-in-law.

❦

Septimus Crescant sat at the corner of the bar with Hamish O'Brien, talking. Purl stood behind the bar painting her fingernails while Fred, Bobby Pickett and Scotty Pullit sat at the card table, sipping, smoking and shuffling. Finally Fred looked at Teddy's empty chair and said, 'May as well start.' Reginald dealt the cards and every man threw ten two-shilling coins onto the table.

The telephone rang. Purl walked to the far wall and gingerly lifted the receiver, careful not to smudge her nails. Bobby waved his cards at Purl and mouthed, 'Tell her I've just left.'

'Hello, Station Hotel . . .'

The poker players stared.

'Look, love, I appreciate it very much but I'll be busy on Sunday all right, 'bye.' Purl hooked the phone back into its cradle.

'That was poor suffering Mona-by-name-Mona-by-nature phoning on behalf of the Dungatar Social Club inviting me to their inaugural meeting out at Fart Hill, to discuss their first ever fund-raising croquet day and tea party – and there's to be a "presentation night".'

'Now there's something to look forward to,' said Fred.

Purl closed her eyes and shook her head slowly from side to side. 'I can hardly wait.'

The men resumed their cards and Hamish and Septimus resumed their discussion. 'O'course,' said Hamish, 'it all started to go wrong when man domesticated crops so there was a need to protect the crop and to gather in groups, build walls to stave off hungry neoliths.'

'No,' said Septimus, 'the wheel sank humanity the deepest.'

'Och, you've got to have the wheel for transport.'

'Then the industrial revolution followed, mechanisation that did the rest of damage –'

'But steam machines, steam's harmless, a steam train at full pelt is a sound to behold –'

'Diesel's cleaner.' Septimus drank his beer.

The card dealer stopped shuffling, and the players shifted their eyes to the two sparring regulars at the corner of the bar.

Hamish turned to face his companion. 'And the world is round!'

He quietly poured his remaining half glass of Guinness into Septimus's hard hat sitting squarely on the floor by the bar. Septimus in turn splashed the contents of his beer glass onto Hamish's head, leaving his walrus moustache dripping. Hamish raised his clenched fists, took a classic, menacing Jack 'Nonpareil' Dempsey pose and started dancing, moving his arms like wheel rods on a train. Purl hastily waved her wet fingernails about and Fred sighed.

'Come on then, Septimus, up with ye dooks, outside . . .' Hamish took a jab just as Septimus reached down to the floor for his hat. Hamish swung two more air-jabs and the third landed when Septimus rose, lifting his arms to put his hat on.

There was a soft but audible splat like a raw egg hitting a kitchen table. Septimus buckled, holding his bleeding nose.

'Hamish,' said Fred, 'it is time for you to remove yourself.'

Hamish put on his station master's hat and waving cheerfully from the door called, 'See you tomorrow.'

Purl handed Septimus a handkerchief.

Septimus moved towards the door. 'In this town a man can covet his neighbour's wife and not get hurt, but to speak the truth can earn a bleeding nose.'

'It can,' said Fred, 'so I wouldn't say too much more if I were you or else you'll end up with a *broken* nose next time.' Septimus left.

Purl enquired if Reg was donating meat to the footy club again this year.

'Doing the time-keeping as well,' said Scotty.

♯

Ruth and Miss Dimm, Nancy and Lois Pickett, Beula Harridene, Irma Almanac and Marigold Pettyman were also approached by the Dungatar Social Committee. Faith was not at home. She was rehearsing, with Reginald. Mona asked the ladies to attend the inaugural meeting at Windswept Crest and to please bring a plate. The newly recruited members of the Dungatar Social Club immediately rang Ruth at the exchange and told her to put them through to Tilly Dunnage.

'Elsbeth's got her by the ear at the moment,' she said. 'I'm next then I'll ring all youse.'

♯

When Ruth arrived at the top of The Hill, she banged on the back door and called, 'Anyone home?'

'We'd hardly be out visiting, would we?' came Molly's reply.

Then the others arrived and had to wait in the kitchen with Mad Molly, who sat hunched in her decorated wheelchair poking at a burning log with her walking stick. She blew her nose into her fingers and flicked the green slime onto the embers, watching closely as it bubbled and hissed and vanished.

Tilly, professional and gracious, took each of her clients one by one to the dining room to discuss their needs and visions. She noted the members of the newly formed Dungatar Social Club had acquired an accent overnight – an enunciated Dungatar interpretation of queenly English.

As customers, their demands were simple – 'I've got to look better than everyone else, especially Elsbeth.'

❦

Out at Windswept Crest the new man, Lesley Muncan, sat petitely, knees crossed in the kitchen, peering at Mona's back as she leaned over the sink washing dishes.

Lesley had been working in the laundry at the hotel where the Beaumonts stayed for their honeymoon when he encountered William in the foyer, reading the paper.

'The girls out shopping, spending all your money, are they?' he joked.

'Yes,' said William, surprised.

'Enjoying your stay?'

'Yes,' said William. 'Are you?'

Lesley adjusted his cuffs. 'It's a nice hotel,' he said. 'You're from the country, aren't you?'

'Yes,' said William, smiling.

Lesley looked about the foyer quickly then sat on the lounge beside William. 'I've done a lot of equestrian work and I've got my eye open for a suitable placement. I don't suppose you know of anyone who needs a riding instructor, do you?'

'Well . . . ,' said William.

Lesley glanced towards the reception desk. 'Strapper? Stable hand even? I can start right away.'

Just then Elsbeth, Trudy, and Mona bustled through the door, bringing with them the smells from the perfume counter at Myers. Lesley leapt to his feet to help with their parcels.

William said, 'This is a fellow guest . . . Mr . . . ?'

'Muncan, Lesley Muncan, delighted to meet you all.'

'Mr Muncan is an equestrian,' said William.

'Oh really?' Gertrude had said.

❦

'Mona,' Lesley said now, and tapped the end of his cigarette with his forefinger, 'if I can get my foot in a stirrup, so will you – it's very, very early days yet, my dear.'

Mona was afraid of horses but she wanted Lesley to like her. 'I'll try,' she said, running the dish-cloth around and around the clean plate. Mona wanted someone, a partner. Her mother and Trudy were best friends now and Mona often found herself alone in the big house, sitting at the bay window, watching the stables where Lesley worked. He'd set up quarters in the loft, but in the past few days would arrive in the kitchen when he saw her at the window.

'Good,' he said, 'that's what your mother wants – and we can't let the boss down, can we?'

❦

Elsbeth and Trudy were relaxing with William in the library which up until that day had been 'the spare room' – a room in the middle of the badly designed house with no windows that was used to store junk. William had taken to smoking a pipe. He found taking it from between his teeth and sweeping it about a useful gesture to emphasise an idea. Most of his points were actually Trudy's, but she let him have them. That way she could say, 'But, William, you said a leather lounge suite would last longer.' *South Pacific* played softly on the new record player, 'Bali Haiiiiiiii, come to meeeeeee'. Without warning Trudy froze, clutched her mouth and ran from the room. Elsbeth and William raised eyebrows at each other.

Mona tripped down the hall, calling, 'Mummy, William, come quickly!'

Lesley cried, 'She's just been sick into the dishes!' and he closed his eyes and raised the back of his hand to his forehead.

'Why, Trudy,' said William, and went to her. Elsbeth put her fingers to her lips and steadied herself on the refrigerator.

'I'll put the kettle on,' said Mona.

'Have you been feeling unwell of late, dear?' asked Elsbeth, suddenly important.

'A little tired, that's all.'

Elsbeth looked knowingly at her son and they looked down upon Trudy with love and overwhelming gratitude. They reached for her while Lesley muttered to the ceiling, 'OhmyGod. She's preg-nnt.'

Mona held the teapot tightly to her chest and said, 'You'll want my room for a nursery!' Elsbeth stepped towards her daughter. 'Selfish little wretch,' she snapped, and slapped her viciously on the cheek.

eula Harridene was out walking one evening when she discovered Alvin shining a torch into a travelling salesman's boot, sorting through cheap materials. In the morning she found the materials on Muriel's counter, for sale at inflated prices. The haberdashery counter had expanded its range of buttons, zips and beads, which Alvin imported from specialist shops in Richmond, while he purchased accessories from wholesalers in Collins Street then sold them at 100 percent markup to the highly competitive locals. These days women made their housecoats from 'imported' brocade with ivory or diamanté buttons, and swanned about their country bungalows in pastel silk chiffons or tapered velvet pants with cummerbund waists and high-necked jerseys, like movie stars.

Tea-chests kept arriving for Miss T. Dunnage, Dungatar, Australia. Sergeant Farrat arrived at The Hill one evening as Ruth struggled to drag one from the postal van to Tilly's veranda. 'Dear me,' said the sergeant, 'what's in it – gold?'

'Supplies,' said Tilly, 'cottons, patterns, sequins, magazines, feathers –'

'Feathers?' Sergeant Farrat clasped his hands.

'Oh yes,' said Ruth, 'all different sorts of feathers too.'

Tilly looked coolly at her and raised an eyebrow. Ruth's hand flew to her mouth. Sergeant Farrat caught everything that passed between the women. 'Ostrich feathers?'

'I don't know really, sergeant,' said Ruth, 'I'd *imagine*, there is, I mean I wouldn't *exactly know* what's in the box but everyone's been talking about their new frock for the social club presentation night . . .'

They all looked down at the tea-chest. The seals were torn and there were raw holes where nails had been newly pulled and about them brand-new nails inexpertly hammered in. The original tape had been torn away and new standard postal tape applied in its place. 'Well,' said Ruth, 'I'd better get on then, Purl'll be waiting for her new shoes and Faith's got new sheet music to practise.' They watched her putter away in her van, then the sergeant smiled at Tilly and asked, 'How is your mother these days?'

'These days she's far from neglected.' Tilly crossed her arms and looked at him.

Sergeant Farrat removed his policeman's cap and placed it over his heart. 'Yes,' he said, and looked at the ground.

'It's amazing what a little bit of nourishment will do,' she continued. 'She has good days and not-so-good, but she's always entertaining and things come back to her from time to time.' They dragged the tea-chest into the kitchen.

'I was under the impression Mae looked out for her,' said the sergeant.

Molly shuffled into the kitchen in her dressing gown and slippers, dragging a piece of rope. She stopped and looked closely at Sergeant Farrat. 'In trouble, is she? I'm not surprised.'

'Would you like to join us for a cup of tea and some cake, Molly?'

She took no notice of Tilly but leaned closer to Sergeant Farrat. 'My possum's gone missing,' she said, 'but I think I know what happened to it.' She inclined to a large pot simmering on the stove.

'I see,' he said, nodding gravely. Molly shuffled on. Tilly handed the sergeant a cup of tea. He tapped the tea-chest with the side of his shoe then walked around it. 'You'll need pliers to get this undone,' he said. Tilly handed him the pliers and he put down his cup of tea, then fell to his knees in front of the chest. He levered the top off and dug inside, grabbing packages and holding them to his nose, inhaling. 'Can I open them, please?'

'Well, I was going to –'

He tore lasciviously at the corners of the paper, tugging fabrics out and rubbing them between his thumb and fingers, then he placed them along her small work table. Tilly sorted through the drawings and measurements she'd made and placed them with the material. Sergeant Farrat came to the last package at the bottom of the tea-chest. He clutched it to his heart then ripped the brown paper apart and freed yards and yards of brilliant magenta silk organza. 'Oh,' he cried, and buried his face into the boiling mass. He stopped abruptly and gaped at Tilly, smacking his hands against his reddened face, appalled at his abandonment.

'Gorgeous, isn't it?' said Tilly. 'It's mine.'

The sergeant stepped to her, took her hand in his and looked into her eyes. 'Can I please have one of your ostrich feathers?'

'Yes.'

He kissed her hand then wrapped the magenta silk organza about his shoulders like a giant Trailing Bertha and walked gracefully to the mirror in imaginary stilettos. He twirled, enjoying his reflection, then looked at Tilly and said, 'I'm brilliant at sequins and diamantés and I bet I can hemstitch just as fast as you – I'm a whiz with zippers, gauging and frogging too.'

'How do you feel about ruffs and flounces?'

'I hate them.'

'So do I,' she said.

❦

Beyond Windswept Crest the neat, cut stubble stretched to the horizon, like a new coir mat. On the Beaumont property, cattle stood stomach-deep in the low, grey stubble, which was the remains of last season's crop. There was a green oasis that was the homestead, surrounded by gums, its roof red against the bright sky. Parked cars glittered in the sun and small striped marquees stood in front of the green island. In one paddock a horse skipped stiffly around at the end of a rope held by a small figure in a red coat – Lesley demonstrating dressage. People stood about on the mowed paddock that fell away to the Dungatar creek, which was lined with grey drowned gums. William was explaining to Bobby and Reg the new developments. 'We had Ed McSwiney build a new yard and stables for the equestrian. The tennis court is under renovation and we've a new irrigation system dug for the gardens, the poultry and so on – and of course you're all here to try out the new croquet lawn and I believe Mother is going to announce a new project when she awards the various prizes for the cakes . . .' The smile fell from William's face and his voice trailed away, '. . . and I have plans for the agricultural side of things, when I get the machinery . . .' He shoved his hands in his pockets and wandered away.

Scotty Pullit said, 'That's why we're here, to pay for it all.'

'Nice lawn,' said Bobby. The footballers looked at the croquet field and smiled.

Muriel passed along the stalls collecting the profits, bundling them into a brown paper bag. She limped over to Trudy with her canvas stool beneath her arm. She unfolded it, kicked off her dusty white sandals and plopped down beside her daughter, who lay in her deckchair on the homestead veranda. Trudy looked about her nervously. Lipstick sat on the ends of each hair of Muriel's pale moustache, like tiny redhead matches. She needed a tint and a perm and her feet were dry and cracked, like big long warts.

'I have some new relatives here today, from Toorak,' said Gertrude.

'Elsbeth's cousin Una?' said Muriel.

'You didn't introduce yourself!'

'We actually met a long time ago, Gert –'

'*Trudy*, my name is Trudy I keep telling you.'

'They don't live in Toorak, they live next door – Prahran.' Muriel stood abruptly, took up her stool and tossed the paper bag onto Trudy's lap. 'I ought to know, I'm South Yarra born and bred.' Muriel limped away with her sandals swinging in her hand and her skirt stuck between her buttocks. She watched the ground pass between her feet. 'My own daughter has turned into the sort of person I moved here to avoid.'

❦

Graham raised his long, dusty, velvet nose and turned to look behind him. He'd crunched his way through half a row of carrots, about fifteen iceberg lettuce, one or two tomato plants – not ripe yet – some beans and a cucumber or two. Finding he wasn't partial to the cucumbers he returned to the carrots and ripped them from the earth by their green tops, shaking them and shunting them

between his soft, fat lips. Faith strolled past heading for a ren-
dezvous with Reginald and smiled. 'You're a naughty horse.'

Hamish was at the far side of the homestead adjusting his
model railway signals, the miniature steam train chugging and
tooting around and around on tiny steel tracks. 'You mustn't get too
close,' he growled to the watching children. 'It's a very fine delicate
piece of machinery, tuned, balanced . . . listen to the rhythm . . .
magnificent. There was of course a better model than this, the D
class, Type 4-6-0. Now it had two nineteen-inch cylinders, coupled
wheels, 11/16 inch diameter OCH, I TOLD YE NOT TO
TOUCH, NOW PUT THAT WATER TOWER BACK!'

❧

Six of Lesley's young pupils rode into the middle of the paddock
on hacks and Shetlands. 'Ladies and gentlemen, parents . . .' Lesley
smiled at the pastoral people from far-flung properties, sitting in
jodhpurs beside horse floats, picnicking at fold-up tables. They
nodded back. Behind him the ponies moved diagonally sideways
in an uneven line. 'The foundation of dressage is rhythm, sup-
pleness, contact, impulsion, straightness and collection in a horse.
Rhythm is the beat and tempo is the measure of time between the
beats, or steps. A rider must feel the music the horse is playing.' The
pastoral parents were pointing their thermos cups and laughing.
Lesley turned to find the hacks and Shetlands had walked sideways
into a bunch in one corner of the arena where they milled about,
biting, kicking and bucking, the children bawling in their saddles.

❧

Teddy removed the hoops from the croquet lawn and started a
game of kick-to-kick. Someone kicked a wobbly and the ball
bounced towards the creek but was picked up by Faith, who was

wandering up the slope brushing grass from her hair and clothes. She shot back a powerful short punt right into Scotty Pullit's lowered forearms, then remained where she was at the back line, close to the creek. Nancy joined the lineup in front of the homestead, then Ruth. Teddy gathered all players to the centre and they nutted out two teams. Bobby, Reginald and Barney stood horse jump poles in forty-four-gallon drums for goalposts. A coin was flipped and the players trotted off to their positions. Barney was given a white shirt and told to wave it whenever the ball came between the posts. He stood proudly at his position with the shirt held high, ready. Teddy kicked the first try and as the ball sailed towards the posts, he called, 'Watch it, Barney.' Barney dropped the shirt and marked the ball. Reginald Blood declared it a no-ball. Teddy lightly biffed the back of Barney's head so Reg announced Teddy's team would forfeit another point. There was an argument, the shouts echoing over the creek, the raucous laughter bouncing off gum trees and lifting the crests on roosting galahs. Elsbeth Beaumont turned her cousins towards the horse floats and station owners. 'It's always the way with the rabble,' she sniffed.

While the townsfolk played football Trudy Beaumont counted the money.

Mona and Lesley rested on hay bales in the gloom of the stables. 'I suppose I'll wear my bridesmaid's dress again,' said Mona, and sighed.

'What's it look like?'

'It's rust –'

'Oh that one, the cowl neckline. Why don't you get that scandalous creature Tilly what's-her-name to make you some new things? She's cheap, I hear.'

'Mother says I haven't had enough wear out of the orange one.' They picked at bits of straw and swung their riding boots. 'Are you, um, going to the presentation tonight with anyone special, Maestro?'

'Why of course!' squealed Lesley. 'I'm picking up Lois Pickett at seven.'

'I see.'

Lesley rolled his eyes. It dawned on Mona that her friend, her Maestro, had made a joke. They fell all over the hay cackling.

❀

When Mona stepped through the hall door on Les's arm that evening she was shining. She wore a plain blue rayon dress with a full skirt and a centre-front box pleat which she'd had for years, but she had draped a red floral scarf about her shoulders and pinned a red flower behind her ear. She blended with the other women who still favoured their long black gloves, waistlines and pleated skirts, taffeta, glazed printed cotton, princess-line skirts all in contemporary designs. But they'd been renovated, European-touched, advanced to almost avante-garde by Tilly Dunnage. The tempo in the hall was fast, the tone high and excited. Lesley turned to Mona and said, 'Now hold your shoulders back and walk like I showed you.'

When Trudy and Elsbeth stepped onto the stage and took their place at the microphone a hush swept across the room. All heads tilted to them. Elsbeth wore an exquisite gown of rubescant shot taffeta. The collar was off-the-shoulder and very deep and wide, and Tilly had created a clever and complicated bodice in the modern wrap-over style.

Pregnancy had added almost three stone to Trudy. Her face

had swelled so that her cheeks were spinnakers. Fluid bobbed about her stern like lifebuoys on rough waves, then cascaded down her legs to gather about the ankles. To distract the eye from Trudy's appearance, Tilly had created a design that was very *Vogue*, all line and finish. It was calf-length navy silk taffeta, with a strapless underbodice, high-boned and gathered to accommodate her swollen midrift, and swept in wide, unpressed pleats to the hem.

Mona moved towards the stage with Lesley following. He leaned to her and said from the corner of his mouth, 'It's snowing down south.'

She looked out the door. 'I'm not cold.'

'Your slip's showing.' He indicated her hemline with his eyebrows then inclined his head to the door. They moved quietly towards it and stepped outside into the darkness. Lesley held Mona's shawl while she fumbled about with her petticoat strap and a safety pin she kept fastened to her panties.

'Quickly,' said Lesley, 'they're about to make the welcoming speech.'

Mona removed her dress and shoved it at Lesley, saying, 'Hold this.'

❦

'Ladies and gentlemen,' trilled Elsbeth, 'welcome to the presentation night of Dungatar's first-ever Social Club.' She paused as everyone clapped. 'Tonight we'll be presenting the members of the committee and discussing our plans to raise funds for the Dungatar Social Club! Our fund-raising afternoon of tea and croquet has been a very thrilling start and it proved to be a very popular day!' She smiled broadly but no one clapped, so she carried on. 'Naturally we could not have raised enough money to assist us towards our big fund-raising ball without the help of the ladies who make up the Social Club Committee. And so, without further ado, it gives me great pleasure to present the committee members to you. Firstly, our secretary and treasurer, Mrs Alvin Pratt.' The guests clapped and Muriel stepped onto the stage, smiled and bobbed.

'And a special thanks goes to our tireless typist and odd jobs girl, Miss Mona Beaumont . . .'

But Mona was nowhere to be seen. The crowd murmured, their heads swayed. Nancy was leaning against the doorjamb at the back of the hall so waved at Trudy and ducked outside, 'Psst, Mona.'

'What?'

'You're on.' Nancy came inside. 'They're coming,' she yelled, and Trudy and Elsbeth smiled at the waiting crowd.

Mona and Lesley stumbled back into the hall and the crowd began to clap. They moved to the stage and Mona stepped up to stand between her mother and her sister-in-law. The clapping dwindled and someone giggled. There was a murmur from the crowd as feet shuffled, ladies covered their mouths and men looked at the ceiling.

It was then that Lesley noticed. Mona's frock was inside out.

✂

Tilly stood in her cottage, surrounded by colourful debris. The past two weeks had been a period of intense hand-stitching, draping and shaping, and there was the ball to come. Teddy arrived wearing a pair of new blue denim Levi jeans, a brilliant white T-shirt and a leather jacket with lots of zippers and studs. His hair shone with Brylcream and he had developed an insolent, upper body lean and matching pout. It suited him. She looked at him and smiled. 'You're going to wear leather and denim to the Social Committee's first-ever event?'

'What are you wearing?'

'I'm not going.'

'Come on.' He stepped towards her.

'I've got nothing to wear.'

'Just whip something up, you'll look better than any of them anyway.'

She smiled and said, 'That won't do me much good, will it?'

'Let's just sit in a corner and watch all those beautiful creations swinging about the hall on Miss Dimm and Lois and Muriel.' He stopped. 'I see what you mean.' He slumped into the chair by the fire and put his boots up on the wood box.

Molly looked over to Teddy, lifted her top lip and sent a fine line of spittle into the flames with her tongue. 'You think you're good-looking, don't you?' she said to him.

'We could go to Winyerp to the pictures,' said Teddy, 'or we could sit here with Molly all night.'

'What's on?' asked Tilly brightly.

'*Sunset Boulevard*, with Gloria Swanson.'

'You two go ahead to the pictures and have a lovely time,' said Molly. 'Don't worry about me, I'll be all right here . . . alone, by myself. Again.'

Molly insisted on sitting in the front of Teddy's Ford for her first-ever ride in a car. 'If I'm going to die I'd like to see the tree I'm going to splatter against,' she said, then demanded that they sit right at the front of the picture theatre directly under the screen. She sat between them, hooting and laughing at Tom and Jerry, then made loud, detracting comments about everything else. 'That's not really a car they're in, it's pretend . . . He's not very convincing is he? . . . She's just kissed him and her lipstick's not smudged and her eyes look like armpits . . . Stand up and get out of the way – I need to get to the lav, quickly!'

At home they offered to help her to bed but she was reluctant. 'I don't feel sleepy,' she said, and looked above at the starry sky to stifle a yawn. Teddy went inside and got a glass, poured firewater from his flask and handed it to Molly. She drank it and held her glass out for more. He looked at Tilly, who looked down at the hall lights from where fragments of conversation drifted up, so he gave Molly another splash of watermelon wine. Very shortly they were lifting her onto her bed.

They sat out under the stars again, watching the Dungatar hall flicker to darkness and the socialites disperse.

Teddy turned to her. 'Where did you go from here?'

'To Melbourne, to school.'

'And then where?'

She didn't reply. He looked impatient and said, 'Come on – it's me, not them.'

'It's just I've never really talked about it until now.'

He kept his eyes on her, willing her. Finally she said, 'I got a job in a manufacturing factory. I was supposed to work there forever and repay my "benefactor" but it was horrible. At least it was a clothing factory.'

'Did you know who your benefactor was?'

'I always knew.'

'Then?'

'I ran away. I went to London.'

'Then Spain.'

'Then Spain, Milan, Paris.' She looked away from him.

'Then? There's more, isn't there?'

She stood up. 'I think I'll go inside now –'

'All right, all right.' He caught her by the ankle, and she didn't seem to mind, so he stood and slid an arm about her shoulders and she leaned against him, just a little bit.

*M*ona eventually stopped crying because Lesley started to giggle about it. By then Trudy and Elsbeth had thought of a solution.

'You'll have to marry her . . . ,' said Elsbeth.

The way to solve everything.

Lesley sat down suddenly, 'But I don't want to get –'

'. . . or leave town,' said Trudy.

⚜

Lesley had Tilly run him up new riding attire – sky blue and pink silks and close fitting, immaculate white jodhpurs. He sent to RM Williams in Adelaide for new knee-high riding boots with Cuban heels. Mona wore her bridesmaid's dress with a white rose pinned behind her ear. It was a quiet ceremony in the front garden at Windswept Crest. Sergeant Farrat conducted the brief ceremony. William drove Mr and Mrs Lesley Muncan to the railway station. They waved to him as their train moved out, standing there with his pipe in his teeth with Hamish and Beula. The Dungatar Social Committee had donated two railway tickets as a wedding gift, so Mr and Mrs

Lesley Muncan were to spend a night in the Grand Suite at the Grand Hotel overlooking the river at Winyerp.

When the newlyweds returned to the reception counter a mere five minutes after the publican had shown them to their suite, he was very surprised.

'We're off to see the sights,' said Lesley. 'We'll collect the key about 5:30 and will be down for dinner at 6:00.'

'Zup to youse,' said the publican, and winked.

After dinner, they went upstairs. At the door of the Grand Suite – the big corner room with the arched window situated nearest the bathroom – Lesley turned to his new wife and said, 'I have a surprise for you.'

'Me too.' Tilly had run up two items for Mona's trousseau, one of which was a rather 'fast' negligee – Tilly's design.

Lesley flung open the door to the Grand Suite. On a pot plant stand next to the bed sat an enamel jug packed with icecubes and a bottle of sparkling wine. Two seven-ounce beer glasses sat beside it and between the glasses a card was propped. Embossed gold wedding bells and streamers spelled 'Congratulations'. Inside the card the publican's wife had written,

> *'Congrats + Good Luck*
> *from all us X X X'.*

'Oh Maestro,' said Mona, 'I'll be back in one moment.' She grabbed her suitcase and disappeared next door into the bathroom. Lesley ran to the men's, leaned over the toilet bowl and started dry retching. He returned eventually, sweaty-palmed and ashen to the Grand Suite where Mona reclined nervously on the chenille bedspread in her new negligee.

Lesley was overcome. 'Ohmygod, Mona.' He took her hands

and pulled her up then stood back and walked around her twice. Then he rustled into her fine silk peignoir up to his elbows and said, 'Mona it's just GOR-gess!' He opened the wine, filled their glasses and they twined arms and sipped. Mona flushed.

'I don't think I'll have too much wine . . . darling.'

'Nonsense,' said Les, and pecked her cheek. 'You'll do as you're told you, naughty wife, or I'll make you whip me with your riding crop.' They squealed and clinked their glasses.

Halfway through the first bottle Lesley produced another from his suitcase and plunged it into the ice. Halfway through the second bottle Mona passed out so Lesley finished the last of the champagne, wrapped folds of his wife's peignoir about his neck and shoulders, popped his thumb in his mouth and slept, nuzzling deep in silk folds which were tinted with fragrance of lily-of-the-valley.

❦

Mona woke feeling headachy. The first thing she saw was her new husband posing in the window – dressed, spruced and ready to catch the train home. Mona's heart was sluggish, saturated with hurt, her chin quivered and a sad lump as big as a quince stuck at her tonsils. She could hardly swallow. Not even so much as a cuddle.

'Come now, wife,' smiled Les, 'there's a nice hot cuppa waiting for us downstairs.'

Back at Windswept Crest Trudy showed her her old room – it was a nursery now – then her mother handed her a cheque.

'Mother . . .' Mona's face lifted.

'It's not a gift, it's your inheritance. I've been to a great deal of trouble for it. As you can see it's made out to Alvin Pratt Real Estate, a deposit for that vacant cottage in town.' She turned on her heel and as she passed through the stable doorway she called behind her, 'You're Lesley's responsibility now.'

❦

That afternoon Mr and Mrs Lesley Muncan moved to the workman's cottage between Evan and Marigold Pettyman's orderly house and Alvin and Muriel Pratt's comfortable weatherboard.

❦

Faith cut out letters from a *Women's Weekly* and painstakingly pasted them together on pink cardboard to make up the words, then she drew balloons and streamers weaving through the letters and sprinkled glitter on Clag. She cut out a bell from a Christmas card and pasted it on an angle next to the word 'Bell'.

Come one come all
start the football season dancing
Dungatar Social Club Ball
Featuring the new music of the new
'Faithful O'Briens',
AND
BELL OF THE BALL
Bookings – Bobby or Faith.

Hamish was waving the afternoon train in as Faith glanced over on her way to Pratts. When the train had stopped he assisted a strange woman to step down from the carriage onto the platform. She looked around anxiously before asking, 'When is the next train out?'

'Day after tomorrow, 9:30 sharp, it'll be a D Class Steamer –'

'Is there a bus?'

Hamish put his hands behind his back and crossed his fingers. 'No,' he said.

'Thank you,' she said, and stepped away.

Hamish pointed at Edward McSwiney waiting at the doorway with his cart. 'Ye can catch a ride to the hotel with our cab there,' he said. The woman placed a gloved finger under her nose and pointed to her pigskin suitcases standing on the platform between the mailbags and the crated chickens. Hamish handed them up to Edward and the stranger picked up her attache case and walked cautiously around Graham, giving him a very wide berth. She picked her way along the broken cement footpaths in her alligator skin court shoes, and at last stood in the foyer of the Station Hotel, removing her sunglasses and gloves, and clearing her throat. Fred looked up from his paper and searched the bar. She cleared her throat again and Fred wandered through to the residential entrance. He considered her over the rim of his bifocals: the dusty slippers, skinny but shapely calves, the pencil line skirt and tent jacket which she removed to reveal a white shirt tailored entirely of broderie anglaise. He could see her underwear.

'Are you lost?'

'I'd like a room for two nights, please . . . with a bath.' She held out her coat to him. Fred put down his form guide, folded the coat over his arm and smiled graciously. 'Certainly, madam, you may have the room next to the bathroom. It's a share bathroom but you're the only customer along with Mr Pullit and he hasn't bathed in nine years, so it's all yours. It's a nice room, west-facing windows which will give you a view to the setting sun, a featured hilltop cottage and sweeping vista beyond.'

Edward came through the front door and placed her suitcases gently at her knees. 'Thank you,' she said, and smiled faintly at him, then looked back at Fred, who bowed, took up her cases and led her upstairs. She inspected the room, opened the cupboard doors, sat on the bed, lifted a pillow to check the linen and then looked at herself in the mirror.

'Travelling far?' asked Fred.

'I thought a night or two in the country would be refreshing.' She looked at Fred. 'That is what I thought anyway.'

'Will you be eating this evening?'

'That depends,' she said, and wandered out onto the balcony.

Fred told her that if she needed anything just to yell out, and rushed downstairs to find Purly.

The stranger sat in the afternoon sun. She lit a cigarette and inhaled, then glanced down at the people in the main street, noticed their dresses and stopped, agape. The women of Dungatar dressed astonishingly well, strolling from the library to the chemist and back again in luxurious frocks, showing flair in pant suits made from synthetic fabric, relaxing in the park in sun frocks with asymmetric necklines common to European couture. She went downstairs to the Ladies Lounge and found a group chatting at a table, drinking lemon squash and wearing Balenciaga copies with astrakhan trims. She peeped out the residential entrance door and studied a group of women holding common cane baskets, reading something in the general store's window. A fat woman with unsightly hair wore a streamlined, waistless wool crepe, princess-cut frock with a standaway collar and magyar sleeves, which hung like cold honey and flattered her fridge-like form. A small, pointy woman wore a soft pink suit, double-breasted and wide-collared with revers and purple trim, all of which softened her leather-like complexion. Next to her, leaning on a broom, a girl with a boyish figure wore a design she was sure had not yet even been invented. It was a fine black wool dress with a shallow boat-shaped neckline and short sleeves. The bodice bloused gently into a wide, black calfskin belt with a huge black buckle. The skirt was narrow and knee length! There was a blonde showing great panache in satin-velour pedal-pushers, a shopkeeper in a smart faille tunic suit, and a small, taut woman in silk capri pants and a very chic sleeveless paletot. The stranger went back to her room to smoke her cigarettes. She wondered how Paris had found its way to the dilapidated confines and neglected torsos of banal housewives in a rural province.

❦

'Faith's done a good job with the notice,' declared Ruth.

They all nodded.

'Very artistic,' said Marigold.

'Doesn't say how much it costs,' sniped Beula.

'It's always the same,' said Lois.

'Not this time,' said Beula, nodding vigorously. 'The club needs new umpires' outfits and Faith's charging for the band – they've been practising a lot, they've got new songs . . . and another new name.'

'Well, you'd know,' said Purl.

Beula put her hands on her hips. 'And, Winyerp's coming.'

They stared at her.

'Winyerp's comink?' asked Lois.

Beula closed her eyes and nodded slowly.

'Better book a table . . . ,' said Muriel.

'. . . next to each other,' added Lois.

They looked again at the notice.

Nancy, standing at the rear with her broom, said, 'She got in another tea-chest lately.'

'Where from this time?'

'Spain?'

'France?'

'Neither – New York,' said Sergeant Farrat. The women started and turned around. 'Yes,' he said, 'New York. I was there when she opened the crate.'

'I've picked mine,' said Purl, 'you should see what I'm wearing.'

'Me too.'

'Of course mine's quite different!'

'I'm having something very original!'

'But oh my,' said the sergeant, and raised his shoulders and closed his eyes in rapture, 'you should see the material Tilly's got for herself!' He placed his hands on his cheeks. 'Silk organza – magenta! And the design – she's a *real* couturier,' he sighed. 'The structure of Balenciaga, the simplicity of Chanel, the drapery of Vionnet and the art of Delaunay.' He walked away with his hat perched smartly and his shoes sparkling.

'She always saves the best for herself,' said Beula. The women turned to look up at The Hill and narrowed their eyes.

❦

Purl waited, her pen poised over the order book. The stranger studied the three items on the menu board.

'What'll it be, love?'

The woman looked up at her and said, 'Where did you get your frock?'

'Local girl. I suggest either the steak and salad or the soup if you're not real hungry. I can heat a pie or even make you up a sandwich –'

'Is this "local girl" open after hours?'

Purl sighed. 'She'd be at home, I'd say.'

'Where does she live?'

'Up The Hill.'

'Perhaps you could show –'

'I'll tell you how to get there after you've had your steak – how would you like it done?'

❦

The traveller stood in her slip and stockinged feet in front of the fire flicking through Tilly's sketch book, her Chanel suit slung over a chair. Tilly stood next to her with her note book and tape measure and admired her soft permanent wave, her slender manicured hands.

'Right,' said the traveller, and smiled. 'I definitely want the wild silk frock with the Mandarin collar the barmaid has, and I'll have this Dior interpretation, and this pant suit – one of yours, I take it.' She continued flicking through Tilly's designs.

'What about alterations?' said Tilly.

'They'll only be minor. If there are any I'll manage them myself.' She looked at Tilly. 'Some of these are original designs.'

'Yes – my original designs.'

'I understand.' She closed the book and looked at Tilly. 'Why don't you come and work for me?'

'I have my own business here.'

'Here? And where exactly is "here"?'

'Here is where I am, for the time being.'

The traveller smirked. 'You're wasted here –'

'On the contrary, I'm used a lot. And anyway, I'm worth a small fortune on paper but until I'm paid I can't move to Collins Street.'

The traveller looked at the closed door behind Tilly. 'I'd like to see what's in your workroom.'

Tilly smiled. 'Would you let me into *your* workroom?'

Some time later Tilly showed the traveller to the back door and handed her a torch. 'Leave it in the letter box at the foot of The Hill. You'll have street lights from there on.'

'Thank you,' said the traveller. 'You'll forward a bill?'

'I will.'

'And I will pay it.' They shook hands. 'Should you ever reconsider . . .'

'I appreciate your suggestion, thank you, but as I said, at the moment I'm in no position to consider a move for several reasons. I know where to find you,' said Tilly, and closed the door.

※

As the time for the ball drew nearer they arrived at The Hill in waves, banging on Tilly's back door and making sharp demands about unique designs and individual accessories. She showed them photographs of famous European beauties and tried to explain style and how it differed from fashion. She suggested they either cut their hair (there were an astonishing number of Louise Brooks look-alikes as a result) or brush it one hundred times every night. She demonstrated back combing, pompadour and other coiffure styles. She got them to send away for hair clips and beaded shells, false flowers, postiches and plaits, ribbons, stone-headed hair pins and combs, fake vegetable costume jewellery and coloured glass beads, and buttons shaped like cigarettes. She had them thread earrings and bracelets from beads and old necklaces, she had them buy tinctures and hennas from Mr Almanac (who'd had them since the Belle Epoque) and she demonstrated the correct way to apply Chadlee and Ambre Solaire, or pale foundation makeup and indigo kohl. She prompted them to order new lingerie, and quoted Dorothy Parker – *Brevity is the soul of lingerie.* She told them about body shape and what complemented theirs and why. She constructed patterns and designs especially for them and warned them they would need three fittings each, and then she told them they must choose fragrances that reflected the mood of their clothes. Again they rushed down to Mr Almanac's, so Nancy summoned a Perfumer to call for an afternoon of sniffing and dabbing. Tilly tried to enlighten them, draping them in luxurious material and folding it against their bodies so that they knew how it felt to be caressed and affluent and they had an inkling of deportment when swathed in fine crafts created by genius.

The Faithful O'Briens arrived – Faith and Hamish, Reginald Blood and Bobby Pickett – wanting new costumes. Faith fancied two-tone red with sequined lapels for the men and neck-to-toe sequins for herself. Bobby Pickett stood in the kitchen with his arms out while Tilly stretched a tape measure around sections of his large form and wrote numbers in her note book. Reg and Faith sat patiently at the kitchen table, silently exclaiming over fashion pictures in international magazines and nudging each other. Molly glided in and sat at the table close to Hamish, put her hand on his knee then ran it up his thigh to his crotch. He turned his walrus face to her and raised two bushy orange brows, so she smiled and pursed her lips for a kiss. He moved quickly to sort through Tilly's record collection.

'Put one on,' said Tilly.

Hamish carefully placed a disc on the turntable, lifted the arm and placed the needle gently on the record. There was scratching, and then the sound of soulful music filled the room.

'What sort of bloody awful music is this?' asked Faith disapprovingly.

'Music to hang by,' said Hamish.

'Blues,' Tilly said.

'I like it,' said Reg. 'She's got a tinny voice but it's got something . . .'

Hamish grunted. 'Pain, I reckon.'

'What's her name?' Reg asked.

'Billie Holiday.'

'Sounds like she needs one,' said Hamish.

❦

Sergeant Farrat called after dusk to collect long, flat boxes containing lace, silks, beads and feathers, as well as gently folded gowns, plain and precise and in need only of a final warm press with a damp cloth or a splash of rain water. Tilly said to him, 'I can't talk Faith out of red sequins.'

'Faith's a red sequins kind of woman,' said the sergeant, and moved to the dress stand.

Tilly threw her hands in the air. 'This is a town of round shoulders and splayed gaits.'

'And always will be, but I appreciate what you make for them. If they only knew.'

'Whose table are you on?' asked Tilly.

'Oh,' said the sergeant, 'I'm compelled to be on the Beaumonts' table with the Pettymans, us dignitaries always sit together.' He sighed. 'I'll ask you to dance, shall I?'

'I'm not going.'

'Oh – the magenta silk organza, my dear, you would look so . . . you must come. You'll be safe with Teddy.' Sergeant Farrat shook the box and said, 'If you don't promise you'll come I won't finish these.'

'You owe it to the gowns to finish them,' she said. 'You won't be able to resist.'

So he left to spend the rest of the evening hemming, tacking down seams and facings and finely camouflaging hooks and eyes.

❦

Lesley Muncan held his wife at arm's length, directing his gaze to the ceiling. On the turntable a record circled, stuck in an outer groove, scratching around and around. Mona tightened her grip on his shoulder, moved closer and kissed her husband's cheek. 'Mona, stop it,' he said, and stepped away from her.

She wrung her hands. 'Lesley, I —'

'I've told you, I can't!' He stamped his foot then buried his face in his hands.

'Why?'

Lesley kept his face hidden. 'It just doesn't . . . work. I don't know why,' he said, his voice miserable behind his hands.

Mona sat on the old couch, her chin dimpling. 'You should have told me,' she said in a wavery voice.

'I didn't know,' Lesley sniffed.

'That's a fib,' she cried.

'Oh all right!'

'There's no need to be angry with me,' said Mona, and dug her hanky out of her sleeve. Lesley sighed and flopped down on the couch next to her, crossing his arms and looking at his slippers. Eventually he said, 'Do you want me to go away?'

Mona rolled her eyes.

He turned to her. 'I've got no family, no friends.'

'But you said —'

'I know, I know.' He took her hands. 'My mother did die, that bit's true. She left me her gambling debts, a disease-ridden, infested stable and some geriatric horses. The horses are either glue or gelatin by now and the stables burned down.'

Mona continued to look at her lap.

'Mona, look at me,' said Les. 'Please?'

She kept looking down. He sighed.

'Mona, you haven't got a true friend in the world and neither have I –'

'So you're not my true friend either?'

Lesley stood up and put his hands on his hips. 'What's got into you?'

'I'm just sticking up for myself,' she said, looking up at him, 'I love you, Lesley.' Lesley burst into tears. Mona stood and held him, and they stayed in the middle of the lounge room for a long time holding each other, the record still scratching round and around. Eventually Mona said, 'No one else wants us,' and they laughed.

'Now,' said Lesley, and blew his nose on Mona's hanky, 'where were we? A waltz, wasn't it?'

'I'm just no good at dancing,' said Mona.

'I'm not very good at a lot of things, Mona,' he replied quietly, 'but we'll do the best we can together, shall we?'

'Yes,' said Mona. Lesley kicked the record player and as the opening bars of 'The Blue Danube' squeaked, Mr and Mrs Muncan began to waltz.

18

*T*illy watched an upside-down beetle try to right itself on the worn floor boards. She picked it up and dropped it onto the grass. Below her, the light in Teddy's caravan burned. She went into the kitchen and checked the clock, then checked herself. She sat on her bed, folded her arms and looked at her lap, whispering *don't, don't, don't*, but when she heard his footfall on the veranda, she said *bugger it* and went out to the kitchen. Lately she'd found herself sitting next to him and reaching for his arm when they walked to the creek. One evening she'd caught three redfin before she realised Barney wasn't with them. Tonight he sat on the floor beside Molly, who sang a tune entirely different from Ella Fitzgerald's. Teddy poured them all a beer, then flopped into his busted armchair and put his boots on the wood box and looked at Tilly, who was stitching tassels to the hem of a lemon, Jacquard jersey shawl for Nancy. 'I don't know why you bother,' he said.

'They want me to make them things – it's what I do.' She put down her sewing and lit a smoke.

'They've grown airs, think they're classy. You're not doing them any good.'

'They think I'm not doing you any good.' Tilly handed Teddy her smoke. 'Everyone likes to have someone to hate,' she said.

'But you want them to like you,' said Molly. 'They're all liars, sinners and hypocrites.'

Teddy nodded, blowing smoke rings.

'There is nothing either good or bad, but thinking makes it so,' said Tilly.

Molly directed her gaze again at Teddy, but the young man was looking keenly at Tilly.

'I'm gunna dig the garden,' said Barney.

'Not now,' said Teddy, 'it's dark.'

'No,' he said, 'tomorrow.'

Tilly nodded. 'Tomorrow, then we'll plant more vegetables.'

'You've got yourself a golf partner *and* a first-class gardener,' said Teddy.

'It's his garden,' said Tilly.

'Freeloaders. You only want food for that rabble down at the tip,' said Molly.

Tilly winked at Barney, who blushed. Later, when the embers nestled in soft ash, when Molly had nodded off and Barney had long gone home to bed, Teddy looked at Tilly with his head on the side and a twinkle in his eye. She found it unsettling, he made her palms sweat and her feet itch when he looked at her like that.

'You're not a bad sort of a sheila, are you?' He suddenly put his boots to the floor and leaned close to Tilly, elbows on his knees. 'You could make some bloke pretty happy.'

He was about to take her hands when she stood. 'I pray you, do not fall in love with me, for I am falser than vows made in wine. I must put Molly to bed now.'

'I don't know that one,' said Teddy.

'Ah ha,' said Tilly. 'Good night, good night, parting is such sweet sorrow . . .'

She threw a seat cushion which hit the door as it closed behind him. His head appeared again. He blew her a kiss then vanished.

Tilly blew a kiss at the closed door.

❦

He came to collect her for the ball wearing a new dinner suit, bow tie and patent leather shoes. She was not dressed.

'You're wearing your dressing gown?'

'What if no one talks to you, like last time?' she asked, grinning.

Teddy shrugged. 'I can talk to you.'

'They'll make it uncomfortable –'

He took her hand. 'We'll dance.'

When she looked doubtful, he put his arms around her waist and she leaned into him.

'I knew you couldn't resist me.'

She laughed. He could make her laugh these days. He pulled her to him and they tangoed around the kitchen table. 'We'll do a jitterbug that'll send them running from the floor!'

'And they'll hate me even more!' she cried, and arched back over his arm, her hair hanging to the floor.

'The more they hate you the more we'll dance,' said Teddy, and pulled her up, holding her close. They looked at each other, their faces close, the tips of their noses almost touching.

'Sickening,' said Molly.

❦

Teddy zipped up the back of her dress and shoved his hands into his pockets, looking closely at the perfect way the zipper sat over her backbone, the way it raised mounds of skin, the way she'd scooped up her hair, admiring her lovely earlobes and the fine down across the top of her lovely lip. He stepped back and looked at her standing there in her fabulous dress. Tilly had copied one of Dior's most famous gowns – the Lys Noir, a strapless, floor-length creation conceived as a sarong – but she had shortened the hem, so the magenta silk organza sat just above her knees at the front and swung behind to catch between her shoulder-blades and then fell away to a short train that frothed along the floor behind her. 'Dangerous,' said Teddy.

'You said it.' She held her hand out to him. He took it, folding it in his strong hands. He was her good friend and he was her ally. She gathered her train, draping it over her free arm. He pulled her to him and kissed her. It was a warm, soft, delicious kiss that found its way to the soles of her feet, curled her toes and melted her. It made her knees want to lift and her legs open, it pulled her hips against his and made her groan in the back of her throat. He kissed her slowly all the way across her neck and back up to her ear, then to her lips where he found her a little breathless.

'What am I doing?' she whispered.

He kissed her again.

Molly wheeled quietly up to them. They turned to look down at the old woman with the tea cosy on her head, the wool threads and ribbons dripping from her chair like soiled horsehair and the dried geraniums clinging to the spokes of her chair.

'My intentions are only honourable,' said Teddy.

'You know perfectly well girls who wear dresses like that don't warrant honourable intentions,' said Molly.

They laughed out loud together and she felt her breasts press against him, felt his heart beat and his belly shimmer gently against hers when they laughed. Teddy held her as though she were crystal and she smiled. He drove down The Hill holding her hand.

❧

The couturiered ladies of Dungatar arrived late and entered the hall at three-minute intervals, poised, their noses aimed at the lights and their mouths creased down. They moved slowly down the centre of the hall through the gaping guests from Winyerp.

Usually Marigold sent her measurements and a picture of what she wanted to Tilly via Lois, but this time she had gone for a fitting. Tilly had swathed her tightly-sprung and trembly form in long, soothing lines of pastel blue silk crepe, very closely cut on a bias with a saucy short train. A high, fine net draped softly over her throat (to hide her rash) and was sprinkled with light diamantés. The sleeves were slightly angel cut, three-quarter-length net. She had dressed her hair in a high, curled fringe. Evan told her she looked 'like a seraph', and rubbed his hands together.

Lois Pickett had brought a drawing to Tilly and said, 'What about this?' Tilly looked briefly at the long-sleeved cuffed blouse with a neckline featuring a high stand-up collar and flounced peasant skirt, then made her a sculpted, floor-length black crepe gown with a lifted front hem which exposed her slim ankles. The sleeves were bangle-length Magyar, the decolletage horse-shoe shaped and low, exposing a respectable but alluring show of Lois's cleavage. Tilly stitched a pink satin rose at the front, just inside her hip, softening her barrel appearance. Lois floated down the centre of the hall looking quite the *bon vivant* and three sizes smaller, her hair bobbed and waved and sprinkled with glitter. For Miss Prudence Dimm, Tilly had tailored royal blue wool crepe close to her body and inserted a sky

blue silk double pleat down one side which kicked and shimmered when she moved. She followed Nancy, who oozed in
only just wearing a silver lamé halter-necked backless gown that
clung like warm toffee over an apple. She was unable to swagger
since the skirt was firm, and she held herself erect (unaided by a
broom handle) in case the lamé lapels curled and exposed the
side of her breasts. Ruth followed Prudence. Tilly had created
the perfect outfit to hide Ruth's sun-baked shoulders: a long-
sleeved, high-necked diaphanous black top with light beading
that started at her nipples and accumulated at her waist. The silk
skirt was long and soft, split to the top of her slim thigh. She
looked like someone normally seen at New York's Cotton Club.

Purl had pointed to a picture of Marilyn Monroe in *Bus Stop*
and said, 'I want to look like that.' She stood in the doorway on
Fred's arm, milky white and sparkling in an itty-bitty frost-green
satin bodice with thin beady shoulder straps. A frothy ice-green
tulle skirt curled seductively from her tiny waist to hang in jagged
handkerchief triangles about her beaded ankle straps and spike
heels. She had gone platinum and copied Jean Harlow's shoulder-
length creases and curves. Fred's smile equalled her glow.

The fashion parade continued. Tilly had chosen pastel pink
satin for Gertrude. The bodice was chic – boat-necked with cap
sleeves – and the waist dipped at the back, rising gently at the
front to accommodate her fecundity. The skirt fell to a bias
A-line that kicked happily about her ankles. William had grown
a Clark Gable moustache and escorted his wife down the centre
of the hall, one hand behind his back, the other raised slightly,
Trudy's palm resting on it. They followed Elsbeth, who glided
as though she had a vase balanced on her head. Her gown was
lush, bottle-green velvet, sleeveless, with a black satin-trimmed
square neck. A wide satin belt, fitted low across her pelvis, tied

over her bottom in a huge knot that trailed the floor behind her. Tilly had made her elbow-length black satin gloves to match. Elsbeth and Trudy both dressed their hair in a French pleat coiffure.

Sergeant Farrat arrived in top hat and tails and went straight to his table. Evan and Marigold sat opposite. Trudy and Elsbeth were on either side of William and leaned across him talking. 'When shall we have Belle of the Ball?' asked Trudy.

Elsbeth looked about the hall. 'Can you see a magenta dress?'

'She's not here yet,' said William.

Elsbeth turned to her son. 'What table is she on?'

Evan patted his wife's hand and said, 'I don't think the judges will have much trouble finding Belle of the Ball tonight.' He winked at Elsbeth and Trudy.

Beula Harridene came marching through the door. Her cheeks were flushed and her hair untidy and she wore a white cardigan over a floor-length, pale green button-through with a dusty hem.

'They're on their way!' she said, and sat down next to Sergeant Farrat.

Elsbeth, Trudy and Evan stood and moved to the stage. The Faithful O'Briens played 'My Melancholy Baby'. Lesley turned to Mona and said formally, 'Shall we dance, my dear?' and they moved to the dance floor, followed by Sergeant Farrat and Marigold and the remaining Dungatar couples. They swished and shuffled in circles with their chins high. The ladies from Winyerp and Itheca remained in their seats hiding their frothy frocks and net shawls. When Nancy visited the ladies' powder room, a woman in a stiff, strapless bird's-eye gown stood beside her at the mirror and asked, 'Who makes your enchanting gowns?'

'That's our secret,' said Nancy, and turned her back.

Evan Pettyman stood in front of the microphone and wiped the sweat from his brow with a square white handkerchief. He welcomed the guests from out of town, then went on to speak about good neighbours and competitors, and begged the entrants for Belle of the Ball to rise and parade the floor just once more so the judges could make their final, very difficult decision. Purl, Lois, Nancy and Ruth, Miss Dimm, Mona and Marigold crossed the floor, stiff and smiling in front of Trudy and Elsbeth, who leaned together, nodding and whispering. Evan leaned down to them as Hamish played a drum roll.

'Oh my,' exclaimed Evan, putting his hand to his heart. 'This is indeed the right judgement. Tonight's Belle of the Ball is . . . my good lady wife, Marigold Pett-e-mon!' He moved towards his blushing wife, took her small hand and ushered her onto the dance floor to lead the evening's first waltz.

At the end of the waltz, Beula moved to Marigold and assisted her to the powder room to catch her breath and splash cold water on her wrists. Beula stood over her fanning her with a thick wad of toilet tissue. 'So, you won Belle of the Ball, in a dress *she* made,' she hissed. Marigold nodded.

'You know who her father is, don't you?' said Beula.

'A travelling repair man, a Singer Sewing-machine man,' replied the Belle.

'Wrong. Molly gave her his name, it's her middle name.'

Marigold leaned closer to Beula, who whispered into her ear, then stood back to make sure she had heard, watching her rash turn purple.

❦

Tilly and Teddy stood holding hands, smiling in the open doorway. They tapped their feet to the music, watching Tilly's gowns float about the floor. 'Oh Lord,' she said when Faith tried for F sharp. There was no one at the door – just two empty seats, the raffle book and the door prize – a new thermos and a collapsible canvas stool.

Tilly reached for the floor plan of the tables and leaned over the diagram. There were six tables with about a dozen names listed on each. She peered hard at the names.

'Look for where table six is,' said Teddy. Fred Bundle beckoned to him from a crowd of footballers lounging by the entrance, so Teddy stepped just inside the door, letting her hand slip from his.

'Table six,' said Tilly. 'Norma and Scotty Pullit, Bobby Pickett and T. McSwiney . . .' T. Dunnage was printed lightly beneath T. McSwiney but it had been scribbled out. She located her name again on a table with the Beaumonts but they had used a red biro to cover her name. At the primary school table with Miss Dimm, Nancy, Ruth and others, someone had gone to the trouble of using the pinprick-on-felt technique to perforate the plan where a name had been written, then tear the tiny piece out, leaving a jagged little square. On Purl's table, a name tacked onto the very end of the table had been scribbled out in black ink. Down the front at the band table, written in big pencil letters, some of them backward, was BARNEY. Next to his name Barney had added '+ TILLY' in red pencil. Barney was in charge of re-filling the band members' drinks and turning the pages on Faith's music book. But even then, someone had scrubbed out her name.

She straightened and turned to the doorway, but Teddy was not there – only the solid backs of footballers. She stood unsure. Councillor Evan Pettyman turned to her, snorted and spat at the floor near her hem. She gazed down at the grape-coloured splash, then up into Beula Harridene's amber eyes. Beula smiled and said, 'Bastard, murderer,' then pulled the door shut. Tilly stood alone in the foyer in her brilliant magenta Lys Noir gown, then wrapped her shawl tight about her and reached for the handle. Someone held it from the other side.

Teddy found her sitting in the park under a tree, shaking and completely unnerved. He handed her some watermelon firewater.

'They just don't want us to show them up.'

'It's not that – it's what I've done. Sometimes I forget about it and just when I'm . . . it's guilt, and the evil inside me – I carry it around with me, in me, all the time. It's like a black thing – a weight . . . it makes itself invisible then creeps back when I feel safest . . . that boy is dead. And there's more.' She drank again.

'Tell me.'

She started to cry.

'Oh Til,' he said, and held her. 'Tell me.'

❦

He took her back to his caravan by the tip and they sat opposite each other and she told him everything. It took a long time and she cried a great deal so he kissed her over and over and cried with her and pulled her close. He stroked her and soothed her and told her that it wasn't her fault, that nothing was her fault, that everyone was wrong. In the end they made close and tender love and then she slept.

He covered her in her magenta gown and sat naked next to her and smoked cigarettes, pondering her disturbed sleep, with tears sliding over his cheeks. Then he woke her. He handed her a glass of champagne and said, 'I think we should get married.'

'Married?' She laughed and cried at the same time.

'It's what they'd hate most – and besides, you're the girl for me. There could never be anyone else now.'

She nodded, smiling through her tears at him.

'We'll do it here. We'll have a big wedding in Dungatar then we'll move away to somewhere better.'

'Better?'

'Away from bad things, to a good place, where the Saturday night dances are better –'

'And will you take my mad mother as well?'

'We can even take my slow brother.'

'Barney,' she laughed again and clapped, 'yes, Barney!'

'I'm serious.'

She didn't reply so he said. 'It's the best offer you're ever going to get 'round here.'

'Where would we go?'

'To the stars,' he said, 'I'll take you to the stars, but first . . .' She stretched out her arms to him, and he lay down with her again.

❦

Later they lay together on top of the silo looking up; two silhouettes on a corrugated silver roof under a velvet black sky shot with starshine and a cold, white moon. The air was chilly, but the Autumn sun had warmed the iron.

'You never played with me when I was little,' said Tilly.

'You never came near us.'

'I watched you play here, you and Scotty and Reg. You used binoculars to search for rockets from "out of space". Sometimes you were cowboys scouting for conquering Indians on horseback.'

Teddy laughed. 'And Superman. I got into real trouble once,' he said. 'We'd jump into the grain trucks as they pulled out of the loading dock then stay on top of the wheat until we crossed the creek, where we'd jump in. The sarge waited one day with Mae. Boy, did she kick my bum.'

'Fearless,' said Tilly softly.

'Fearless,' he said, 'and I still am.'

'Are you?' She sat up. 'What about my curse?'

'I don't believe in curses. I'll show you,' he said, and stood.

Tilly sat up and watched him inch down the sloping roof to the edge. 'What are you doing?' He looked down to the grain trucks lined up beside the loading dock.

'They might be empty,' she called.

'No,' he said. 'They're full.'

'Don't,' she cried, 'please don't.' He turned and smiled at her and blew a kiss.

❧

Evan Pettyman stopped his car outside his house and helped his drunk wife inside. He lay her on her bed and was sliding her stockings from her limp feet when he heard someone in the distance, calling. He listened. It came from over at the railway line.

'Help, I need your help . . . please.'

He found Tilly Dunnage edging up and down the rim of a railway truck with her gown torn and electric hair flapping in the night wind as she stirred the seed in the truck with a long pole.

'He's in there . . . ,' she called, in a voice that came from somewhere after death,

'. . . but he won't take hold of the pole.'

III

Felt

A nonwoven fabric made from short wool
fibres lying in all directions, which become
interlocked with steam, heat and pressure into a
dense material. Dyed in plain, clear colours.
Used for skirts, bonnets and gloves.

———————

Fabrics for Needlework

19

Tilly sat opposite Sergeant Farrat. He held a biro poised over paper and carbon on a clipboard. His police uniform was crumpled, soft and limp, and in places his white hair stood on end.

'What happened, Tilly?'

She spoke in that voice that came from far away, looking at the floor. 'No,' she said, 'my name's Myrtle, I'm still Myrtle . . .'

'Go on.'

'Remember when they built the silo?'

Sergeant Farrat nodded, 'Yes,' and smiled a little, remembering the excitement the new construction caused. She crumbled a little so Sergeant Farrat said softly, 'Go on.'

'The boys would climb to the top and jump . . .' She stopped.

'Yes, Tilly,' he whispered.

'Like Superman.'

'They were foolish boys,' said Sergeant Farrat.

She still looked at the floor. 'Just boys. The people of Dungatar do not like us, Sergeant Farrat, me and Mad Molly and they never will forgive me for that boy's death or my mother's mistakes . . . they never forgave her and she did nothing wrong.'

Sergeant Farrat nodded.

'I didn't stay at the ball. Teddy found me and we went to his caravan and stayed until . . . well, for a long time but we ended up at the silos . . . we wanted to watch the sun come up on a new day . . .'

Sergeant Farrat nodded again.

'I told him my secrets and he promised he didn't care. "I am Morgan Le Fay," I said, "a banshee". We were happy – he said it was going to be all right . . .'

She crumbled a little bit more but wrenched herself back again. 'It was as if I had made the right decision after all. That to come home was right because when I got here, I found something golden – an ally. He took more champagne and we climbed up on the silo roof.'

She stopped, and stared at the floor a very long time. Sergeant Farrat let her, because she was turning to liquid inside and he needed her to hold on, he needed to be able to understand.

Finally, 'There was of course the boy . . .'

'When you were ten,' said Sergeant Farrat in a soft teary voice.

'Yes. You sent me away to that school.'

'Yes.'

'They were very good to me. They helped me, told me it wasn't really my fault.' She caught her breath. 'But then there was another . . . everyone I've touched is hurt, or dead.' And she folded in half on the wooden police station chair and shook and sobbed until she was weak and aching all over. Sergeant Farrat put her to bed in his four-poster and sat beside her, crying.

♯

Edward McSwiney had seen what happened to Stewart Pettyman. He had watched what had gone on between him and

Myrtle Dunnage from the top of the silo twenty years before. Edward was mending the roof. Kids had been playing up there and they'd broken the guttering. Edward McSwiney heard the school bell and he stopped working to watch the little figures in the distance leave school and head home. He saw Myrtle cornered and he watched the boy assault her, but by the time he got there the girl was standing frozen, terrified, against the wall. 'He was running at me like a bull . . . ,' she said in a high-whistle voice and put her fingers either side of her ears to make horns, '. . . like this.'

Edward McSwiney reached out for her then because she started to shake, but she shrank away and hid her face, and Edward saw what she had done. She had stepped aside and the boy had run head-first into the library wall, and now lay with his neck broken and his round podgy body at right angles to his head.

Later that day Edward had stood with Molly and Evan Pettyman in the police station and Sergeant Farrat said, 'Tell Mr Pettyman what you saw, Edward.'

'They used to follow her and tease her,' he said to Evan, 'call her a bastard. I caught them many times. Your Stewart had the poor little thing cornered beside the library, she was just trying to save herself –'

Evan turned away. He looked to Molly. 'My son, my son has been killed by your daughter –'

'Your daughter!' called Molly.

Edward always remembered the look on Evan's face at that moment . . . when he realised fully what it all meant, what it had come to.

Molly read his face too. 'Yes. How I wish you'd just left me alone – you followed me here, tormented me and kept me as your mistress . . . you ruined our life. We would have had a chance, at least a chance, Myrtle and I could have had some sort of life . . .' Molly had covered her face with her hands and cried, 'Poor Marigold, poor stupid Marigold, you'll send her mad,' then she flew at him with bared fingernails and kicking feet.

And Sergeant Farrat had grabbed her and held her and said, 'Stewart Pettyman is dead. We will have to take Myrtle away.'

❧

And now the sergeant had to stand by while Edward said to his own family, 'We have lost our hero, Teddy.'

They crashed before him like sugar lace. He wasn't able to offer any sense of anything from his own heart to them, no comfort, and he understood perfectly how Molly Dunnage and Marigold Pettyman could go mad and drown in the grief and disgust that hung like cob-webs between the streets and buildings in Dungatar when everywhere they looked they would see what they once had. See where someone they could no longer hold had walked and always be reminded that they had empty arms. And everywhere they looked, they could see that everyone saw them, knowing.

❧

Sergeant Farrat asked God many questions as he sat by Tilly but he received no answers.

❧

When finally he wrote his report he did not write about the champagne or the two twined beneath the close stars or that they had made love over and over again and were made one person in their intentions and that they should be sharing a life now, not just have shared a few hours. He did not say that she knew she was a cursed woman who caused boys to die with the sound of her cry and he did not say Teddy was trying to prove to her no harm would come to him when he jumped, even though she begged him not to tempt fate.

Teddy was determined, so he jumped into the full waiting grain bin sitting in the dark, the wheat bin that would be pulled away in the morning to empty its load onto a ship bound over high seas to distant continents.

But it wasn't a bin brimming with wheat. It was a bin filled with sorghum. Fine, shiny, light, brown sorghum. It wasn't bound for other continents. It was fodder. And Teddy vanished like a bolt dropped into a tub of sump oil and slid to suffocate at the bottom of that huge bin in a pond of slippery brown seeds like polished liquid sand.

☙

Instead he wrote that Teddy McSwiney had slipped and that it was his own terrible mistake, and that the witness, Myrtle Evangeline Dunnage, had indeed warned him against it and was innocent.

Sergeant Farrat found Molly by the fire, quiet and pondering. He stepped inside the door and she did not look at him, but said, 'What is it?'

He told her and she wheeled herself to her bed in the corner and pulled the blanket over her head.

☙

Tilly knew she must stay in Dungatar for a kind of penance. If she went anywhere else the same thing would happen. She was bankrupted in all ways and all that was left for her was her frail, infirm mother.

Sergeant Farrat knew that he had to step forward and

embrace his flock – to save them from themselves, and to try and make them see something to salvage in it all. He asked if she would go to the funeral and she looked at him, her soul empty and said, 'What have I done?'

'It will be better if you face them,' he said, 'show you have nothing to hide. We will go together.'

❧

It was a severe, cruel burial that trembled with things no words could describe. It was a black and shocking time and grief sickened the air. The people failed to find the strength to sing, so Reginald accompanied Hamish on bagpipes and they played a dirge by Dvořák called 'Goin' Home', which took the congregation's breath away and voiced their grief. Then Sergeant Farrat left Tilly's side to stand and deliver a sermon of sorts. He spoke of love and hate and the power of both and he reminded them how much they loved Teddy McSwiney. He said that Teddy McSwiney was, by the natural order of the town, an outcast who lived by the tip. His good mother, Mae, did what was expected of her from the people of Dungatar, she kept to herself, raised her children with truth and her husband, Edward, worked hard and fixed people's pipes and trimmed their trees and delivered their waste to the tip. The McSwineys kept at a distance but tragedy includes everyone, and anyway, wasn't everyone else in the town *different*, yet included?

Sergeant Farrat said love was as strong as hate and that as much as they themselves could hate someone, they could also love an outcast. Teddy was an outcast until he proved himself an asset and he'd loved an outcast – little Myrtle Dunnage. He loved her so much he asked her to marry him.

Sergeant Farrat walked now, back and forth in front of

the mourners, speaking sternly, 'He wanted you to love her, forgive her, and if she had been loved on that night . . . but of course you couldn't love her, you are not as large as he in heart, nor will you ever be, and that is the sad fact. Teddy thought it unforgivable – so unforgivable that he was going to leave with Myrtle and you would have lost him. If you had included her, Teddy would have always been with us, instead of trying to prove the might of his love that night. He made a terrible mistake, and we need to forgive him for that mistake. He loved Tilly Dunnage as strongly as you hate her, please imagine that – she said that she would marry him and I know that without exception all of you, along with your secrets and mistakes and prejudices and flaws, would have been invited to witness the occasion. It would have been a soothing occasion, a right and true union. In fact, it was . . .'

A sound came from deep inside Mae. It was a sound only a mother can make.

Tilly heard all of this but it was as though she were watching through a motion picture camera. She saw that the coffin was white and covered by a mountain of wreaths and that there was row after row of neat backs shuddering and bunches of tearful faces turning away from her – the Almanacs crippled together, the Beaumonts all stiff and severe and held, fat Lois blotched and scabbed and blowing her nose, her big baby Bobby crying and Nancy and Ruth clutching him. Marigold sipped from a flask of something and there was Evan, red with anger but not looking at anyone. The footballers stood in a line with their backs rigid, holding their jaws high and tight, their eyes red and brimming.

Sergeant Farrat took Tilly home after the burial and Molly rose to sit in her chair by her daughter.

❦

The wake was an awful affair that stayed soaked in stunned rage and wretchedness. Fred and Purl stood at the bar like orphans at a bus stop, since no one felt much like drinking and the sandwiches would not go down. The McSwineys sat as one, grey-faced and stiff and shocked in their chairs. Behind them on the wall hung photographs of their cheeky boy along with the Grand Final victory flag. The team said time and time again, 'He won it single-handed for us,' and tried to press the flag into Edward's crossed arms.

❦

Barney laboured up The Hill the next day with the galah on his shoulder, the cow at his heels and the chooks pecking along behind him. He tied the cow to the fence and put the galah on the post then stood in front of her with his hat crushed in his hands. He tried to raise his head to look at her, but he couldn't get his eyes to meet hers.

She felt sick – bile rose in the back of her throat and her body ached from crying. She was exhausted, but her mind raced with venom and hate for herself and the people of Dungatar. She'd prayed to a God she didn't believe in to come and take her away. She looked at Barney and wished he would hurt her, or embrace her, but he just pointed at the animals and said in a high, thin voice, 'Dad said you'll need 'em and they need a home.' She stood unsteadily and held out a hand to him but his mouth screwed open and he turned and stumbled away, yowling, holding his arms across his chest. Tilly felt her heart turn and squeeze in her chest and she sat down heavily on the step, her face twisted and crying.

✤

Graham stood harnessed and waiting, the cart behind him loaded with boxes and bundles and small brown and white dogs. Edward and Mae, Elizabeth, Margaret and Mary, Barney, George, Victoria, Charles, Henry, Mary, and Charlotte holding the baby, just stood close together, like sad rag dolls leaning each other upright. They watched the caravans and railway carriages burning. First there was smoke, then flames burst with a roar and a low wall of spitting red and orange rolled through the winter grass to the edge of the tip. The fire truck wailed from behind the shire offices and drove to park at the edge of the burning pyre. Some men got out of the truck and went to stand by the McSwiney family, then shook their heads and drove away.

When Edward was satisfied he'd rendered their happy family home a crumpled shrouded black heap, the family left. They followed Graham, the first rays of morning sun on their backs. They didn't look back, just stumbled away slow and bent to find a new place to start, their faint moans to reach at her forever.

✤

The afternoon grew bitterly cold but still she couldn't go back inside. The place was full of material – coloured bolts and rags, loose threads and cotton reels, needles and frayed edges, mannequins shaped like snobby old Elsbeth and canvas water-bag Gertrude, and puny Mona or putrid gossiping Lois, leathery old stickybeak Ruth, venomous Beula. The floor was a mattress of pins, like dead pine needles under a dark plantation. She lit another cigarette and drank the last watermelon firewater from a bottle. Her face was puffy, her eyes purple and swollen from crying. Her hair stuck out in clumps about her shoulders like strands of aloe vera leaf, and her legs and feet were bruised with cold. Deathly pale and shuddering in the smoke rising from the tip, she stared down. The town was dormant, the eye closed.

She remembered Stewart Pettyman's eyes staring up and the sound, *crack*, the groan then another sound like a cow falling on hay. When she opened her eyes Stewart Pettyman lay in the hot summer grass with his head all twisted to the side, very suddenly. There was a smell, and blood came from between his red, sloppy lips. Liquid poo filled his shorts and crept out under his thighs.

Sergeant Farrat said to her, 'His neck is broken. He is dead now and gone to heaven.'

ॐ

Tilly shifted her gaze to the square dark silo that sat like a giant coffin beside the railway line.

The people of Dungatar gravitated to each other. They shook their heads, held their jaws, sighed and talked in hateful tones. Sergeant Farrat moved amongst his flock, monitoring them, listening. They had salvaged nothing of his sermon, only their continuing hatred.

'She made him jump.'

'She murdered him.'

'She is cursed.'

'She gets it from her mother.'

Very early one morning she snuck down to Pratts for matches and flour. Purl and Nancy stopped to stare as she passed, their hate piercing her heart. Faith shoved her when she saw her standing searching the shelves, and someone ran up behind her and pulled her hair. Muriel snatched the flour and money from her hand and threw them out onto the footpath. They drove up The Hill to throw rocks onto the cottage roof in the middle of the night, driving around and around, revving, calling, 'Murderers! Witches!'

Mother and daughter stayed behind their locked door cuddling their desolation and sorrow, moving about very little. Sergeant Farrat brought them food. Molly buried toast and jam and hid boiled eggs in the folds of her blankets or shoved steamed vegetables into crannies about her chariot. On warm days flies circled her. She was silent, rising each day only to sit staring at the fire, her scarred old heart beating on and on. Tilly left her only at night to roam the plains or scout along the creek for dry gum branches to burn. They stayed together by the fire staring at the flames, and wound themselves tightly under their blankets to listen for sounds in the night's blackness. Bitterness rested on Tilly's soul and wore itself on her face. Her mother let her head drop and closed her eyes. People threw their rubbish into the smouldering pit so that the stench wafted up The Hill and filled the house.

21

*L*esley swung down the deserted main street between Mona and her mother's cousin, Una Pleasance, who was shivering. 'Of course, I'm used to European winters. I was in Milan for many, many years,' he said. 'I was working with the Lippizzaners.'

Mona slipped her arm through her husband's. 'He taught the horses, didn't you, Lesley?'

'And now you are in Dungatar?' Una looked at the few shabby shops along the main street.

'I was forced to return to Australia upon the death of my dear, dear mama. Her affairs had to be settled and just as I was on the verge of returning to Europe, I was snapped up by the Beaumonts.'

Mona nodded. 'Snapped up, by us.'

'But Dungatar's hardly –'

'Snapped up just like you, Una!' sang Lesley, and smiled sweetly at her.

'So,' he continued, 'here we all are! That's the Station Hotel – miles from the railway line,' and he laughed, nudging Una.

'They do a lovely steak and chips,' said Mona.

'If you like steak and chips,' said Lesley.

Una pointed to The Hill. 'What's up there?' They stopped, looking at the smoke curling up to shroud the vine-covered walls and creep away to the plains. Smoky fingers stretched around the chimney and up into the clouds.

'That's where Mad Molly and Myrtle live,' said Mona gravely.

'Oh,' said Una, and nodded knowingly.

'This is Pratts Store,' said Lesley, breaking the trance. 'The only supply outlet for miles, a gold mine! It's got everything – the bread monopoly, the butcher, haberdashery, hardware, even veterinary products, but here comes Dungatar's richest man now!'

Councillor Pettyman was walking towards them, smiling, his eyes on Una.

'Good morning,' he cried. 'It's the Beaumont family with my special guest.' He grabbed Una's hand and kissed her long white fingers.

'We're just giving Una a guided tour of her new home –'

'You must allow me!' said Evan, rubbing his hands and licking his lips, his warm breath visible in the winter air. 'I can drive Miss Pleasance in the comfort of the shire car, after all – she is my guest.' He looped her arm through his and spun her off towards his car. 'We can drive along the creek to some of the outlying properties and then . . .' He opened the car door and helped Una settle in the front seat, lifted his hat at Mona and Lesley left standing on the footpath then drove the new girl in town away.

'The cheek!' said Lesley.

♯
𝄐

Tilly sat against the wall looking down through the grey mist to the round green and grey mud-smudged oval fringed by dark cars, the supporters standing between them like caught tears. The small men washed from one end of the field to the other, black bands on their flaying arms as they grabbed at the tiny ball, the supporters howling their scorn at the opposition. She knew anger and woe propelled them. Their cries bounced off the great silo and shot up to her and out across the paddocks in the smoke.

Rain started and fell from the clouds in sheets, pelting and drenching, pounding the cars and the iron roof above her. It bashed at the windows and bent the vegetable leaves in Barney's garden. A diesel engine groaned away from the Dungatar station, the passenger carriages empty. The cow, tethered halfway down The Hill, ceased munching to listen, then turned her rump to the weather and folded her ears forward. The players stopped and stood about, blinded and confused in the grey flooded air until the rain eased, when they started playing again.

Tilly feared football defeat would send the people to her, that they would spill wet and dripping from the gateway of the oval to stream up The Hill with clenched fists for revenge blood. She waited until there was a scattered clapping from the crowd and a horn tooted. The galah bobbed, raising his crest, and lifted a claw from the veranda rail . . . but it was Dungatar who had lost, failed at its last chance to make the finals. The cars drove out the gate and dispersed.

She went inside where Molly sat turning the pages of a newspaper. 'Oh,' she said, 'it's only you.'

Tilly looked at her mother, her skeleton shoulders under her tattered hessian shawl. 'No,' she said, 'it's me *and* you; there is only you and you have only me.'

She sat down to sew but after a while she shoved the needle safely in the hem of Molly's new dress and leaned back to rub her eyes. She gazed at Teddy's empty seat and the wood box where he always put his boots and let her mind rest in the orange flames dancing in the stove. Molly spread the paper on the kitchen table, squinted through the bifocals perched at the end of her nose and said, 'I need my glasses, where have you hidden them?'

Tilly reached over and turned *The Amalgamated Dungatar Winyerp Argus Gazette* the right way up. 'Well,' Molly said, and smiled slyly, 'they got another seamstress, from Melbourne. There'll be trouble now, she'll have a trail of Singer Sewing Machine men after her, roaming the countryside leaving broken hearts and hymens in their wake.'

Tilly peered over her mother's shoulder. The one item in 'Beula's Grapevine' column read, 'High Fashion Arrives'. There was a photograph of the president, secretary and treasurer of the Dungatar Social Club – wearing creations by Tilly – smiling at a severe woman, whose middle part dissected her widow's peak.

'This week Dungatar welcomes Miss Una Pleasance, who has brought to us her considerable dressmaking talents. The Dungatar Social Club, on behalf of the community, welcomes Miss Pleasance and we look forward to the grand opening of her dressmaking establishment, *Le Salon*. Miss Pleasance is at present a guest of Councillor and Mrs Evan Pettyman. Her business premises will be temporarily located at their home. The grand opening will be celebrated on Friday 14th July, at 2 p.m. Ladies bring a plate.'

❦

First thing in the morning they heard the Triumph Gloria arrive and sit idling on the lawn. Tilly crept to the back door and peeped out. Lesley sat behind the wheel and Elsbeth waited in the back seat with a hanky held to her nose. The new seamstress sat beside her, staring at the wisteria climbing the veranda posts and up and over the roof. Mona stood on the veranda, twirling a riding crop around and around in her hand. Tilly opened the door.

'Mother says she wants . . . all the things you've got half made, mine and hers and Trudy, Muriel . . . Lois . . .' Her voice faded.

Tilly folded her arms and leaned on the doorjamb.

Mona straightened. 'Could we have them, please?'

'No.'

'Oh.' Mona ran back to the car and leaned in to talk to her mother. There was a small conversation in spatting tones then Mona stepped hesitantly back to the veranda.

'Why?'

'Because no one's paid me.' Tilly slammed the door. The frail building creaked and leaned an inch closer to the ground.

❦

That evening, there was a knock at the door. 'It's me,' called Sergeant Farrat, sotto voce. When Tilly opened the door she found the sergeant standing on the veranda in black linen gaucho pants, a white Russian Cossack shirt and red quilted waistcoat with a black hat with flat brim balanced at a scandalous tilt on the side of his head. He held a white paper package and from beneath his waistcoat he produced a long brown bottle which he held high, moths fluttering about his shoulders. 'One of Scotty's finest,' he said, smiling broadly.

Tilly opened the screen door.

'Nightcap, Molly?' asked the sergeant.

She looked at the sergeant, horrified. 'Don't wear them,

they're the sort of thing that'd get wrapped around your neck while you're asleep.'

Tilly placed three chilled glasses on the table and Sergeant Farrat poured. He unwrapped the package he'd brought. 'I have a challenge for you. I've been reading up on the Spanish invasion of the South Americas and I have here a costume for my collection which needs alteration.' Sergeant Farrat stood and pressed a diminutive matador's costume against his round form. It was bright green silk brocade, heavily beaded, bordered with elaborate gold lamé binding and tassels. 'I thought perhaps you could improvise some inserts, similar or at least blending with the general glitter of the costume. They could be disguised quite cleverly by Dungatar's only real creative hands, don't you think?'

'I see there's a new seamstress in town,' said Tilly.

Sergeant Farrat shrugged. 'I doubt she's travelled, or received any sophisticated training.' He looked down at his shiny green outfit. 'But we'll see – at the fund-raising festival.' He looked back up at her expectantly, but she merely raised an eyebrow. Sergeant Farrat continued, 'The Social Club have organised it, there'll be a gymkhana and a bridge competition during the day with refreshments of course . . . and a concert – recitals and poetry. Winyerp and Itheca are participating . . . there will be prizes too. It's in this week's paper, and Pratts' window.'

Tilly reached to feel the beading on the matador's costume. She smiled. Sergeant Farrat beamed down at her. 'I knew a bit of needlework would lift your spirits.' He sat down in the old armchair by the fire, leaned back and put his leather slippers up on Teddy's wood box.

'Yes,' she said, and wondered how her teachers in Paris –

Balmain, Balenciaga, Dior – would react at the sight of Sergeant Farrat sailing down a catwalk sparkling in his green matador's costume.

'Poetry and recital you say?' Tilly swallowed heavily from her glass.

'Very cultural,' said the sergeant.

22

William was slumped in a battered deckchair on what was now called 'the back patio', formerly the porch. His heavily pregnant wife sat inside, filing her nails, the telephone caught in the fatty folds of her chins and shoulder. '. . . Well I said to Elsbeth today that there's no hope at all of getting any of our mending back, lunacy is hereditary, you know – Molly most likely murdered someone before she came here so Lord knows what they get up to in that slum on that hill . . . Beula's seen her milking the cow and she sneaks along the creek to steal dead wood, like a peasant, in broad daylight! Doesn't look the least bit guilty, Elsbeth and I were just saying the other day, thank heavens we've got Una . . .'

'Yes,' muttered William, 'most important.' He reached under his chair for the whisky bottle, slopped a generous amount into the thick glass, held it up to his eye and viewed the horse jumps in the front paddock through the amber liquid. Inside his wife talked on. 'I'll get William's cheque book but I really shouldn't have a new wardrobe until after the baby . . . must dash, here's Lesley with the car, see you there.'

William waited until the scurrying heels had ceased and the

front door slammed. He sighed, drained his whisky, refilled the glass, banged his pipe against the wooden armrest and reached for his tobacco.

❦

Una Pleasance stood at Marigold's front door wearing a navy A-line with matching pumps featuring a striped bow at the toes.

'Please remove your shoes,' she said to the arriving guests before they walked on Marigold's bright, white floor.

Beula cruised the parlour, peering at photos, searching for dust on the skirting boards and picture rails. 'What an unusual sideboard,' she said, opening the top drawer.

'It's antique – my grandmother's,' said Marigold, worrying Beula would leave fingerprints on her polish.

'I chucked all my grandmother's old junk out,' said Beula.

Just then Lois lumbered past pushing Mrs Almanac in her wheelchair: there were bindis in the tyres and oil traces on the axle. Marigold shuddered, and ran to her room, grabbed a Bex powder sachet, flung back her head and opened her mouth. She winced as the powder slid from its paper cradle onto her tongue, then reached for the tonic bottle on the bedside table, unscrewed the cap and sucked. Just then Beula barged in. 'Oh,' she said, 'your nerves again, is it?'

She smiled and backed out. Marigold put her hand to her neck rash and took another long swig, then popped two tin oxide tablets onto her tongue just for good measure. In the parlour, Beula selected the chair in the corner for a prime view and sat with her chin tucked down, her arms folded over her white blouse and her skinny legs under her kilt. The rest of the ladies sat on plastic-covered sitting room chairs sipping tea from cups that tasted faintly of ammonia, tsk-tsking at the offered cream cakes.

When Lois landed on the couch next to Ruth Dimm stale air billowed, and Ruth pressed a hanky to her nose and moved to stand by the door. Then Muriel Pratt caused a stir when she arrived wearing a frock made by 'that witch . . . just to show you what we're used to,' she said to Una, who looked closely at it then went to stand next to her display.

For the opening of *Le Salon*, Una had provided a sample of her work. A mannequin stood in the corner wearing a button-through seersucker peasant floral frock with a flounce-collared neckline and small puffed sleeves. The mannequin wore vinyl Mexican moccasins to match and a small straw bonnet. It was an outfit straight from Rockmans of Bourke Street catering for the 'not-so-slim figure'.

When Purl arrived she dumped a concave sponge on the table and said, 'Lovely day,' then turned to Una and looked her up and down. 'Get sick of Evan or Marigold, you just come and camp at the pub.' She lit a Turf filter tip and, looking about her for an ashtray, spotted the mannequin in the corner. 'That one of the first things you made back at sewing school, is it?' she asked with interest.

Beula turned to the Beaumonts standing together by the window like a grim wedding photograph from 1893 and said loudly, 'My, you're big, Ger, I mean Trudy. When *exactly* are you due?' Mona offered the cake plate around again. Soon everyone's saucer was crammed with thick bricks of lemon slice, hedgehog, cinnamon tea cake and pink cream lamingtons, and they were picking the crumbs and coconut flakes from their bosoms.

When Marigold stepped red-faced and shaking back into the crowded room, Mona handed her a cup of tea with a cream scone on the saucer. Nancy marched through the door behind her, bumping Marigold and sending her cup and saucer splashing onto the carpet. Marigold collapsed, her face resting in the tea and cream puddle, the two fluffy pods of scone dough resting at her ears. The clucking, floral women assisted her to bed, and when finally they returned, Elsbeth stepped to the table, clapped loudly and began the formal proceedings. 'We welcome Una to Dungatar and wish to say –'

At that moment Trudy bellowed like a distressed cow and doubled over. There was a noise like a water bag bursting. Pink, steamy fluid flowed from her skirts and a circle of carpet around her feet darkened. Her belly was lurching as if the devil himself was ripping at her womb with his hot poker. She folded down on all fours, yelling. Purl finshed her tea in one swallow, grabbed her sponge and left hastily. Lesley fainted and Lois grabbed his ankles and dragged him outside. Mona watched her sister-in-law labouring at her feet. She put her hand over her mouth and ran outside, retching.

Elsbeth turned crimson and cried, 'Get the doctor!'

'We haven't got a doctor,' said Beula.

'Get someone!' She knelt beside Trudy. 'Stop making a scene,' she said. Trudy bellowed again.

Elsbeth yelled, '*Shut up*, you stupid grocer's girl. It's just the baby.'

Lesley lay on the lawn, flat on his back with Lois hosing him down. His toupée had washed off and lay like a discarded scrotum on the grass by his bald head. Mona stalled the Triumph Gloria three times before lurching up onto the nature strip, shattering Marigold's front fence and roaring away with the hand brake burning, the front fender left behind, swinging from a denuded fence post. Just then Purl jogged back around the corner calling, 'He's coming, he's coming.'

Lois called to Una. 'He's coming,' and Una called to Elsbeth, 'He's coming.'

Trudy yelled and howled.

Elsbeth shrieked, 'Stop screaming.'

Through clenched teeth between contractions Trudy growled, 'This is all your son's fault, you old witch. Now get away from me or I'll tell everyone what you're really like!'

Twenty minutes into the labour Felicity-Joy Elsbeth Beaumont shot from her mother's slimy hirsute thighs into the bright afternoon and landed just beside Marigold's sterilised towels with Mr Almanac standing in distant attendance.

Beula Harridene leaned close to Lois. 'She's only been married eight months.'

❧   •

When Evan got home that evening he found his nature strip ploughed, his front fence demolished, all the doors and windows open and an odd smell permeating the house. There was a large stain on the carpet and, in the middle of it, a pile of soiled towels. On top of the towels was a fly-blown lump of afterbirth, like liver in aspic. Marigold, fully clothed, was unconscious in bed.

23

*T*hree women from Winyerp stood at Tilly's gate-posts, tiny flakes of ash from the burning tip settling on their hats and shoulders. They were admiring the garden. The wisteria was in full bloom, the house dripping with pendulous, violet flower sprays. Thick threads of myrtle crept around the corner, through the wisteria and across the veranda, netting the boards with shiny green leaves and bright white flowers. Red, white and blue rhododendron trumpets sprang up against the walls and massive oleanders – cerise and crimson – stood at each corner of the house. Pink daphne bushes were dotted about and foxgloves waved like people saying farewell from a boat deck. Hydrangea, jasmine and delphinium clouded together around the tank stand and a tall carpet of lily of the valley marched out from the shade. French marigold bushes, squatting like sentries, marked the boundary where a fence once stood. The air was heavy, the garden's sweet perfume mingling with the acrid smoke and the stink of burning rubbish. A vegetable garden faced south: shiny green and white spinach leaves creaked against each other in the breeze while fuzzy carrot-tops sided against straight, pale garlic stalks and onions, and bunches of rhubarb burst and tumbled against the privet hedge, which contained the garden entirely. Bunches of herb bushes lined the outside edge of the hedge.

Molly opened the door and called, 'There's a bunch of old stools from out at Fart Hill trespassing out here.'

Tilly arrived behind her. 'Can I help you?'

'Your garden . . . ,' said an older woman. 'Why, Spring isn't even here.'

'Almost,' said Tilly. 'The ash is very good and we get the sun up here.'

A pretty woman with a baby on her hip turned to look down at the tip. 'Why doesn't the council do something about the fire?'

'They're trying to smoke us out,' said Molly. 'They won't, though, we're used to being badly treated.'

'What can I do for you?' asked Tilly.

'We were wondering if you were still seamstressing?'

'We are,' said Molly, 'but it'll cost you.'

Tilly smiled and put her hand over her mother's mouth. 'What would you like?'

'Well, a christening gown . . .'

'Some day wear . . .'

'. . . and a new ball gown would be nice, if you're . . . if it's at all possible.'

Molly shoved Tilly's hand away, pulling a measuring tape from within her blankets, and said, 'Yes – now take your clothes off.'

❦

Again Molly woke to the sound of pinking-shears crunching through material on the wooden table, and when she got to the kitchen she found no porridge waiting, only Tilly bent over her sewing machine. On the floor about her feet lay scraps and off-cuts from satin velour au sabre, wool crepe and bouclé, silk faille, shot pink and green silk taffeta, all perfect to decorate her chair with. The small house buzzed with the dull whirr and thudding of the Singer and the scissors rattled on the table when Tilly let them go.

Late one afternoon Molly sat on the veranda watching the sun draw in its last rays. A mere breath after the last tentacle of light had been pulled below the horizon, a skinny woman marched up The Hill towards her hauling two suitcases. Molly scrutinised the severe woman's widow's peak, the mole above her dark lipstick. Ash settled on the tips of the pinpoint nipples pressing against her sweater and the pencil-line skirt she wore stretched over her hip bones. Finally she spoke. 'Is Tilly here?'

'Know Tilly, do you?'

'Not really.'

'Heard about her, though?'

'You could say that.'

'Figures.' Molly turned her wheelchair to the screen door. 'Tilly – Gloria Swanson has come to stay,' she called.

Una's hand went to her throat and she looked afraid. The veranda light flicked on.

'We saw *Sunset Boulevard* earlier this year,' said Tilly from behind the screen door. She had a tea towel flung over her shoulder and a vegetable masher in her hands.

'I'm Una Pleasance,' said the woman.

Tilly said nothing.

'I'm the –'

'Yes,' said Tilly.

'I'll get to the point. I'm afraid I'm rather inundated and need some sewing done for me.'

'Sewing?'

Una paused. 'Mending mostly, hems, zips, darts to alter. It's all very simple.'

'Well then I'm afraid you've made a mistake,' said Tilly. 'I'm a qualified tailoress and dressmaker. You just need someone handy with a needle and thread.' She closed the door.

'I'll pay you,' called Una.

But Tilly was gone and Una was left on the veranda in the yellow light with a few moths and the sound of night-crickets chirping and frogs croaking.

'Oh,' said Molly, beaming up at her, 'that's very good, it worked very well in the film too, the way you open your eyes, bare your teeth and curl your top lip like that. It suits you.'

❧

Mrs Flynt from Winyerp stood in front of Tilly's mirror admiring her new outfit – a white silk satin jumpsuit with flock printed roses. 'It's so . . . so . . . it's marvellous,' she said, 'just marvellous. I bet no one else is game to wear one of these.'

'It suits you,' said Tilly. 'I hear there's to be a concert?'

'Yes,' said Mrs Flynt, 'poetry and recitals. Mrs Beaumont has been teaching elocution – wants to show off. She's determined to beat us at bridge as well.'

'Nothing like a bit of one-upmanship,' said Tilly. 'You should challenge her to a bit of singing and dancing as well.'

'We're not much good at either, I'm afraid.'

'What about a play then? Best actress, best set design, best costume . . . ,' suggested Tilly.

Mrs Flynt's face lit up. 'A play.' She opened her purse to pay.

Tilly handed her the bill. 'Plays are such fun to put on. They bring out the best and worst in people, don't you think?'

❧

Purl was being a good barmaid. She patted William's wrist.

'It's horrible,' said William. 'I didn't know it would be like this. She smells like stale milk and there's pink, crusty secretions all over the bed, the baby's all floppy and gooey, I feel so . . . alone. I wanted a boy.'

'She might grow up to be just like her grandfather – on your side that is, like your dad, eh, William?' said Purl.

William raised his head from the bar cloth and tried to focus on her. 'You knew him well, didn't you?' he said.

'I certainly did.'

Fred and the drinkers at the end of the bar nodded. She had known him very well.

'He wasn't a very good father either,' said William. The men at the bar shook their heads. They watched William drain glass after glass until he focused on Purl again and said, 'There's more.'

'What?'

William curled his finger at her and when she leaned closer he whispered very loudly to her earring, 'I don't really love my wife.'

'Well,' said Purl, and patted him again, 'you're not alone there.'

The men at the other end of the bar nodded.

'Oh God,' he cried. The men looked tactfully out the window and sent more cigarettes and beer down the bar with Fred.

24

Marigold wasn't in the front yard so Lois crept to the door and knocked softly.

'Have you got an appointment?'

Lois jumped. Marigold had appeared in front of her wearing a blue housecoat with kneeling pads bound to her knees with elastic bands, a shower cap on her head and elbow-length canvas gloves. She had a handkerchief tied across her nose like an outlaw and held a tin of polishing wax and a greasy cloth.

'Did you make an appointment?' she said.

'Yes.'

'Have you got velvet?'

'No,' said Lois, 'a fitting – didn't she tell you?'

'It's already cut out then?'

'Just some adjusting to do.'

'As long as it's not velvet – it gets everywhere. I hate it when she cuts velvet, or linen. You can see the bits in the air.'

Lois picked her fingernails.

'Well you'd better go on in, but mind you take your shoes off – I've just vacuumed. And walk along the edge of the hall carpet because the middle's wearing. I've had to put her rent up.'

Which means the prices'll go up again, thought Lois.

Marigold took a clean hanky from her pocket and twisted the door knob open then watched Lois edge along the wall to Una's room where she knocked quietly. Una opened the door a little and peeked out, 'Where is she?'

'Polishing the veranda.'

Una looked away while Lois eased on her new frock. It had a fitted bodice, a dropped waist and gay accordion pleats. When Una turned to look her eyes began to brim brightly and she bit her bottom lip. The dress strained across her shoulders and the neckline swam, the bodice drooped in folds where her breasts should have been, the waist stretched across her stomach, flattening the pleats, and the hem rode high above her knees.

'It suits you,' said Una. 'That'll be ten shillings.'

⅋

Evan waited behind the peppercorn tree at the side of the house. Lois, her new frock folded carefully over her arm, stopped on the nature strip where Marigold was hosing leaves from the footpath. Beula arrived and stood talking to them. While the women gossiped Evan crept through the back door and tiptoed to Una's room. She sat in the chair, waiting as Evan rushed to kneel in front of her. He took her hands, pursed his lips to her finger tips then her palms as he kissed his way up to her neck. She swooned back in her chair and he pucked across her cheeks to her lips and pressed his mouth to hers. Una spread her thighs and undid her blouse. 'Quickly,' she gasped, and tugged her skirt up to her waist. Evan seized his member in his hands and shuffled forward on his knees, aiming.

There was a sudden, loud, thruuppppp as the water-jet from the hose ripped across the windowpane. Una jumped and sat up, wrenching her knees together, catching Evan's testicles and squashing them so they shot up, leaving his scrotum crawling and empty. He bent double, folding like tinfoil, his forehead cracking dully on Una's. They held their foreheads screaming silently, then Evan fell to lie staring at the fine threads and flux in the carpet nap, purple-faced and winded. He felt his mighty penis melt to a damp heavy mass.

Outside, Marigold stood on the front lawn running the hose back and forth, back and forth across the dusty windowpane.

❦

That night, a year after Teddy McSwiney met his death, Lois lumbered up The Hill and pounded at the back door calling to Tilly and Molly as though she had visited only yesterday. Tilly opened the door.

'I must say, Til,' she said, and stepped into the kitchen, 'that garden you got sure is lovely.' She placed a bag and an envelope on the table. The envelope was from Irma Almanac and when Tilly opened it a pound note fluttered to the table.

'You got any of them cakes you used to make her? She's all stuck up again, stiff as a board with terrible pain. You know what to put in them,' said Lois, and winked.

'Herbs,' said Tilly, 'and vegetable oils, from my garden.'

'You got any I can take for her now?'

'I'll have to make some.'

Lois reached into the bag and dumped a packet of flour and half a pound of butter on the table then made her way to the door. 'I'll tell her you'll bring them tomorrow, shall I?'

When Tilly hesitated she put her hand on the door knob and added, 'If we still had Ed McSwiney we could send them around wif him couldn't we, eh?'

She closed the door firmly behind her.

❦

The next afternoon Tilly made her way down The Hill, crossed the main road behind the hall and tramped along the soft, mossy creek bank behind Irma's.

'I'm glad to see you,' said Irma, 'and not just for the cakes.'

Tilly put the kettle on then broke one of the cakes into bite-sized pieces, placing them where Irma could collect them in her swollen fingers. 'I have so missed getting out to the front gate,' she said, chewing, 'and as for Lois's manhandling . . .'

She ate slowly and deliberately. While Tilly was making tea Lois rushed in. 'Beula said you was here now,' she said to Tilly. Then she removed her housecoat and stood before Tilly in her ten shilling accordion-pleat frock. 'We've got a drama meeting to-morrow,' she said, 'and I need this fixed up. I'm in a bit of a spot.'

Tilly was still gazing at the dress.

'I won't say nothing to Mr A about you being here if you do it by tomorrow.'

Tilly raised an eyebrow. 'Turn around,' she said. Lois turned.

'I could do something with it,' she said.

Lois clapped her hands and started removing the dress. 'I'll collect it tomorrow then,' she said.

'It'll cost you,' said Tilly.

Irma stopped chewing and looked over at Lois, frozen with her skirt pulled up over her head, her grubby step-ins squashing folds about her knees and her shins shining maroon and pock-marked blue against the lino floor. 'How much?'

'Depends how long it takes,' said Tilly.

Lois removed the frock. 'I'll need it by four.'

'Pick it up about ten to,' said Tilly, reaching for the bundle of beige pleats.

That night she sat by the fire and sewed darts into the neckline and let the bodice seams out. Then she unpicked the skirt and sewed it back on again, front to back, back to front.

❦

Una, Muriel, Trudy and Elsbeth watched the visitors from behind the curtain. The Winyerp and Itheca Drama Club dignitaries stepped from their automobile and paused to admire the homestead and surrounds. They looked like a group of European aristocrats' wives who had somehow lost their way. A statuesque woman with Veronica Lake hair wore a strapless jersey top with a scarf tied neatly about her throat like a choker, and a floral-printed silk organza pareo. Another wore a fitted skirt featuring an asymmetrical peplum and a polo-necked blouse and there was a trumpet skirt – afternoon attire – of black silk faille. A buxom lass wore wrap slacks and her top featured a keyhole decolletage and mitred corners. There was even a jumpsuit. The Dungatar Social Committee women smoothed the full circle skirts of the cotton seersucker sun dresses Una had made especially for them and frowned. Elsbeth took a deep breath and flung the front door open. There were loud introductions all around and the Dungatar committee welcomed them cheerily, squeaking and cooing and being very gay. William heard them in the nursery where Felicity-Joy gurgled in her cot, bubbling and reaching for her toes. William shoved his fists deep into his Bombay Bloomers and kicked the skirting board then leaned his head against the wall and banged it softly.

Lesley and Mona arrived. Mona looked crisp and summery in a lemon Nankeen sun dress with a crossover top and pegged skirt – one of Tilly's.

The socialites sat on the new leather lounge suite chatting

as Lois came through the door pushing a tea trolley, the cups and spoons rattling. 'Thank you,' said Elsbeth in her most dismissive voice, but Lois remained. 'Hello,' she said, smiling and nodding at the visitors. 'My, don't you look lovely in your smart outfits?'

'Thank you,' chorused the ladies.

'I've got a new frock myself!' she said beaming, nodding to Una, 'our town dressmaker made it for me.'

Lois held her arms away from her sides and turned slowly, saying, 'I'll just fetch the semmiches, cucumber they are, real thin.' As she walked across to the kitchen the accordion pleats rose and dropped on her cliff hips and because the hem rose alarmingly in the centre, the ladies glimpsed the bulge where her step-ins ended and the flesh behind her knees quivering like a baby's bottom.

Una paled and Elsbeth excused herself, following Lois to the kitchen. A short time later the back door slammed and Elsbeth returned to calmly discuss the program for the concert.

'We have an idea,' said Mrs Flynt.

Elsbeth blinked at them. 'An idea?'

'An eisteddfod,' said Mrs Flynt, 'a *drama* eisteddfod. That'll test your elocution, and everything else, won't it?'

Elsbeth stiffened. Trudy looked afraid.

'What's an eisteddfod?' asked Mona.

'I'll explain, shall I?' said Mrs Flynt, graciously.

'If you would,' said Muriel.

🎵

It was agreed the Winyerp hall was the most suitable venue. Trophies would be awarded to best actor, best actress, best play and best costumes . . . Elsbeth's hand went nervously to her marcasite brooch and Trudy cleared her throat.

Muriel said, 'I guess we'll get Una to make ours –'

Mrs Flynt from Itheca slapped her knee and cried, 'Splendid, because we want your Tilly.'

'No!' said Trudy, and stood up. Her hem caught in the heel of her sandals and her full skirt peeled away from her waist like greased paper from a warm cake, exposing her off-white nylon slip. 'She's ours. I've spoken to Myrtle Dunnage, this morning in fact,' she lied.

'You could ask her to fix your skirt then,' said Mrs Flynt. 'They just aren't made the way they used to be, are they?'

25

Hamish slid the one-way ticket across the slippery leather counter to 'Miss Unpleasant', as Faith called her. Miss Unpleasant picked up the ticket with her fingernails, turned wordlessly away and went to the end of the platform to look down the tracks towards the setting sun, her suitcases about her knees.

The station master approached the Beaumonts. He checked his watch, twisted the ends of his moustache and said, 'It's a steamer t'night, R class, type 4-6-4. A "Hudson" it's called, running to time, o'course. It'll be a grand trip.'

'Yes,' said William, and bounced on the balls of his feet. Hamish ambled down the track towards the signal levers. William wandered down to Una and said, 'It's a steamer, an R class, a "Hudson", on time as well. You should have a pleasant journey.' He puffed on his pipe and wandered back to his family.

Hamish moved back to the edge of the platform and held out his flag, the whistle between his teeth.

A tear welled and slid down Una's cheek to plop between the dots on the rayon scarf tied at her throat.

⅋

Evan Pettyman stood over his wife's bed and carefully poured thick syrup tonic into a teaspoon.

'I think I need two spoonfuls tonight, Evan,' said Marigold.

'Will two be enough do you think, dearest? Mr Almanac said you could have as much as you needed, remember?'

'Yes, Evan,' said Marigold. He poured her another spoonful then fluffed her pillows, adjusted the photo of Stewart and tucked the bedclothes in. Marigold folded her hands across her ribs and closed her eyes.

'Marigold, I have to go to Melbourne soon, just for a few days,' said Evan.

'Why?'

'Shire business, very important.'

'I'll be alone in the evenings –'

'I'll ask Nancy to call.'

'I don't like her.'

'I'll get Sergeant Farrat to call, or someone . . .'

'You're so important, Evan,' she muttered. Soon her mouth fell open and her breath came evenly, so Evan left her. He closed himself in his office and took a photograph of Una from his locked safety box and propped it on his desk, then leaned back in his leather chair, loosened the tie on his pyjama pants and reached in.

*T*illy was dreaming. Pablo came and sat above her bed in his nappy, the down on his perfect round head haloed in the light. He looked at his mother and laughed, wet-mouthed, showing two short round teeth. He flapped his cushion-arms and Tilly reached for him, but he hugged his pale round tummy and looked serious. He frowned, puzzled. It was the same expression he had worn the day he heard the new sound – the fluid chocolate noise of a street busker's oboe. He had been perched on her hip when he turned his clear blue eyes to hers with a look of wonderment and touched his ear where the sound had caught the side of his head. His mother had pointed to the oboe and he understood and clapped.

Tilly held her arms out to him again but he shook his head – no – and her singing heart fell flat.

'I have something to tell you,' he said in an old voice.

'What?'

He faded – she cried out but he was moving away too quickly. Baby Pablo looked down at her and said, 'Mother.'

It was daylight, the sun shining on her through the window,

so she got up and went to find her mother. Molly sat upright in her wheelchair by the stove, dressed, her hair brushed. She'd re-kindled the fire and was gently pulling the fibre threads and material strips from the armrests of her chair and throwing them into the flames. The hard dirt-shiny cushions that were usually stuffed about her thighs and back were gone. In the flames old boiled eggs, serviettes wound tight in lumps and chicken legs caught the golden flames and melted to embers. Molly ceased working and looked up at her daughter. 'Good morning, Myrtle,' she said in a soft voice. Tilly paused with the kettle at the stove to look down at her mother, amazed. She picked some lemon grass and was standing watching the lemon bits float about on the hot water in her cup when Molly spoke again. 'I had a dream last night,' she said, 'about a baby. A bonny, round baby with dimples in his knees and elbows, and two perfect teeth.' The old lady looked closely at Tilly. 'It was your baby.'

Tilly turned away.

'I lost a baby too,' said Molly, 'I lost my little girl.'

Tilly sat down in Teddy's chair and looked at her mother. 'I was working in Paris,' she said haltingly. 'I had my own shop and lots of clients and friends, a boyfriend, my partner – his name was Ormond, he was English. We had a baby, my baby, a boy we called Pablo, just because we liked the name. We were going to bring him here then take you back with us, but when Pablo was seven months old I found him one morning in his cot . . . dead.' Tilly stopped and took a long deep breath. She had only ever told this story once, to Teddy.

'He died, he just died. Ormond didn't understand, he blamed me and couldn't forgive me – but the doctors said it must have been a virus, although he hadn't been sick. Ormond left me so I had to come home – I had nothing anymore, it all seemed so pointless and cruel. I decided I could at least help my mother.' She stopped again and sipped her tea. 'I realised I still had something here. I thought I could live back here, I thought that here I could do no more harm and so I would do good.' She looked at the flames. 'It isn't fair.'

Molly reached out and patted her daughter's shoulder with her flat soft hands. 'It isn't fair, but you may never have gotten out of this place, you could have been stuck here hiding with me on top of this hill if you hadn't been sent away, and there is time for you yet.'

'It hasn't been fair for you.'

'I suppose. I was a spinster when your . . . well, I was naive. But I don't care, I ended up with you. To think I almost married that man, your "father". We could have been stuck with him as well! I've never told you who –'

'No need,' said Tilly. 'Miss Dimm told me in primary school. I didn't believe her at first but then when Stewy . . .'

Molly shivered. 'I wouldn't give my baby away so I had to leave my home and my parents. He came after me and used me. I had no money, no job and an illegitimate child to support. He kept us . . .' Molly sighed. 'Then when he couldn't have his son anymore, I couldn't have you.' Molly wiped tears from her eyes and looked directly at Tilly. 'I went mad with loneliness for you, I'd lost the only friend I had, the only thing I had, but over the years I came to hope you wouldn't come back to this awful place.' She looked at her hands in her lap. 'Sometimes things just don't *seem* fair.'

'Why didn't you ever leave?'

She said very softly, 'I had nowhere to go,' and she looked at Tilly with love, her soft, old face with its high cheekbones and creamy, creased complexion. 'He wouldn't let them tell me where you were. I never knew where you were.'

'You waited?'

'They took you away in a police car and that's all I knew.'

Tilly got on her knees in front of her mother and buried her face in her lap, and Molly stroked her head fondly and they wept. Sorry, so sorry, they said to each other.

❦

In the afternoon Molly fell. Tilly was in the garden picking soapwort for salad when she heard the thack of Molly's walking stick slapping the floor boards. Tilly lay her flat gently, then sprinted down to Pratts. She found Sergeant Farrat at the haberdashery counter.

She ran back to squat by her mother and soothed her and held her hand, but even breathing caused Molly distress and any slight movement sent her face into contortions. She fell in and out of consciousness.

❦

Sergeant Farrat brought Mr Almanac. He stood over Molly, lying on her back on the kitchen floor boards.

'I think she broke her femur or something when she fell,' said Tilly. 'She's in terrible pain.'

'Didn't trip on a rug so it must have been a stroke,' said Mr Almanac. 'Nothing to be done, just keep her still. God will see to her.'

'Can you give her something for the pain?'

'Can't do anything for stroke.' Mr Almanac inched away.

'Please, she's in pain.'

'She'll be in a coma soon,' he said, 'be dead by morning.'

She stood quickly and raised her hands, lunging at him to shove him and send him rolling and cracking down The Hill to smash into fifty fractured pieces, but Sergeant Farrat caught her and held her to his big warm body. He helped her put the broken old lady to bed while Molly howled with pain and hit out for anything she could hurt back, but her clenched fists fell like light hail on Sergeant Farrat's wool coat. Then he drove Mr Almanac away.

He returned with some pills for Molly. 'I phoned the doctor but he's away from Winyerp, thirty miles out at a breech birth.'

❧

He watched Tilly grind hemp in a mortar and pestle then scrape it into boiling honey. When the mix had cooled she spilled it onto Molly's tongue so that it slid down her throat. She squatted by the poppies with a razor blade and a cup but the seed pods were too ripe and the white liquid wouldn't dribble, so they ripped the poppies from the earth and chopped the seed pods until they were like gravel then boiled them in water. Tilly spooned the poppy tea between Molly's soft lips but Molly frowned and flung her bony head from side to side. 'No,' she whispered, 'no.'

He helped her rub Molly's tissue-skin with comfrey oil, he mopped her cold brow with dandelion water and he wiped green-tinted mucus from the corners of her eyes with salt water. They sponged and powdered her with lavender dust and held her hands while they sang hymns – 'Be thou my Guardian and my Guide, And hear me when I call; Let not my slippery footsteps slide, And hold me lest I fall.'

Near to dawn Molly shoved the sheets away from her rattling breast and began to pluck at them. She sucked air through the dry black hole that was her mouth, rasping in out, in and out, and by the time dawn broke, had slipped further. Only her breathing remained. Her body had turned limp and still in her bed, her chest rose and fell, rose and fell with shallow sparse breaths answering the life-long impulse, but finally her chest fell and did not rise again. Tilly held her mother's hand until it was no longer warm.

❦

Sergeant Farrat left her and when the sun was high he returned with the undertaker and the doctor from Winyerp. They brought with them the smell of whisky and antiseptic. They arranged a funeral. 'The burial will be tomorrow,' said the undertaker.

Tilly was astonished. 'Tomorrow?'

'Health regulations – the only place to keep corpses here is in Reg's coolroom behind Pratts,' said the doctor.

Tilly sat on her smoky veranda until night came, trembling in waves, sad fever washing through her. The tip ash skipped down to settle in her hair, and the fire lines at the tip glowed in the dark like a city miles away. She could tie up the loose ends, leave, go to Melbourne, take a job with the traveller who'd visited last autumn.

Yet there was the matter of the sour people of Dungatar. In light of all they had done, and what they had not done, what they had decided not to do – they mustn't be abandoned. Not yet.

Some people have more pain than they deserve, some don't. She stood on top of The Hill and howled, wailed like a banshee until lights flicked on and small dots glowed from the houses.

She walked to the meat safe behind Pratts. She stood looking at her mother's casket, lying darkly, a shadow in a sad place, as Molly's presence had always been.

'Pain will no longer be our curse, Molly,' she said. 'It will be our revenge and our reason. I have made it my catalyst and my propeller. It seems only fair, don't you think?'

❧

It rained cats and dogs all night as Tilly slept lightly in her mother's bed. They came to see her, just briefly, and filled her heart. Teddy waved then looked to Pablo in Molly's arms and they smiled a silver smile. Then they were gone.

IV

Brocade

Opulent fabric woven from a combination of
plain and silky yarns to produce a striking texture
on a dull background. Raised floral or figurative
patterns, often emphasised by contrasting colour.
Used for decorative wraps and upholstery.

Fabrics for Needlework

Sergeant Farrat put his hand across his forehead and leaned over his log book to write.

'What time is the funeral?' said Beula.

'Two pm.'

'Are you going, Sergeant?'

He took his hand away and looked up into her eager, pine-coloured eyes, 'Yes.'

'Can anyone go?'

'Anyone can go, Beula, but only good people with respectful intentions should attend, don't you think? Without Tilly's tolerance and generosity, her patience and skills, our lives – mine especially – would not have been enriched. Since you are not sincere about her feelings or about her dear mother and only want to go to stickybeak – well it's just plain ghoulish, isn't it?' Sergeant Farrat reddened but held her gaze.

'Well!' she said, and headed to Pratts. 'Hello, Muriel.'

'Morning, Beula.'

'Is she out there?' she said, jerking her head towards the meat safe.

'If you want to look –'

'Going to the funeral?' Beula asked sharply.

'Well I –'

'Sergeant Farrat said if she hasn't enriched our lives in any way and since we haven't been patient and respectful it would be insincere and we're just being ghouls and stickybeaks.'

Muriel crossed her arms. 'I'm no stickybeak.'

Alvin came out from his office. His wife kept her eyes on Beula and said flatly, 'Beula says that Sergeant Farrat said if we went to the funeral we'd only be ghoulish and that we never had any patience or respect for Molly so we'd just be stickybeaking.'

'We should by rights shut the door when a hearse and procession goes past, but I doubt there'll be one,' said Alvin, and picked up the docket book.

Lois Pickett lumbered in through the front door and up to the counter, saying, 'I fink we should go to the funeral, don't youse?'

'Why?' said Muriel. 'Are you Tilly's friend or are you just going to go for a "stickybeak" as Sergeant Farrat says?'

'She's still got mendin' of mine see –'

'It would be insincere to go, Lois,' said Beula.

'Ghoulish, according to Sergeant Farrat,' said Muriel.

'Well I suppose . . . ,' said Lois, and scratched her head. 'Do youse fink there's somethink going on between the sarge and Tilly?'

'What do you mean?' shot Muriel.

'An affair,' said Beula. 'I always suspected it.'

'Nothing would surprise me,' said Muriel.

Alvin rolled his eyes and walked back to his office.

❧

Sergeant Farrat arrived to collect Tilly wearing a black knee-length wool-crepe frock with a draped neck, a stylish lampshade overskirt cut assymetrically, black stockings and sensible black pumps with a discreet leather flower stitched to the heel. 'Molly would disapprove,' he smiled, 'can't you just see her expression?'

'Your dress will be ruined in this rain.'

'I can always make another one and besides, I have a nice blue cape and umbrella in the car.'

She looked at him and frowned.

'I don't care, Tilly,' he said. 'I'm beyond caring what those people think or say anymore. I'm sure everyone's seen what's on my clothes line over the years, and I'm just about due to retire anyway.' He offered her his elbow.

'The rain will keep the crowds away,' said Tilly, and they stepped from the veranda to the police car.

Reginald drove Molly to her resting place in Pratts' grocery van, then leaned on it to watch the two mourners, their hair plastered to their foreheads and their faces screwed in the rain. Sergeant Farrat clasped his hands together under his cape and raised his voice above the grey din. 'Molly Dunnage came to Dungatar with a babe-in-arms to start a new life. She hoped to leave behind her troubles, but hers was a life lived with trouble travelling alongside and so Molly lived as discreetly as she possibly could in the full glare of scrutiny and torment. Her heart will rest easier knowing Myrtle again before she died.

'We bid Molly farewell and in our sadness, our anger and our disbelief we beg for Molly a better life hereafter, a life of love and acceptance and we wish for her everlasting peace – for I suspect that is all she ever wished for herself. That is what, in her heart, she would have wanted for anyone.'

Councillor Evan Pettyman, on behalf of the Dungatar Shire Council, had sent a wreath. Tilly scooped it from the top of the coffin with the shovel then dropped it on the sodden clay at her feet and sliced it into tiny wedges. Reginald stepped forward to help them lower Molly to rest. Flat raindrops plopped, smacked a rat ta tat tat at the coffin top, as Tilly dropped the first clod of earth onto her mother's final bed.

The men stood respectfully in the rain either side of the thin girl in the big wet hat. She leaned on the shovel, shuddering in a grey crying sky, mud stuck to her boots and caked to the cuffs of her trousers. 'I will miss you,' she cried. 'I will just go on missing you as I always have.'

Reginald handed Sergeant Farrat the bill for the cost of the casket and hire of Alvin's van. The sergeant put it in his pocket, took the shovel from Tilly and said, 'Let's tuck Molly in, then go and drink laced tea until we feel some understanding has been reached on behalf of Molly Dunnage and the life she was given.'

Tilly held the umbrella over the sergeant as he shovelled, the blue cape stuck in folds about him, his black pumps sinking in the clay. The rain trickled down, darkening his stockings.

♮

Much later Beula heard them singing as she crept up The Hill. She crouched at the back window and saw Tilly Dunnage leaning with Sergeant Horatio Farrat, who was wearing a frock. The kitchen table was littered with empty bottles, discarded clothing and old photograph albums, and the Holy Bible lay open, its pages stabbed and ripped – they'd found no understanding in it, so had killed it. The two mourners swayed together with their heads back singing, '*You made me love you, I didn't want to do it –*'

'No no no, not that one. That's exactly what happened!' said Tilly.

So Sergeant Farrat sang, '*Ma, he's making eyes at me, Ma, he's awful nice to me –*'

'*No*, definitely not that one either.'

'*Who were you with last night? Out in the –*'

'No.'

'I've got one, Til, howbout *When I grow too old to dream –*'

'Yes, yes, that's one she'd've liked. Lesgo, onetwo-tree . . .'

They steepled together again and sang, '*When I grow too old to dream, I'll have you to remember, when I grow too old to dream, your love will live in my heart –*'

'Oh shit,' said Tilly, 'she would have hated that one. All those songs are corruptive, pornographic.'

'No wonder she got into trouble.'

'That's exactly right. That's it!' said Tilly, and took the tea cosy from her head and threw it in the air.

'What?'

'It's all the fault of persuasive popular song, and a lecher.'

'Solved,' said the sergeant, and sat down at the table. He poured them a glass of champagne and they toasted.

'Lessing Loch Lomon' again.'

'No more singing,' said Tilly, 'it's corruptive!' She went to the lounge room and toppled back through the kitchen with the radiogram in her arms.

Beula jumped away from the window light and lay flat in the dark on the grass. Tilly braked on the veranda and with a grunt slung her radiogram out into the black night. There was a sickening uugghh sound and a muffled thud as Tilly went back inside. She grabbed her records and ran back out with them, stacked them beside her on the veranda, then stood in the oblong yellow light from the doorway, flinging them one by one to the wind.

❦

When the edge of the flying radiogram hit Beula it dented her forehead, broke her nose and gave her a mild concussion. She felt her way home along the worn tracks, along the fences she knew so well, and lay down. Her wound started to seep, and a black and green bruise swelled from the raw fleshy cavity in the middle of her face all the way down to her undershot chin and over the creased brow to her hairline.

On Monday morning Sergeant Farrat took his preparatory bath and waited for Beula. He waited again on Tuesday morning until half past nine, then went looking. There was no response to his knock so he opened the door to Beula's grease-and-dust-caked kitchen, immediately dancing backwards, coughing. He rushed back to the police car, took a bottle of eucalyptus oil from the glove box and poured it onto his handkerchief. Back at the kitchen door he pressed the scented cloth against his nostrils and entered. He found her, a stiff, black-stained tea towel draped over her head, lifting and sucking back in the middle where a nose should have peaked the material. 'Beula?' he breathed. There was a noise like rattling drops in a drinking straw and her arms raised a little. He pinched the edge of the towel and jumped back quickly, dropping it onto the floor. Beula's eyes were bulging purple-red slits and there was a crusty, blackened hole in the middle of her face. Two brown stumps jutted where her eye teeth had snapped off at the gums.

The sergeant led her to his car and drove her to the doctor at Winyerp. They sat in the surgery. Beula could make out the fuzzied outline of a white-ish figure moving about in front of her. It said, 'Hmmm.'

'I tripped and fell,' said Beula through her rotting face and burst adenoids, pink bubbles boiling through her lips.

'You tripped?' The doctor looked at the sergeant and made a gesture to suggest she'd been drinking.

'It was dark,' she said.

'You may have suffered internal optical damage – it looks like the eye casement is shattered,' said the doctor, and handed her a letter addressed to a specialist in Melbourne.

'The nasal bone has crashed against the lacrimal bone splintering it. This in turn has severed the lacrimal duct, damaging the sphenoid bone and therefore the optic foramen and, unfortunately, the all-important macula luteras. It's too late to do anything about it now of course . . .'

The lights had gone out for Beula.

Sergeant Farrat gave her dark glasses, tied a scarf around her chin, placed a white cane in her hand and put her on a train to Melbourne with a tag pinned to the back of her cardigan which said, 'Beula Harridene, C/- police station, Dungatar, Ph: 9 (trunk call)'. Then he went to see Tilly, stepping from his car in the orange glow of dusk, his green-beaded, silk brocade matador's costume glinting. Tilly had altered it to fit the sergeant by adding gold silk inserts and the sergeant had attached green tassels to them. They stood in her garden, waist deep in flowers and bushes, herbs and vegetables, the air around them clear and fresh from the recent rain.

'I see Molly has put the tip fire out,' joked the sergeant.

'Yes,' said Tilly.

'Did you hear about poor Beula?'

'No.'

'She's gone to the sanatorium.' The sergeant rubbed his hands together.

'Tell me everything,' said Tilly.

'Well . . . ,' he began, and ended by saying, '. . . it must have been an awful fall, she looks like she's been hit by the corner of a flying fridge.'

'When did it happen?' said Tilly.

'The night of Molly's funeral.'

She looked up at the heavens and smiled.

❦

That afternoon Nancy arrived to fetch Mr Almanac. She found him in the back room stuck fast, his head bent into the cupboard where he kept his apothecary measures, his round shoulders resting against the ledge. Nancy carefully backed him out and shunted him out the door, checked for traffic and gave him a gentle shove. He tripped down the kerb and across the road while Nancy switched off the lights, padlocked the refrigerator and secured the front door. Mr Almanac accelerated towards his wife, who was dozing in the sun. He tumbled past her and continued through the house, whose hallway ran from the front door to the back. Nancy glanced across at Mrs A, then up and down the street. She frowned, cupped her hands around her eyes and peered back into the gloomy shop. She looked at Mrs A again, then bolted across the street, past Mrs Almanac, who felt the passing breeze and opened her eyes. 'Holy Mary, mother of God,' she heard Nancy say.

Sergeant Farrat followed Mr Percival Almanac's foot scrapes all the way across the back yard to the creek's edge. He stood on the bank looking sadly at the brown water, mosquitos singing around him. He removed his blue cap and rested it over his heart before dropping it despondently on a log and carefully removing and folding his clothes. When all that remained were his red satin boxers he eased into the still creek. In the centre his white head sunk and small bubbles circled on the watery surface, then Mr Almanac's head rose. The sergeant held him over his shoulder like a rigid upright question mark with slimy green cumbungi streaming from his bent neck, yabbies clinging to his earlobes and leeches hanging from his lips.

❦

Tilly stood by the muddy mound of her mother's grave and related the details of Beula's and Mr Almanac's accidents. 'Like you said, "Sometimes things just don't *seem* fair".'

❦

She heard the galah before she reached the crest of The Hill. The committee members of the Dungatar Social Club were being held against the veranda by the bird, which was dancing at them, screeching, wings outstretched, crest rigid. The women wore 'Tilly originals' and looked afraid. She strode to the veranda, looked at the galah and said, 'Shsss.'

He stopped, cocked his head at her and closed his beak. His crest flattened and he waddled pigeon-toed to the gatepost, climbed to the top, then turned and hissed once more at the intruders.

'Your garden, Tilly,' said Trudy, 'so pretty, such a big job you've done and still managing to sew so well!'

They were all smiling at her.

'A very fragrant garden indeed.'

'You have some very unusual plants.'

Tilly plucked a blade of grass and chewed it.

Trudy cleared her throat. 'We're putting on a eisteddfod –'

'We're doing *Macbeth*,' snapped Elsbeth, 'Shakespeare's *Macbeth*. It's a play. Itheca and Winyerp Dramatic Societies are doing *A Streetcar Named Desire* and *H.M.S. Pinafore* –'

'Light entertainment,' said Muriel disparagingly.

'So we're doing *Macbeth*, and we've chosen *you* to do the costumes.'

Tilly looked at each of them. They were all nodding at her, smiling. 'Really?' she said. '*Macbeth*?'

'Yes,' said Trudy.

Elsbeth held up *The Complete Works of Shakespeare*, and *Costumes Throughout the Ages*. 'We have some ideas about what we want . . .'

'Show me,' said Tilly. Elsbeth hurried towards her, the page open at drawings of men dressed in dull togas with rope looped around the waist, full sleeves and scalloped collars and women in tight, draw-string vests.

'I like the ones over the page,' said Trudy. Tilly turned the page. The pictures showed men costumed in skirts with layers and layers of petticoats and yards and yards of lace dripping from arms covered in voluminous cuffed ruffles and frills. They posed on the page in stockings, below-knee pantaloons with godet bell-bottoms or deep flounces above high-heeled Cromwell slippers tied with large satin bows. Their hats were oversized and heavily plumed. The women wore three-tiered full skirts with ruffled bustles, elaborate multi-storied architect-designed fontanges, feather muffs and jackets with complicated jabots or frilled revers.

'But this is Baroque,' said Tilly, 'seventeenth century.'

'Precisely,' said Elsbeth.

'It *is* Shakespeare,' said Trudy.

Muriel was incredulous. 'You've heard of him, haven't you?'

'She may not have,' said Mona. 'I hadn't until last week.'

Tilly raised an eyebrow and recited,

'Double, double, toil and trouble;

Fire burn and cauldron bubble.

Fillet of a fenny snake,

In the caldron boil and bake;

Eye of newt and toe of frog,

Wool of bat and tongue of dog . . .'

The committee members looked at each other, confused.

Tilly raised an eyebrow. 'Act four scene one, three witches at the cauldron? No?'

The women remained blank. 'We haven't actually read the play yet,' said Muriel.

'I prefer the costumes I selected, don't you?' asked Trudy.

Tilly looked directly at Trudy and said, 'They'd definitely be the most effective.' Trudy nodded emphatically at her friends.

Elsbeth took a step closer to Tilly. 'Can you manage them?'

'I can, but –' said Tilly.

'How soon can you start?' interrupted Elsbeth.

Tilly studied the pictures, thinking. The women looked at each other and shrugged. Then she smiled at them. 'I'd be more than delighted to contribute to your drama by making these costumes . . . provided you pay me.' She snapped the book closed and held it to her breast. 'You still have outstanding accounts that go back twelve months and more.'

'We'll bring the matter up at the next meeting,' said the treasurer lamely.

'Well, that's settled then,' said Elsbeth, wiping her hands down her skirt and starting off down The Hill.

'I won't start until I've been paid the outstanding accounts and I want cash up front. Otherwise I'll offer to take on Itheca's and Winyerp's costumes instead. They always pay me.'

Elsbeth and Trudy looked to Muriel, who looked back at them evenly. 'He'll never lend it to us,' she said.

'Mother!' said Trudy, and stepped up to the treasurer, and poked at her nose, 'You *have* to ask Father.' Alvin had ceased extending credit to his daughter and her family again, charging only food to the Windswept Crest account – they even had to do without soap.

Muriel folded her arms. 'No one's paid Alvin either, he's got accounts go back ten years. We can't feed everyone for nothing forever,' she said haughtily, and glared at Elsbeth. Elsbeth and Trudy looked accusingly at each other.

'Well,' said Elsbeth, 'William will just have to wait another year for his new tractor.'

'He can play Macbeth!' said Trudy.

'Yes!' they said, and the committee moved as one towards the gatepost.

As she watched the women waddle off down The Hill, Tilly smiled.

❦

Tilly rose early and dressed for gardening, then attacked the French marigold bushes, cutting the branches from the thick stem and carrying the bundles inside. She selected a big bunch of flowering heads and put them in a vase of water, then she stripped the remaining stalks of leaves and flowers, chopped them roughly, and threw them all into a huge pot of boiling water. The kitchen filled with steam, boiled wood and a sweet burned scent. When the marigold water cooled she bottled it. That night she packed a bag and headed for the shire offices.

Two mornings later Evan woke depressed and moody. He checked his comatose wife in her cot, then lay down and conjured lewd images of Una, but the only thing he felt was an uneasy numbness – a faint plegia contaminating his limbs and appendages. He stood up and looked down at his penis, hanging like a strip of wet chamois. 'I'm just anxious,' he said, and started packing.

Mid-morning Evan threw his Gladstone bag onto the back seat and ducked down behind the wheel of his Wolseley. The curtains on all the neighbours' windows fell back into place. He set off for Melbourne, eager for Una.

☙

Tilly's stomach lurched but she stayed, and when Marigold answered the door she handed her a bunch of French marigolds.

Marigold's hand flew to cover her rash. 'What do you want?'

'I've brought flowers,' she said, and swept into the Pettymans' house.

Marigold sneezed and said, 'How unusual.'

'*Tagetes patula*,' said Tilly. 'They deter white fly from tomato plants, and they're good for repelling eelworm in roses and potatoes as well. The roots have a component that deadens the detector that triggers eelworm release – numbs it completely,' said Tilly.

Marigold looked at Tilly's feet. 'You should have taken your shoes off.'

Tilly sat down in the lounge room. Marigold studied her features; a fine-looking girl with a pale complexion, Evan's complexion, but Mad Molly's thick hair and full mouth. 'I'm sorry about your mother,' she said.

'No you're not,' said Tilly.

Marigold's eyes bulged and the tendons in her neck rose like a warring lizards, 'Evan sent a wreath!'

'The very least he could do,' said Tilly. 'Shall I find a vase?'

Marigold grabbed the flowers and rushed out to the kitchen holding them at arm's length. They were dropping pollen on the carpet. 'What do you want?' she called again.

'Nothing – just visiting.' She picked up a photograph of Stewart on the table beside her and was studying it when Marigold returned and sat down opposite. 'It's all very hazy now, but you left I seem to remember, because your mother became unwell?'

'Not quite in that order, however –'

'Where did you learn to sew?' Marigold fiddled with the button of her dressing gown.

'Lots of places.'

'Like where?' Marigold's eyes darted across Tilly's face, searching.

'I returned to Dungatar from Paris but before that I was in Spain and before that in Melbourne, at a clothing factory. While I was at school in Melbourne I took sewing classes. It wasn't a very good school, my benefactor –'

'Who was your benefactor, your father?' Marigold was

tugging at the button at her collar now and the veins on her temples pulsed.

'He'll be paid back,' said Tilly.

'I had quite a bit of money put aside for Stewart's education,' Marigold said, and looked out the window, 'but it's all gone.' The button popped off into her fingers.

Tilly continued, 'Apprentices don't get paid much but I managed to travel and keep on with my learning so –'

'Well,' said Marigold, 'no one was ever displeased with anything you made for them here, not like that Una . . .' She slapped her hands over her mouth. 'Don't tell Elsbeth I said that!'

'Never,' said Tilly. 'Would you like me to make you a new frock for the eisteddfod?'

'Yes!' she said, and sat forward. 'I'd like something special, very special. Better than everyone else. I won Belle of the Ball, you know. Do you want a cup of tea?' Marigold flitted into the kitchen, returning a short time later with an afternoon tea tray.

'There's one thing I'm going to say. I know you didn't mean to murder that boy.' She sipped her tea and Tilly's stomach twisted. 'That Teddy McSwiney, but I know how Mae felt. You see, my son fell out of a tree and died. Landed on his head.'

Marigold showed Tilly all her photograph albums – Evan and Stewart when Stewart was three weeks old, Marigold and her parents before they died, the house before the front fence was built, and there was even one of Tilly in a school photo, with Stewart. Marigold glanced at Tilly and said, 'Where did your mother come from?'

Tilly looked directly at Marigold and said, 'Would you like to hear the whole story?'

'Yes,' she said, 'I would.'

Tilly took a deep breath. 'All right,' she said, 'Molly was an only child and still unmarried, quite late in life for the times. She was very innocent, and easily swept off her feet by an ambitious, conniving and charm-wielding man. The man wasn't very successful at anything, but told everyone he was. Her good Christian parents believed him with all the might of their open hearts and closed imaginations, and they let her go on a walk with him. The charming man was very persuasive. She found herself in a position where her parents would be deeply hurt and embarrassed unless she married quickly –'

'I know this story!' said Marigold, her voice shrill.

'I know you do,' said Tilly.

⁊

Evan lay on his back with the bed sheets pulled up to his chin. Around his knees the sheets humped, buckled and bulged, then Una emerged from under them and fell on his shoulder, breathless, red faced and moist. She lifted the sheet and looked down at Evan's squishy, orange, wet conger lolling on his thigh. She giggled. Evan began to cry.

He arrived home early, undressed on the back sleep-out and headed for the bathroom. His wife sat calmly by the radiogram, knitting. 'Hello, Evan,' she said softly. 'How were things in Melbourne?'

'Oh,' he said absently, 'a little disappointing.' He was sitting on the toilet with a wad of crumpled Sorbent wrapped around his right hand when the door kicked open. Marigold leaned casually on the doorjamb, still knitting. 'You've been in here a long time, Evan.'

'I'm sick. There's something wrong with me,' he said.

'I used to be sick, Evan, you used to make me sick, but Tilly Dunnage has cured me.'

'What?'

She sighed. 'You've had a lot of affairs, haven't you, Evan?'

'She's mad, we can have her committed –'

'She's not mad, Evan. She's your daughter.' She smiled down at him and said very sweetly in a baby voice, 'Poor Evan is miserable and I know why and I think she's a clever, clever girl, that Tilly.'

Evan stood up and closed the door but Marigold kicked it open again. 'It's in your electric jug, at the office – poison, so you can't do those things you used to do to me at night anymore, can you, Evan?' She walked away, chuckling softly.

He followed her to her immaculate kitchen where she stood gazing at a speck of fly shit on her otherwise spotless windowpane.

'She murdered Stewart, did you know? Your new friend –'

'You mean Tilly, your daughter, murdered *your* son?' Marigold turned and looked at Evan. 'Your son the bully. The fat, freckled, rude and smelly little boy who elbowed me when he passed, spied on me in the shower and assaulted little girls. If it weren't for him I wouldn't have had to marry you, I may have woken up to you.' She shuddered.

'Why don't you fall down, Marigold, faint, have one of your headache fits – you're insane.'

'You stole all my money!'

'You're unstable, drug dependent and neurotic, the doctor knows all about you!'

'Certifiable,' she said peacefully. 'Beula says it's nice in there.' She sighed and fell gently to her knees. Evan looked down at her. He caught a flash of light as she reached behind his ankles and slid the razor-sharp carving knife across his calcanean tendons. They tore and snapped, making a sound like a wooden tool-box lid slamming shut. Evan hit the linoleum, trumpeting like a tortured elephant as his Achilles tendons shrunk to coil like snuggled slugs in the capsular ligaments behind his knee joints.

'This is very wrong, Marigold,' he cried.

Marigold looked at Evan twitching, smearing a red puddle across her polished linoleum. 'I've been under a lot of pressure for many years,' she said, 'everyone knows that, and they know all about Una Pleasance. They'd understand completely. But that doesn't matter.' She stood spread-legged over him and wiped the knife on her apron, then dropped it in the drawer.

'Please,' cried Evan. 'Marigold, I'll bleed to death.'

'Eventually,' she said, and wrenched the telephone from the wall.

'Marigold!' he screamed.

She closed the door behind her and Evan was left in agony on the floor, his shins like loose thread at the ends of his knees and the door knob unreachable.

'Marigold, please?' he squealed. 'I'm sorry.'

'Not as sorry as I am,' she said. She sat on her bed and poured the whole bottle of her sleeping tonic into a jug, topped it up with sherry, stirred it, closed her eyes and drank.

The galah called 'Wallopers' as quick steps crossed Tilly's veranda. The back door burst open and a haystack-sized bundle of brilliant coloured frocks, feather boas, hats, shawls, scarves, satins and sequins, cotton, chiffon, blue gingham and matador brocade – the contents of Sergeant Farrat's secret wardrobe – stood rustling in her kitchen. Tilly looked down at the sergeant's navy pants and shiny shoes. 'The district inspector's coming to stay with me,' he said, and rushed out to Tilly's front room. He dumped his load and rushed outside again, then came back and put his photo albums, some wall paintings, his gramophone and record collection on her table. 'He might think I'm queer,' he said, but stopped at the table to rub some cloth he'd never seen between his fingers and thumb. 'Silk or Peau de soie?' he asked.

'What exactly is the district inspector going to do?' asked Tilly.

'First Teddy, then Molly, then Beula's incident and Mr Almanac, but it was my report on the Pettymans that sparked his interest. Committing Marigold was bad enough, but Evan – the things we found in that house! Drugs . . . pornographic books, even blue films. And he was an embezzler!' Sergeant Farrat rushed out to his car for another load.

'I'd like to meet the inspector,' said Tilly.

'Why?'

Tilly shrugged. 'Just to see if he's . . . smart.'

'Not in the least. He wears brown suits – and I'm sure they're made from slub.'

❦

She fell asleep in the empty, busted armchair and dreamed of her round soft babe suckling at her breast, and of Molly when Molly was her mother, young and smiling, strawberry blonde and walking down The Hill to greet her after school. She was there with Teddy again on top of the silo, on top of the world. She saw his face, his mischievous grin in the moonlight. His arms stretched up to her and he said, 'Now quick desire hath caught the yielding prey, And glutton-like she feeds . . .'

Then her round soft babe was still and blue and wrapped in cotton-flannel and Molly, pained and cold in her rain-soaked coffin turned stiffly to her, and Teddy, sorghum-coated and gaping, clawing, a chocolate seed–dipped cadaver. Evan and Percival Almanac stood shaking their fingers at her and behind them the citizens of Dungatar crawled up The Hill in the dark, armed with firewood and flames, stakes and chains, but she just walked out to her veranda and smiled down at them and they turned and fled.

❦

A fart drummed through Sergeant Farrat's station, then a loud yawn. The district inspector was still in bed, in the cell. He was a scruffy middle-aged man with slovenly habits and very bad manners. At dinner time, Sergeant Farrat moved close to the wireless and turned the volume up so that he could eat his meal without retching, because the district inspector propelled his dentures about his mouth with his tongue, to suck out remaining food particles. He used his sleeve as a serviette and did not swish out the hand basin after shaving, he left drips on the floor after using the toilet, he never switched off lights or taps, and when Sergeant Farrat asked if he needed clothes washed – 'since I'm just about to do a load myself,' – the inspector lifted his arm, sniffed and said, 'Narrr.'

The district inspector – 'call me Frank' – talked a lot. 'I've seen a lot of action – been shot at three times. Had to leave my wife – broke her heart – but it was to keep her out of strife. Freed me up to solve a heap of unsolvable crimes – single handedly – caught a bunch of fugitives in me time, they'd done the crime, I made them pay the fine. Wasn't fair on the cheese-and-kisses at all, the danger of it all. You understand, don't you, Horatio?'

'Oh yes,' said the sergeant, 'that would explain why they've put you here, in rural Victoria.' Sergeant Farrat just wanted his evenings back – his radio serial, his books and records, his sewing . . . and his 9:00 pm drive around, in peace.

'What's for tea tonight, Horry?'

'We're going out. We'll be having tripe,' said Sergeant Farrat, and dropped his pencil onto the counter.

'My favourite, love a tripe in parsley sauce.' The inspector wandered out to the bathroom. 'I like this place,' he called, and started whistling.

Sergeant Farrat closed his eyes and pinched the bridge of his nose.

❧

They arrived early for dinner. The inspector removed his hat and bowed when he caught sight of Tilly posing in the doorway. She wore a clinging black swanskin fishtail with a neckline that ended at her waist. The sergeant poured champagne and Tilly made conversation. 'I hear you're quite an effective crime fighter, Inspector?'

The inspector blushed. 'Caught a few crims in me time.'

'Are you a good detective as well?'

'That's why I'm here.'

'To solve the Pettyman case?'

The district inspector was captured by Tilly's plunging décolleté. She placed her finger under his chin and raised his head, made his eyes meet hers. 'Have you had forensic training?'

'No, I mean, not yet.'

'The inspector is more of a "gatherer of facts" and report writer, wouldn't you say, Inspector?' The sergeant handed him a glass of champagne.

'Yes,' he said, and sunk his flute of sparkling wine in one gulp. 'Tripe for tea, is it?'

'Gigot de Dinde Farcie with stuffed lovage and vine leaves, globe artichokes with ravigote sauce,' said Tilly, and placed the roasted fowl on the table.

The inspector looked disappointed and shot a questioning glance at Sergeant Farrat, pulled the chair at the head of the table out, sat down and rolled his sleeves up.

The sergeant carved, Tilly served and the inspector started eating. Sergeant Farrat poured the wine, sniffed his glass then toasted Tilly.

'You're a very noisy eater, Inspector,' said Tilly.

'I'm enjoying your stuffed . . .' The inspector caught sight of the galah, preening itself on the curtain rail.

'It's turkey,' said the sergeant.

'We're not enjoying ours, so eat with your mouth closed,' Tilly scolded.

'Yes ma'am.'

They polished off all there was to drink (the inspector brought beer) and Tilly offered cigarettes to the men. The sergeant lit his and inhaled, while the inspector sniffed his and said, 'Unusual. Peruvian?'

'Close,' she said. 'British Honduras.'

'Aaahhh,' said the inspector appreciatively. She held a match to his cigarette. Tilly played loud music and they danced – an independent, jumping, goose-stepping twirl around the kitchen table, to the sound of Micky Katz playing an accelerating rendition of 'The Wedding Samba'. They danced on top of the table to every other tune that featured on the record *Music for Weddings and Bar Mitzvahs*. Then they dived off the kitchen table into each other's arms and danced flamenco on the cement hearth, they played drums with wooden spoons and saucepans and they danced some more – rumbas and sambas and a Highland fling – then collapsed into a chair each, puffing and laughing, holding the stitches in their sides.

The inspector suddenly stood and said, 'Well, we must be off,' and rolled out the door. Tilly's mop-head sat over his bald patch. Sergeant Farrat shrugged and followed, serviettes poking through the epaulets on his red Eton jacket.

Tilly stood, her hands on her hips and her brow creased. 'Where are you going?'

'I'm compelled to do my 9:00 pm drive around,' said Sergeant Farrat regretfully, and rolled his eyes at the inspector.

Frank swayed knee-deep in her small purple hemlock tree, its white flowers bleeding small droplets of foul perfume onto his trousers. 'Wanna come?'

'You can't be seen with me,' said Tilly. 'I'm the town murderess.'

Frank laughed and waved and fell into the police car. Sergeant Farrat tooted farewell as they drove off. Tilly wandered back inside. She looked at the galah and said, 'I can start now, there's nothing to be afraid of.' She surveyed the soft-coloured piles – calico, boxcloth, satin, silk, vicuña and velveteen, petersham ribbon, lace ribbons, paper flowers, plastic gems and gilded cardboard, all for the Baroque costumes. She wandered to her mother's bedroom where she kept the soft creamy beiges and blue-white piqué, the poplin, ninon, lisle, organdie, silk, lace and duchesse for the balls, christenings and weddings, then went back to look at the tape measures, pins, buttons and mannequins in corners, waiting, between the rooms. Sergeant Farrat's secret wardrobe hung in a locked cupboard next to the front door. Her foot rested on scissors lying on the floor where she did her cutting. Baroque sketches were pegged to the curtains and her concertina file containing the cast's measurements sprang open on the floor.

She swapped her swanskin for overalls and found a mallet and a jemmy. She tore down the curtains and covered all the materials and machines with them, then stood in front of the wall that divided the kitchen from the lounge room, spat on her palms, lifted the mallet and swung. She hammered until she'd made a sizable hole, then jemmied the boards from their bearers. She repeated the process until all that was left between the kitchen and lounge room were old pine beams, covered in fine black dust. She removed the doors and walls from between the bedrooms and the lounge room in the same way then unscrewed the door knobs. She wheeled the splintered planks with rusty nails and her old bed down to the tip in her mother's wheelchair. She returned to her remodelled house and nailed two doors together, then attached them to her kitchen table. At dawn she stood next to the great big cutting table in the huge open plan workshop and smiled.

She was covered in dirt and cobwebs, so drew a hot bath. While she soaked she hummed and held her toe against the nozzle, blocking the drips until water forced its way around her toe and sprayed out in a thin sharp thread.

The residents of Dungatar assembled at the hall to audition for the Dungatar Social Committee's production of *Macbeth*. Irma Almanac rolled in and positioned her chair at the end of the aisle next to Tilly. Nancy nudged Ruth and said *Hmph* and the auditioners looked sideways at them. Irma was not wearing black: her white high heels sat awkwardly on the foot-plates and her dress was fire-engine red.

Most people chose to read a poem or sing for their audition, although the district inspector did a soft-shoe shuffle. The producer and director retired backstage to discuss casting and make their decisions, and then they made the announcements.

Trudy spoke first. 'I am the director so everyone must do what I say.'

'And I am the producer so therefore I am in charge of everything, including the director.'

Trudy turned to her mother-in-law. 'Strictly speaking, Elsbeth, however –'

'Would you please read the cast list, Trudy?'

'I am, as I said, the director and I am also Lady Macbeth. The part of Macbeth – General and future King – goes to . . .'

William braced himself.

'Lesley Muncan!'

There was a general rumble of approval and a smattering of applause. Lesley had put everything into his audition. Mona leaned and kissed his cheek as he fluttered his eyelashes and blushed. William looked at the floor.

Trudy cleared her throat and continued, 'William can be Duncan . . .' Sergeant Farrat, Fred Bundle, Big Bobby, the inspector, Scotty and Reg nudged each other and shook their heads and when Trudy said, '. . . and his sons Malcolm and Donalbain will be Bobby Pickett and Scotty . . .' they rolled their eyes and crossed their arms. 'Septimus Crescant will be Seward and Sergeant Farrat will be Banquo but Banquo gets sort of killed by mistake. Whenever any of you are not Banquo or Duncan or King you are attendants, lords, officers, messengers and murderers. Purl, you are Lady Macduff. The witches are Faith, Nancy and the district inspector.' The cast shuffled and whispered together.

'I wanted to be a witch,' came a faint voice.

'Mona, I told you, you're the ghost and an attendant.'

'But I haven't got a line to say.'

'Mona, there are only three witches in the play.'

Nancy stepped forward, 'My Lady Macduff was better than Purl's –'

'I'm a bloke – I don't see why I should be a witch,' whined the inspector.

Elsbeth sprang. 'There will be no squabbling or you will be told to leave!' She glared at the cast. The inspector cracked the heels of his shoes together and bobbed his head up and down quickly.

Elsbeth looked to Trudy. 'Control your cast,' she snapped.

Trudy sucked in her cheeks and said, 'Mrs Almanac, you are wardrobe mistress.' Irma looked down at her swollen knuckles and loose fingers. 'I'll make some tomorrow,' said Tilly. 'Double strength.'

❧

Several nights into rehearsal, things were progressing slowly.

'Right,' said the director, 'Banquo and Macbeth, enter now.'

'So foul and fair a day I have not seen.'

'How far is't call'd to Forres? . . .'

'*Stop*, stop for a moment, please. Erm, that's very good now, Sergeant –'

'Banquo . . .'

'Banquo then. The kilt is good – but no one else has a Scottish accent and the bagpipes aren't necessary either.'

Hamish was in charge of props and staging. Trudy approached him. 'Why are you building a balcony, Mr O'Brien?'

'For the love scene.'

'That's *Romeo and Juliet*.'

'Aye.'

'We're doing *Macbeth*.'

Hamish blinked at her.

'It's the one about the ambitious soldier's wife who convinces her weak husband to kill the King. It's set in Scotland.'

The high red colour drained from Hamish's cheeks. 'The Scottish play?' he hissed.

'You have to make forests that walk and a ghost,' said Trudy.

'I've been lied to,' cried Hamish, 'by that bloody Septimus!' He dropped his tools and ran from the hall.

❦

February passed quickly for Tilly. She rose early each day to sew costumes in the morning light and organise fittings or alterations. She hummed as she worked. In the evenings she sometimes wandered down to sit at the back of the hall and watch the township of Dungatar rehearse.

The citizens looked increasingly stressed and tired and didn't seem to be enjoying themselves at all. Trudy sat in the front row.

'Begin again, Scene Three,' she croaked – she had lost her voice.

Septimus, Big Bobby, Sergeant Farrat, Reginald, Purl and Fred moved nervously to their places on the stage.

'Enter Porter . . . I can't hear you, Porter,' called the director.

'I'm not saying anything.'

'Why not?'

'Because I can't remember my next line.' Faith burst into tears. The other actors rushed to her.

The director threw down her script. 'Oh jolly good, let's have another five-ruddy-minute break while someone else has a bawl – any other lousy actors here feel like a bit of a bawl? Oh you do, do you?'

'No.'

'Well why are you holding your arm up again?'

'I want to ask another question.'

Trudy blinked at the Attendant – Bobby Pickett – standing on the stage. 'No, you can't ask another question,' she said.

'Why can't he?' Elsbeth walked out onto the stage and stood beside Bobby.

'Because I said so.'

'You're not a very considerate director, *Gertrude.*'

William went and sat in a corner next to Mona and put his head in his hands.

'I suppose you think you could do better?' snarled Trudy.

'I know I could. Anyone could.'

They stared at each other. 'You're fired.'

'You can't fire the producer, you silly girl.'

Trudy stepped close to Elsbeth and, leaning down over her, yelled, 'You're always telling me what I can't do. I can do anything I want. Now get out.'

'No.'

'Go.' She pointed at the door.

'If I go, so does the rest of the funding!'

William looked up hopefully. His mother continued, counting on her fingers. 'There's the hall hire, transport, not to mention the set and we can't have the soldiers' costumes until we've paid the balance.'

'Oh . . . f . . . fiddlesticks,' said Trudy, and clenched her fists at her temples.

Faith started bawling again. The cast threw up their hands or threw down their scripts and William came to the front of the stage. 'Mother, you're ruining it for everyone –'

'Me? It's not *me* that's ruining it!'

Tilly, watching from a dark corner, smiled.

Purl stepped forward. 'Yes you are, you keep interrupting . . .'

'How dare you, you're just a –'

'She knows what you think she is,' bellowed Fred, and stepped to Purl's side.

'Yes,' said Purl, and pointed a red fingernail at Elsbeth, 'and I know what your husband thought you were.'

'And anyway, Elsbeth, I can pay for the soldiers' costumes,

I've still got all the house insurance money in the post office safe,' cried Ruth triumphantly.

Everyone turned to stare at her.

'Haven't you sent it to the insurance company yet?' asked Nancy.

Ruth shook her head.

'See?' cried Trudy. 'We don't need you at all. You can just go and buy William his ruddy tractor.'

'No one's insured?' cried Fred.

Ruth began to look afraid, stepping away.

Nancy put her hands on her hips and glared at the cast. 'Well, there hasn't been an earthquake lately, and I hope you don't think just because she pays it for us every other year it stops fires and floods, do you?'

'That's true!' said Trudy.

The cast looked confused.

'We can't win without the soldiers' costumes . . . ,' said Faith weakly.

'Or a set.' Trudy put her hands on her hips. The cast-members looked at each other, then slowly gathered behind their director.

Elsbeth stamped her foot and yelled, 'You're just a bunch of fools! Hams, dullards, shopkeepers and half-wits, you're uncouth, grotesque and common . . .' She stomped off but stopped and turned at the door. '. . . Loathsome all of you. I hope I never set eyes on any of you ever again.' She marched out, slamming the door behind her. The windows shook and dust fell from the light shades.

'Right,' said Trudy, 'let's start again, shall we?'

'I didn't get to ask my question,' said Bobby.

Trudy clenched her teeth. 'Ask away.'

'Well, when you say "Out, damned spot! out I say!", well . . .
where is he?'

'Who?'

'Spot.'

❧

March arrived. The temperature climbed and the hot northerlies
dusted washing on clothes lines and left a fine brown coating on
sideboards. William Beaumont – Duncan, King of Scotland – was
due at 11:30 am for his first fitting. He stepped onto Tilly's veranda
at 11:23 am. Tilly showed him in. 'Off with your shirt,' she said.

'Right,' he said. He had trouble with his buttons, but eventually she could approach him with a calico vest. She held it up
for him to put his arms through.

'Is that it?' William was disappointed.

'This is a toile. It's customary to make a toile to get a perfect
fit so you don't need lots of fittings.'

'So it will be yellow with lace, like we said?'

'Just like you wanted.'

The underarm curve had to be raised (thin arms) but she'd
got the neckline right. She re-pinned the shoulder seams, lifting
the fullness around the armhole to accommodate William's
rounded back, then helped him off with the toile and went to
her big table.

William was left standing in her kitchen in his singlet with
his arms out. He watched her bending over the yellow cloth
with pins in her mouth, doing clever things with tailor's chalk
and a needle and thread. She glanced up and he quickly looked
up at the light fitting and bounced on his toes, but he was
drawn to watch her again, tacking lace to a collar with her fine

long fingers. She picked up his yellow coat and helped him into it, circled him, tugging and drawing lines with a bit of fine chalk and making titillating sensations on his ribs and backbone so that his scrotum curled and his hair crawled across his scalp.

'Do you know your lines?' Tilly asked politely.

'Oh yes, Trudy helps me.'

'She's taking it all very seriously.'

'Very,' said William, and blew his breath through his bottom lip so that his fringe lifted. 'It's a very complex play.'

'Do you think you've got a chance to win?'

'Oh yes,' he said, 'it'll all come together.' He looked down at the fur on the hem of his coat. 'The costumes are splendid.'

'Splendid,' said Tilly. She tacked the adjustments and he tried it on again. William, admiring himself in the long mirror, said, 'How do you think it's going?'

'Pretty much as I expected,' said Tilly.

He was running his hands over the thick, ornate satin, touching the fur trim.

'You can take it off now,' said Tilly.

William blushed.

That night he found he couldn't sleep so wandered out onto the veranda. He lit his pipe and stood looking out at the moonlit croquet lawn, soft and square, the straight white lines on the tennis court, the new stables and his broken-down tractor sitting in large, separate chunks under the gum tree.

❦

Three weeks before opening night, at the end of the run-through of Acts One and Two, Trudy asked, 'How long did they take tonight, Miss Dimm?'

'Four hours and twelve minutes.'

'Christ.' The director closed her eyes and curled a large chunk of her hair around and around in her fingers. The cast backed away, tiptoeing sideways towards the wings or dressing room, eyeing the exits wildly.

'Right. Everybody back here – we're doing it again.' They had to sweat it out again on Saturday and Sunday afternoon and every week night. At last it was time for costume inspection. Tilly noted that Trudy had lost a lot of weight. She'd bitten her nails down to the quick and there were big, white patches of scalp on her head where she had tugged chunks of hair out. She also muttered lines from *Macbeth* and shouted obscenities in her sleep. She stood before her cast in a soiled dress and odd shoes. Tilly sat behind her, a tape measure around her neck and a serene expression on her face.

'Right,' said Trudy, 'Lady Macduff?'

Purl floated onto the stage in a voluminous satin skirt with a huge bustle. Her face was white-powdered and red-rouged and her hair arranged in storeys of curls, piled high, with a tall, ribboned fontange perched on top. Her pretty face was framed by a wide, wire-framed collar that swung from the top of her fontange to her armpits and was trimmed with bead-tipped ruffles. The sleeves were enormously pumpkin-shaped and the neckline of her gown was straight and low, cutting across her lovely breasts so that they burst out of her very tight, corsetted bodice. The men leered and the witches sneered.

'This costume is very heavy,' gasped Purl.

'I designed it like that, you fool – that's the type of thing they wore in the seventeenth century. Isn't that so, costume maker?'

'Yes. That's definitely what aristocrats wore in the late seventeenth century, at court,' said Tilly.

'I can't breathe very well,' said Purl.

'It's perfect,' said Trudy. The men nodded.

'Next – Duncan!'

William stepped from the wings. Burning red ringlets framed his face which was white-powdered, red-roughed and crimson-lipped, with a beauty spot on each cheek. The curls fell from a fat emerald-encrusted gold crown, like the top of the Taj Mahal. Around his neck he wore a lace bow that plummeted to his waist over a lace bodice. Over that was the fur-trimmed knee-length yellow coat. The enormous deep-folded cuffs of his coat hung all the way to his fur-trimmed hemline. He wore sheer white silk stockings and jackboots with cuffs that turned down and flopped about his ankles. He struck a gallant pose and beamed at his wife, but all she said was, 'Won't that crown topple off?'

'It's attached to his wig,' said Tilly.

'Let's see what you've done to Macbeth then.'

Lesley swept onto the stage wearing a tall sugarloaf hat that supported a forest of standing and sweeping feathers. Lace and ruffles bunched and danced around his earlobes from the collar of a voluminous white silk shirt which had tails that hung about his knees, swinging with the artificial flowers stitched to the trim of several skirts and petticoats. He had a red velvet waistcoat and matching red stockings, and his high-heeled shoes featured satin laces so large it was impossible to tell what colour the shoes were.

'Perfect,' said Trudy.

The soldiers behind her mimicked her, '*Perfect*', and flapped their wrists.

Trudy circled them, her seventeenth-century Baroque cast of the evil sixteenth-century Shakespeare play about murder and ambition. They queued on the tiny stage like extras from a Hollywood film waiting for their lunch at the studio canteen, a line of colourful slashes and frothy frocks, farthingaled frills and aiglets pointing to the heavens, bandoliers and lobster-tailed helmets with love-locks hanging, feathers sprouting from hats and headdresses that reached the rafters, their red-lipped, pancake faces resting in white plough-disc collars and arched white-wall-collars like portraits.

'Perfect,' said Trudy again.

Tilly nodded, smiling.

$\mathcal{T}$illy's back and shoulders were stiff and hurt sharply. Her arms ached and her fingertips were red raw, her eyes stung and had bags that reached her perfect cheekbones, but she was happy, almost. Her fingers were slippery with sweat, so she awarded herself a concession – she used Paris stitch for the lace-trim of the soldiers' red and white Jacquard jersey pumpkin pants when she knew she should use whip stitch. She tied-off the very last stitch and when she leaned to bite the cotton thread she heard Madame Vionnet say, 'Do you eat with scissors?'

Sergeant Farrat was telling her about rehearsals. 'And Lesley! Well if he doesn't think he's important, keeps butting in, telling everyone their lines – which of course upsets Miss Dimm because it's her job to prompt. The inspector over-acts but Mona's very good, she fills in when people don't show up. We've all got summer flu, sore throats and blocked sinus, no one's seen Elsbeth, everyone hates Trudy – I'd be a better director than her, at least I've *been* to the theatre.'

They arrived at rehearsal, their arms piled with pumpkin trousers and ostrich-edged velvet coats, the hot northerly outside wailing through power lines. Inside, the cast were still and afraid.

They were bailed up by the director at the rear of the stage, surrounded by several splintered wooden chairs. Trudy had glazed eyes with large bluish circles around them and her cardigan was buttoned in the wrong holes.

'Do it again,' she whispered menacingly.

Lady Macduff, holding a doll wrapped in a bunny rug, looked at her son. Fred Bundle breathed deeply and began:

Son: 'And must they all be hang'd that swear and lie?'
Lady Macduff: 'Every one.'
Son: 'Who must hang them?'
Lady Macduff: 'Why, the honest men.'
Son: 'Then the liars and swearers are fools; for there
are liars and swearers enow to beat the honest men
and hang up them.'

'NO! NONONONONONONONONONO, YOU'RE HOPELESS . . . ,' Trudy screamed.

'That was right,' said Miss Dimm, 'he said it right this time.'

'He didn't.'

'He did,' chorused the cast.

Trudy walked slowly to the front of the stage and fixed the cast with a demonic gaze. 'You dare to contradict me?' Her voice jumped an octave. 'I hope you develop dysentery and I hope you all get the pox and die of dehydration because enormous scabs all over your body ooze so much, I hope all your dicks turn shiny-black and rot off and I hope all you women melt inside and smell like a hot rotted fishing boat, I hope you –'

William moved to his wife, took a big backswing and slapped Trudy's face so hard that she spun 360 degrees. The curtains across the stage shifted in the whirling air. He spoke softly into

Trudy's blotchy, sweaty face. 'I happen to know the doctor is at the Station Hotel this very minute. If you make one more sound tonight we'll tie you to this chair with fishing line, fetch him and all swear on Bibles that you're mad.' He turned to the cast and in a wavery but confident voice said, 'Won't we?'

The cast nodded.

'Yes,' said Mona, and stepped towards her sister-in-law. 'You're an unfit mother – William'll get custody of this poor baby and you'll go to the asylum,' she said, and handed the baby to William. The cast nodded again. Felicity-Joy lay back in her father's arms and put the end of his lace bow in her mouth, then reached up with her hand and placed her fat little middle finger gently in his nostril.

'I think,' said Mona, 'we should take the night off, don't you?'

'Yes,' said William. 'Let's go to the pub. We'll postpone dress rehearsal until tomorrow.' The cast left, talking and laughing, traipsing off down the dark main street, feathers bobbing and lace kicking about their wrists and knees.

Trudy turned to Tilly calmly sitting across the aisle and viewed her with fixed and dilated orbs. Tilly raised an eyebrow, shrugged, then followed the others.

Later the cast ambled home and lay rigid in their beds, their eyes fixed to dim shapes in the blackness, doubtful, worried and stewing. They rummaged through the play in their minds, enacting entrances and exits, hoping the audience would not notice that they were playing three characters. No one slept a wink.

32

$\mathcal{E}$isteddfod day arrived unusually hot and windy. Irma Almanac's bones ached so she ate an extra cake with her morning cup of Devil's Claw tea. Sergeant Farrat took an especially long bath laced with oil of lavender and valerian root. Purl cooked breakfast for her guests – the doctor and Scotty – then went to do her hair and nails. Fred hosed the footpath and tidied the bar and cellar. Lois, Nancy and Bobby joined Ruth and Miss Dimm for a hearty cooked breakfast. Reginald dropped in to see Faith and shared Hamish's lamb's fry and bacon. Septimus went for a long walk in the hot wind and marvelled at how lovely the dust looked whipping across the flat yellow plains. Mona and Lesley did breathing and stretching exercises after a light breakfast of cereal and grapefruit. William found Trudy curled under the blankets, trembling and muttering and sucking her knuckles. 'Trudy,' he said, 'you are our director and Lady Macbeth, now act like her!' He went to Elsbeth in the nursery. Elsbeth stood by the cot holding Felicity-Joy. 'How is she?'

'Worse,' said William, and they nodded to each other, resigned. Elsbeth pulled the baby closer.

Tilly leapt out of bed and went straight outside. She stood

knee deep in her garden, watching the town empty as the convoy of spectators drove towards Winyerp.

Bobby was running late. He'd had trouble starting the bus. It revved and leapt along the main street towards the hall, and as it ground to the kerb the director, Lady Macbeth herself, shot from the front doors – ejected like an empty shell from a gun chamber. She fell backwards in the bright sunlight onto the footpath and bounced twice, then with the energy of someone possessed, sprang to her feet like a circus acrobat. She clenched her fists and raised them against the hall doors, screeching and pounding.

'It's mine, mine, none of you would be here without my direction, my planning and guidance, none of you. I *have* to be in the eisteddfod, you can't sack me, I made this play . . .'

Inside, the cast barricaded the doors with chairs and the sand bucket the Christmas tree once stood in. Trudy pushed at the doors. They did not budge. She turned and eyed the bus. Bobby pulled the handle and the door slapped shut, then he grabbed the keys and sprang to fall flat on the floor. Trudy started kicking the bus door, but it wouldn't open so she climbed onto the bonnet and pounded the windscreen with her fists.

The painted faces of the scared Macduffs and soldiers peered from the hall windows. William waved up at the doctor, watching from the balcony. He drained his whisky and put the empty glass on the rail, picked up his bag and was soon saun- tering up behind the energetic lunatic, dancing at the bus. He tapped her on the shoulder. 'What's up?'

Trudy was foaming and gnashing. 'Them,' she screamed, 'that bunch of talentless hams want to sack me!' She swung and pointed at Mona. 'She wants my part, she's just like her mother.'

Then she ran at the locked hall doors, shoulder first, bouncing back and throwing herself bodily against them again. 'Mona Muncan is *not* playing Lady Macbeth. I am!'

The doctor beckoned Bobby, peeping up over the dash. He shook his head. The doctor beckoned again.

'I'll give you a hand,' called Nancy.

'That's my bus too!' screamed Trudy. Bobby ran at her and grabbed her and the cast applauded. He held her wrists with his strong footballers' hands. Trudy screamed, 'I'm Lady Macbeth, I am!'

The doctor held up a large syringe, flicked it with his middle finger, aimed, grinned malevolently, then jabbed it into Trudy's big bottom. He stepped back while she dropped to the footpath to lie like a discarded cardigan, then looked down at her.

'*Full of scorpions is her mind.*' They carried her to his car and lifted her in.

The cast formed a firemen's line, loaded the set onto the top of the bus and tied it down securely. As they got on the bus, Mona stood by the door with a clipboard in the crook of her velvet arm marking them off, Lady Macbeth's frock creasing on the ground about her lacy shoes and Macbeth at her side. Everyone found a seat and sat flapping lace hankies in the heat. Lesley stood at the top of the aisle and clapped his hands twice. The cast fell silent. 'Attention please, our acting director and producer needs to speak.'

Mona cleared her throat. 'We're missing Banquo –'

'I'll be Banquo!' cried Lesley, and shot his hand in the air, 'Me me me.'

'We're picking him up at the station,' said Bobby. He tried to start the bus, which coughed and spluttered. There was a long silence. 'Right,' he said, 'everybody out.'

❧

Tilly looked down at the dull buildings and the slow, brown creek. The roof of the silo shimmered under the sun and dust whipped along the dry, dirt track to the oval. The trees leaned with the hot wind. She went inside. She stood in front of her tailor's mirror and studied her reflection. She was wreathed in a brilliant halo, like a back-lit actor, dust from tailor's chalk and flock floating in shafts of light about her. The skeletal backdrop was cluttered with the stuff of mending and dressmaking – scraps and off-cuts, remnants of fashion statements that spanned from the sixteenth century onwards. Stacked to the roof, shoved into every orifice in the small tumbling house were bags and bags of material bits spewing ribbon ends, frayed threads and fluff. Cloth spilled from dark corners and beneath chairs and clouds of wool lay about, jumbled with satin corners. Striped rags, velvet off-cuts, strips of velour, lamé, checks, spots, paisley and school uniform mixed with feather boas and sequin-spattered cotton, shearer's singlets and bridal lace. Coloured bolts stood propped against window sills and balanced across the armchair. Bits of drafted pattern and drawings – svelte designs for women who believed themselves to be size ten – were secured to dusty curtains with pins and clothes pegs. There were pictures torn from magazines and costume designs scribbled on butchers' paper dumped in clumps on the floor, along with piles of frail battered patterns. Tape measures dripped from nails on studs and the necks of naked mannequin dummies, while scissors stood in empty Milo tins beside old jars brimming with buttons and press studs, like smarties at a party. Zippers tumbled from a brown paper sack and snaked over the floor and onto the hearth. Her sewing machine waited erect on its housing table, an overlocker sitting forlornly at the bottom of the doorless entrance. Calico toiles for Baroque fineries filled a whole corner.

Electrical wire looped through studs and beams, along which sat cotton bobs and reels. In the kitchen area the disused oven stored used teacups, plates and bowls.

She leaned close to the mirror and peered at herself. She saw a thin, tired country-ruddy face with red-rimmed eyes. She picked up the can of kerosene at her feet. 'The night is long that never finds the day,' she said, and started splashing.

❧

Inside the police station, Banquo pondered his big scene, his tongue searching for the end of his nose. He too was haloed by a sun shaft which caught the sheen of the ornamental rose on his patent leather Baroque shoes. He clasped his sword handle as though to draw and bellowed,

'And when we have our naked frailties hid,

That suffer in exposure, let us meet,

And question this most bloody piece of work . . .'

❧

The hot and bothered Baroques pushed the bus backwards into the middle of the road, then adjusted their frothy hats, picked up their skirts and minced to the rear of the bus to push again. It banged, shuddered, and chugged away, oily black smoke wafting.

When Sergeant Farrat heard the explosion he breathed deeply and grabbed his ostrich-trimmed felt hat. He called out, 'Time to go.'

The inspector emerged from his cell in his muddied hessian rags holding a large wooden spoon. 'Think I should use this, Horry? For effect?'

'Please yourself,' said the sergeant.

The bus spluttered to a halt in front of Banquo and witch number three, outside the police station. 'Good morrow,' cried Banquo, sweeping and bowing largely then shoving his hat down hard on his platinum ringlets. No one smiled back.

'Carburettor?' asked the inspector, and climbed aboard. He sat with the other witches.

'Bit of muck got into the fuel, I think, but we'll get there,' said Bobby.

'Well, you go on then,' said Banquo, 'I'd better follow in the police car, it runs perfectly.'

'I'm Lady Macbeth now,' said Mona. 'Gertrude is, um . . .'

'Yes,' said Banquo, and placed his hat over his heart. 'Terrible news.' William looked out the window.

The bus rumbled away from Banquo, who stood waving his plume. Behind him, up on The Hill, a lonely curl of blue smoke wafted from Tilly's chimney.

❦

Tilly untied the cow and slapped her big bony hip, sending her hurrying down The Hill with her bell clanging and her teats swinging. Tilly passed through the empty town for the last time. As she walked she untied tethered dogs, opened chook yard gates and liberated all Bobby Pickett's pets. She removed collars from sheep tied to old railway sleepers on vacant blocks and sent little girls' ponies trotting off to the plains.

❦

Sergeant Farrat gathered his script and admired his reflection one more time then walked to his car. The keys were usually on the floor under the steering wheel, but they'd gone. He patted his thigh then realised he wasn't wearing his uniform. Behind him, blue-grey sheets of smoke streamed from beneath Tilly's rusty corrugated roof, oozing through the budding blue vines covering her house.

❦

Tilly Dunnage sat on her portable Singer sewing machine on the platform at the railway station, watching grey steam clouds chuffing towards her from the golden horizon. For her travelling outfit, she had chosen close-fitting paper-bag pants made of brilliant blue Matelasse and tied at the waist with a red silk rope. Her blouse was delicate and simple, expertly cut from a yard and a half of white nun's veiling sent from Spain. She checked her watch. Right on time. She winked at the galah in the cage beside her suitcase. Behind them, a blue fog drifted to cover Dungatar.

❦

Sergeant Farrat heard the train in the distance. It arrived and stopped, then blew its whistle and pulled away. He waved his plumed hat across his face to dismiss the smoke. He frowned, sniffed, swung around and looked up. His translucent skin purpled.

'My frocks!' he cried. 'Oh my Lord, oh Tilly . . .' He dropped his hat and slapped his cheeks. The members of the fire brigade were heading for the stage at the Winyerp town hall.

He decided to run. For the first time in forty years he bolted, heading for Tilly's burning house, screaming, heat scorching his throat.

At the top of The Hill he staggered to a heaving, wet-red standstill to watch through dripping sweat and running pancake foundation the flames fan past his patent leather high heels, across the dry weeds and stems to the brown grass, then down The Hill towards town. Fire billowed from the doors and windows of the leaning cottage and tiny strands of smoke squirted from holes in the corrugated iron roof. A nice effect, chiffon tulle, something Margot Fonteyn might have worn . . . then he collapsed, prone, where the myrtle patch once bloomed between the oleander stand and the rhubarb patch. Perhaps if he'd changed his shoes he might have made it to the water tap, but it would have been of no use, for Tilly had shut the water off.

❧

Outside the Winyerp hall the cast of *Macbeth* spilled from the bus and stood on the footpath listening to the loud applause. Inside, the curtain had finally fallen on the last encore for the cast of *A Streetcar Named Desire*. The applause went on and on.

When they piled into the foyer the audience paid little attention to the *Macbeth* cast, posing along the back wall near the toilets. They shrieked and laughed about Blanche and Stanley. The canny inspector sensed the taut nerves and low morale and said, 'We're the best, we'll win.'

'You wouldn't bloody know,' snarled Fred.

H.M.S. Pinafore went for a sweltering hour while the Dungatar cast waited, surrounded by glasses, cups and vases stuffed with flowers with cards attached that said, 'Congratulations Itheca', or 'Break a leg, Winyerp'. They listened to the singing sailors and the audience clapping along. Lesley tapped his foot. Mona stood on it. Their pancake began to run, the glue which held eyelashes melted and their costumes became stained with sweat.

'Very effective,' said Lesley. 'They were like that you know. They didn't have washing machines and they never bathed.'

'Some people still don't think they need to wash,' said Faith, and waved her fan at Lois.

'Some people don't think they have to honour their marriage vows either,' said Nancy.

'At least I have a preference for men, some sick people in this town –'

'That's enough!' cried Mona.

'Getting a bit uppity, aren't you, Mona?' said Purl.

'Now now,' said William.

They counted eleven foot-stomping encores for *H.M.S. Pinafore*. When the din subsided Lady Macbeth led her cast onto the stage. The set-dismantler sang, 'I-yam the ve-ry mo-del of a mo-dern ma-jor gen-er-ral . . .'

'Ahem,' she said, glaring, then handed him the stage plan.

'We're going to do a quick run through, then our limbering and stretching exercises but first we'll do our vocal warm-ups.' They stood in a circle and sang 'Three Blind Mice' in rounds. Lesley insisted they end their warm-up with a group hug then they retreated to 'focus'.

The curtain was due to go up and Banquo had not yet arrived. Lesley clapped his hands together and said, 'Attention, please.' Then Mona said, 'We have no Banquo so Lesley will be Banquo.'

'He doesn't know the lines –' said William.

'I've taped them to the column next to the doorway,' said Mona. 'He'll read them.'

'But –'

'He can do it,' said Mona. 'He's an actor.'

❧

The audience – cast members' husbands and wives, mothers and children from Winyerp, Itheca and Dungatar – sat in the seats to the rear of the hall near the exit sign. The judges sat in the first row behind a trestle table. The curtain went up.

An hour or so later, in Act 1, Scene V, Mona writhed on the canopied bed;

> '. . . that croaks the fatal entrance of Duncan
> Under my battlements. Come, you spirits
> That tend on mortal thoughts, unsex me here . . .'

She masturbated through her petticoats, she gasped and sobbed and thrashed. The audience wriggled, chairs creaked, the Act ended and the lights dimmed.

When they came up thirteen seconds later for Act 2, Banquo and Fleance swept onto the stage to find their audience had vanished. Only the four judges remained, leaning together, whispering. A broad matronly woman in a straw hat stood and said, 'That will be all,' then they clattered out together without a backwards glance. The cast emerged from the wings to watch them disappear into the refreshment room for supper and presentations.

33

*T*hey said very little on the journey home. They drank watermelon firewater from the cup awarded to them for Best Costume, and lolled moistly in the rattling bus.

'Sergeant Farrat will be pleased,' said Mona.

'We should have done a musical,' said Nancy, looking back at Mona. 'Who picked Shakespeare?'

'It was the only play in the library,' said Muriel.

'Anyway, no one can sing,' said Ruth.

'No one can act!' snapped Faith.

Late in the afternoon the bus and all the cars of the townspeople stopped outside the hall, or at least where the hall once stood. The cast climbed slowly down from the bus and stood looking about them. Everything was black and smoking – the entire town had been razed. A few smouldering trees remained, and a telephone pole here, a brick chimney there. Anxious pet dogs sat where front gates once swung and chooks scratched between the twisted water tanks and iron roofs littering the black landscape. The cast stood in the wafting smoke, hankies to their eyes and noses, trying to block out the smell of burned rubber, scorched timber, paint, cars and curtains. They had been burned out of existence. Nothing remained, except Tilly Dunnage's chimney. Mona pointed to a figure sitting beside it, moving his arm up and down, waving.

They walked in a pack to the main road where they paused to check for cars before crossing, then along the charcoal footpath, past the creaking shell of Pratts store where tin cans had exploded and cloth bolts still glowed. Reginald went to check his butcher's saw but found only a molten abstract sculpture. When they got to the top of The Hill they stood ankle deep in the hot charred clumps looking down to where their homes had once stood, and saw only mounds of smoking, grey-black coal and rubble. The goalposts at the footy ground were spent matchsticks lying on the black oval, and the willows that once crowded the creek bend were big, bare scaffolds, dead and curled.

Sergeant Farrat, singed and soot-smudged, sat on the chimney hearth, slapping a blackened, withered branch up and down between his blistered patent leather shoes.

'What happened?' asked the inspector.

'There's been a fire.' Sergeant Farrat slapped his twig up and down, up and down.

'My school,' sobbed Miss Dimm. They all started to cry, first slowly and quietly then increasing in volume. They groaned and rocked, bawled and howled, their faces red and screwed and their mouths agape, like terrified children lost in a crowd. They were homeless and heartbroken, gazing at the smouldering trail splayed like fingers on a black glove. It had burned north as far as the cemetery, then stopped at the town's firebreak.

'Well,' said Lois, 'we've all been down to Rufe and gave over our money for our insurance, haven't we?'

They began to calm, nodding, 'Yes,' wiping away their tears and rubbing their noses on their sleeves.

Ruth looked horrified. 'I gave it to Tilly for the soldiers' costumes, remember?'

The people of Dungatar gazed at Ruth. They stood numbly on the black hill, the air around them still and hot, wisps of smoke crawling up their stockings and filtering through their ribboned skirts, the charred wood planks of Tilly's house behind them softly clicking and spatting. The sergeant started to giggle hysterically.

'What will we do now?' asked Fred.

'Have a drink,' said Scotty, and drank. The inspector reached for the bottle.

❦

'I can see Mum's house from up here,' said Mona, and smiled slyly at her brother. He grinned and bounced on the balls of his feet. The people of Dungatar looked out over the ruined town to the homestead, standing whole and perfect, untouched on the slight rise in the distance, its corrugated roof shimmering red in the setting sun.

'Good old Fart Hill,' said William.

'Let's go and see Mother,' said Mona.

They moved silently as one towards Windswept Crest, a motley bunch in very effective Baroque costumes.